FORBIDDEN NEED

A McDADE NOVEL

SCARLETT FINN

Also by Scarlett Finn

TO DIE FOR...
TO DIE FOR TRUTH
TO DIE FOR HONOR
TO DIE FOR VIRTUE
TO DIE FOR DUTY
TO DIE FOR LOVE

GO NOVELS
GO WITH IT
GO IT ALONE
GO ALL OUT
GO ALL IN
GO FULL CIRCLE

KINDRED SERIES
RAVEN
SWALLOW
CUCKOO
SWIFT
FALCON
FINCH

LOVE AGAINST THE ODDS
STANDALONE COLLECTION
SWEET SEAS
HEIR'S AFFAIR
RESCUED
MAESTRO'S MUSE
GETTING TRICKY
THIRTEEN
REMEMBER WHEN...
RELUCTANT SUSPICION
XY FACTOR

EXILE
HIDE & SEEK
KISS CHASE

THE EXPLICIT SERIES
EXPLICIT INSTRUCTION
EXPLICIT DETAIL
EXPLICIT MEMORY

WRECK & RUIN
RUIN ME
RUIN HIM

MISTAKE DUET
MISTAKE ME NOT
SLEIGHT MISTAKE

NOTHING TO...
NOTHING TO HIDE
NOTHING TO LOSE
NOTHING TO DECLARE
NOTHING TO US
NOTHING TO SAY
NOTHING TO GAIN
NOTHING TO YOU
NOTHING TO THIS
NOTHING TO DO

THE BRANDED
SERIES
BRANDED
SCARRED
MARKED

RISQUÉ & HARROW
INTERTWINED
TAKE A RISK
FIGHTING FATE
RISK IT ALL
FIGHTING BACK
GAME OF RISK

FORBIDDEN
PREQUEL DUET
ALL. ONLY.
ONLY YOURS

THE FORBIDDEN NOVELS
FORBIDDEN DESIRE
FORBIDDEN WANT
FORBIDDEN WISH
FORBIDDEN NEED
FORBIDDEN BOND

LOST & FOUND
LOST
FOUND

ONE

"SOUNDS GREAT, TOM. Tulip, what you got?"

Their editor, Steeple, had great relationships with his reporters. Monday morning meetings in his office highlighted that easy rapport every time. He could switch from one person to another and always trust whatever would come from their mouths. Everyone got a fair chance, support, acceptance. Man, she envied his security; his certainty and faith in those around him.

He had a wife, a home, somewhere safe to go back to every night. His life was together, balanced, mature… She needed a piece of that.

"It's a little out of your wheelhouse," Steeple said in response to whatever Tulip just said.

Young Tulip was sitting by the window on the arm of the couch, legs folded beneath her. "It's been weeks and no one has an answer."

The words of her colleagues passed her by. Where was her professional courtesy? Half a dozen people already took their turns and she hadn't heard a word. As the meeting trundled along, she spaced out.

Not that it was anything new. Why had she bothered to show up? These days she struggled to focus on anything. Her erratic lack of concentration didn't have a cure. Not one in her control.

"Sersha's your girl for that."

Her head jerked up from her doodling; the heel of her hand dropped from beneath her chin. The others around the small conference table, and scattered throughout the room, zeroed in.

Steeple and Tulip held the most expectation.

Her attention darted back and forth between them. "I'm what?"

Tulip smiled. "Your work is amazing."

"Thank you," she said, then appealed to Steeple for direction. "What do—"

"The McDades."

A shiver went through her.

Tulip spoke again. "No better guide."

"What do you want to know?" she asked the nightlife reporter.

The audience made her nervous, but even alone, her guard would be high.

"To be honest, I worried about stepping on your toes, but I'd love any support you can offer. You are the expert."

"I'm no McDade expert."

"You were shadowing him for weeks and… nothing," Tulip said, her discerning eye growing acute. "Right around the time the Doherty showed up."

Him. Tulip wasn't talking about the McDades, she was talking about Connel "Ire" McDade. Her McDade, in secret, once upon a time. Oh, shit, suddenly her chest hurt.

"Okay, folks, next Monday same time," Steeple called and people rose. "You've got my number if you need me." Reporters shuffled out. "Ser, Tulip, hang back."

Like they were being pulled in front of the principal, they went to the desk and waited until everyone else departed.

Steeple laid his forearms on the desk, palms flat, looking at each of them in turn. "Tulip, you're on this. We need this. So many have tried to get the story on why Razer McDade and his Doherty showed up in the city. No one can get close."

In the past, or other circumstances, her arm would've shot into the air, waving and bouncing as she begged the teacher to call on her. She had answers. Insider information. And it didn't matter one iota.

Her McDade knowledge never made The Chronicler's pages and it never would. She'd never write it, never share it, him, them, with anyone. Except Strat, her forty-something source and BFF. Strat was the exception; nothing new there.

"We have to go in through Stag," Tulip said, pulling a chair closer to the desk to sit down. "It's the way in."

"Others have tried it," Steeple said.

Tulip disagreed. "No one from this paper."

Once again, Sersha was Ms. Popular. "What?"

"Tonight," Tulip said, leaping to her feet again. "I'll grab a cab and come pick you up around eight?"

Words failed her. Mouthing nothing, she appealed to Steeple, but he just crooked an expectant brow. This was happening whether she wanted it to or not.

"You've gotta back her up," Steeple said. "I can't let her go in alone."

Tulip wouldn't get answers. Still, being present, she could ensure the woman stayed alive.

"Nothing happens in the club before ten," she said on a sigh, retrieving her phone from her pocket. "I'll text you my address."

"Give us a minute, Tulip."

Without question the woman followed their boss's request.

"You need to be honest with me now," he said the moment the door was in the frame. "If the McDades threatened you—"

"They didn't threaten me."

"You dropped the McDade story so fast, and flipped back to the Manzanis, I don't know what to think. It's understandable if the attack knocked your confidence. The paper will cover whatever therapy or rehab you need. Is that what it is? The attack? Because you've been back on the horse, running at full steam recently. I thought you were doing good. But if Tulip's walking into danger—"

"There were no threats. Are no threats."

"I don't want you banged up again."

"That wasn't the McDades either. And, by the way, just for the record, you didn't care about me walking into Stag alone. You didn't send me with backup."

"I didn't know you were going to Stag until after it was a done deal." Good point. "And given your family connections, anyone would be crazy to screw with you." Something they all thought before her attack. "You've also grown up aware of the dangers these families pose. And you know some of the players involved." Evander "Vex" Manzani anyway. "Tulip is enthusiastic and motivated. She's wanted something to sink her teeth into for a while. No offense, but you kind of handed her the opening." Her mouth opened in outrage as she folded her arms. "Everyone expected you to pick up the story of Razer McDade appearing at his cousin's door. It's the biggest story we've had in this arena, in this city, for months. People are hungry to know. Instead, that seemed to be the catalyst for you to cut ties. You've had time to take the story on your own and chose not to do that."

Anyone else would want to get into the nitty gritty of it. She, in contrast, avoided the subject and the family. For reasons. Her reasons. Reasons that couldn't be shared.

"Look…" Steeple continued, "if you really don't want to do it, I won't force you. But if anything happens to Tulip out there on her own—"

"It's on me, right?"

He shrugged. Connel wouldn't hurt Tulip just for showing up. But if she asked the wrong question in earshot of certain parties… Hell, if she got herself cornered by some asshole, it could mean big trouble.

"Have you spoken to him?"

She snapped from her mind's meandering. "Have I spoken to who?"

"Helios Manzani." Shit. That wasn't the man on her mind. Not even close. "You're still trying to engage with him, aren't you?"

"Yeah, it's a process. It's taking more time than I'd like. We're writing, but he won't agree to a call or visit yet."

"Then this is ideal. Something to keep you busy while you work the other story."

Yeah, ideal… providing Connel, or any of his men, didn't see her. If they did, how did she explain showing up at Stag unannounced after all these weeks?

TWO

"YOU LOOK GREAT," Tulip said when she got in the cab.

Anticipatory energy buzzed around her. The woman was psyched liked this was a slam dunk. Nothing was guaranteed. Experience taught her that. Tulip may only be a couple of years younger than her, but her aura suggested a lack of awareness.

"What do you know about the McDade family?"

"What everyone knows. What's been in the news. I searched our archives too." The Chronicler had newspapers in many major cities around the country. "You were attacked."

Right. Sure. That had to be the first thing that came up.

"That's not the beginning of the McDade story. There's background."

"That you never revealed to anyone. You gave the cops minimal information and your father's Police Superintendent. You gave no media interviews, no quote, even to your own paper."

Shifting in her seat, she took a better look at the younger woman. Maybe she wasn't as innocent as it first appeared.

Tulip smiled like there was much more beneath her benign exterior and took a deep breath. "Errol McDade, father to Clancy, Burl, and Amos. Burl had four sons, Biz, Score, Razer, and Play. Score spent a decade on death row after being set up by Biz, who wanted him out of the picture. When this was discovered, Score was liberated. But he's known for settling scores, hence his nickname. He left prison, relocated to Miami and opened a nightclub. From there, he started working with the feds, gathering information on his father and older brother, Biz. His testimony put both of them in prison. He gave no incriminating evidence against Razer or Play, who stayed silent during the trial. They moved to Miami to be near Score and his now wife Shyla. The three brothers have been living there happily; Score has a kid and a second on the way."

"So you know a lot about the McDades who aren't here?"

That part of the McDade family had been the one most publicized in recent years.

"That's the thing," Tulip said, her excitement returning. "Razer is here. He came here with his wife Whisper Doherty. She's basically the only surviving member of the Doherty family. They were the East Coast McDades' greatest rivals. That's a whole other story in itself."

"One we don't have time for," Sersha said. "I need to know that you understand what you're walking into before we get to this club. You can't ask direct questions. You can't be excited or get in anyone's face. We're two women going to the bar for a drink, that's it."

"Why would we choose Stag?"

"Because it's safe... and dangerous at the same

time." Anxiety niggled. How many people might recognize her? How long would word of her presence take to creep up the tree? Only a few weeks ago, she'd been there every day… and in their boss's bed. "I'm your back up, your support, not an active player."

Interest furrowed Tulip's brow. "You're nervous. Reluctant. Steeple said your McDade investigation went nowhere, but word around the office is it ended abruptly. No one really knew why… Straight after Razer and Whisper showed up. What's going on? What's happening in that family? Why did Nicole McDade, Biz's wife, come with them? Why is she even still a part of the equation? Her husband's in prison. For all intents and purposes, Score put him there. Score and Razer are close, I don't understand how Nicole fits in."

"And that's what you hope to do?" she asked. "Fit Nicole in? You won't learn about their intentions in Stag."

"Tell me how to do it? What better way is there?"

In truth, Stag was as good a place as any to begin. If someone wanted information, rumors, gossip, they had to be near the source. Tulip wouldn't get answers ambushing Whisper or Razer directly. That would put her on the enemy list; people on that list never got cooperation.

"We just have to be careful," Sersha said. "One wrong move, one wrong word, and things will get serious fast."

"Are you afraid of them? Your brother's a cop. If you want him to join us—"

"If Lach was with us, we wouldn't get in," she said, unsure if they would anyway.

Connel's mood was volatile. The slightest thing could set him off. If he blacklisted someone, that was it… Until he appeared in that someone's apartment in the middle of the night to change the rules… in her case anyway.

Was she bitter? Pissed? Maybe. She went through cycles of being angry at him, aching for him, crying, cursing, missing him. That last one never really went away. Sometimes she wasn't mad at him, it was herself. Why couldn't she just let him go? Let them go? It's over, deal with it, move on. To whom? Who could possibly follow a man like Connel McDade? Memories tormented her.

The loft. The club. She dreamed of being in his office with him. Still on waking she'd reach for him or grab her phone, but she couldn't contact him.

Communicating would be unfair on them both. And what would be the point of trying? Either he embraced her return and they wound up back where they ended last time, or he shunned her and she'd have to experience losing him all over again.

They rounded the corner and there it was: Stag.

No backing out now. They stopped behind a cab already there. Tulip slid to the front of the seat, hand dipping into her purse.

"No," Sersha said, opening an app on her phone. "This is going on company expenses."

She held her phone to the cab driver's machine and then someone opened the door.

Hock. Shit. One of the guys tasked with protecting her when Connel's bodyguards fleshed out her entourage. They made eye contact as she got out but said nothing. Tulip didn't seem to notice the exchange. Ignoring the line of people behind the rope, Hock led them to the VIP entrance, on the other side of the regular access with its guards and metal detectors.

"Look at this…" Tulip leaned in to mutter, looping her fingers around her wrist. "VIP treatment."

She didn't recognize the bouncers when they moved aside for Hock. Though she spent little time ogling them. Connel rotated his guys regularly, so they'd know every inch of the operation and real estate, and always be on guard. Complacency was dangerous.

Hock moved aside, stopping at the bottom of the stairs shielded by security. Panic hit for a second, did he expect her to go up there?

He winked and side-nodded, indicating they should keep going.

Relief.

Though, yeah, that only lasted a few feet. Then they reached the coat check. A line of people waited for that too, but she glimpsed the counter…

Connel fucked her on that counter… while a bunch of his men listened. The things he'd said… the pleasure he gave…

The curve of her lips was involuntary. Lowering her chin, she tried to hide her reaction to the memory. The shadows of the wide hallway helped with that. Bass from the club drew them closer.

The vast bar and seating area with tables and booths was slightly raised over the dance floor, with the DJ booth in the furthest corner. Somehow the acoustics meant the music filled the space, yet semi-conversation was still possible in that area.

Tulip headed for the bar, but she stalled. Scanning the space, she breathed in the air. The spiral stairs to the apartment stood steeped in darkness. Someone would be there, blocking the route. Would she be granted access? What about the office? Would she get in there?

"What's wrong?" Tulip asked, at her side again. "What do you see?"

"Nothing," she said, holding Tulip's hand to guide her across the room toward the bar. "What do you drink?"

"Where are the restrooms?" Tulip asked as they

sat on adjacent stools.

"You need the restroom already?"

"I like to get a lay of the land."

"There's some by the hallway we just came through and others in the back corner."

She twisted to point across the space at both options. Better to gesture than say something that might pique Tulip's curiosity again. When she turned back, there was a drink in front of her. On an exhale, her shoulders dropped. Biggs was there, right there, waiting.

"What do you drink?" he asked Tulip.

Her colleague didn't miss that she'd been served already.

"Safe Harbor," Tulip said, and Biggs went off to mix it. "It's time to spill…" She put her purse on the bar. "You're a big deal around here?"

"I wouldn't say that," she said. "I spent some time here."

"And they remember you?"

"The reporter? Yeah."

"Good point. They'd have to watch themselves around you. Make sure they didn't do or say anything that could end up in print… or whispered in your father's ear."

She sipped her drink, her eyes traveling to the wall that held up the back of the bar. Behind there, also guarded, was a hidden door. A door that led to stairs. To the basement.

The things she'd done down there… She'd witnessed…

Biggs brought Tulip's drink. "Need anything else?" he asked. She shook her head. "I'm going on break. I'll be back in fifteen."

She smiled at him but was distracted by Tulip raising her glass.

"Sláinte," she said.

They both drank.

"You must have learned something," Tulip said. "About the family, how they work… Something about who they are."

"It's subjective," she said, turning her glass by its base. "Like so much of what we do."

"Did you meet Whisper and Razer?"

"Yes," she said.

In the absence of certainty, she erred on the side of honesty. Who knew what someone else might tell Tulip or what she already knew?

"What are they like?"

"We didn't hang out. We weren't buddies. Like you said I—"

"Oh, my God." Tulip leaped off her stool. "I just saw her. Whisper Doherty. She's headed for the ladies' room."

Before she'd even finished the sentence, Tulip was off the stool, rocketing across the room.

Whisper using the public restroom while the club was in full swing seemed unlikely.

The alone time gave her a chance to absorb the ambiance. Not so long ago, Stag meant safety. Sanctuary. Now being in there, after crossing the threshold and not bringing the roof down on her head, she was beginning to relax.

"Who tipped you off, High Class?"

Someone slid onto Tulip's stool. Not Tulip, the woman she was pursuing. Damn the Doherty was smart.

THREE

"WHISPER," Sersha said. "It's good to see you again."

"That's not an answer to my question," Whisper said. "Who was it?"

"I don't know what you're talking about," she said, twisting her stool toward the Doherty, checking out the room behind her. "But I do know the woman I came with will be back any minute. She wants to know why you and your husband are here. In town."

"And you brought her here?"

"Coming here was not my idea. It was hers. You could say I'm here under duress because my boss ordered me to back her up."

"Because he thinks you know the McDades," Whisper said, assessing her. "Ire's on a kick—"

"I don't want to know," she said, returning to her drink. "You should walk away before—"

"Your friend won't get out of the bathroom until I want her to get out of there." Whisper's smug smile held a power only a mob daughter could own. "The guys aren't here. Ire's on a rampage. Raze is doing what he can. Though, if you ask me, there are certain things he enjoys a little too much for a guy who's supposed to be retired from the game."

"I don't know what that means, Raze is doing what he can?"

"You fucked your guy up good. My guy, he's changed… kinda," Whisper said, picking up Tulip's drink to sip it and scowl before pushing it away. "Some might say it happened years ago. Most of the time, that's the side of him people see. The world sees."

"What are you trying to tell me?"

Everything pleasant or positive was gone from Whisper when her eyes cut around. "My husband isn't squeamish about doing what needs to be done."

"Neither are you."

"Are you?"

"Hey, gorgeous ladies…"

The drawl of a half-drunk playboy was familiar, as was the arm that slid around her waist. Asshole. Of all the women at the bar—

Whisper pounced fast, up to a crouch on her stool. The guy was slammed down on the bar so hard, she jumped off her seat on reflex.

But there was Whisper, a knee between the guy's shoulder blades, twisting his arm up his back, holding a knife to his throat. Honestly, it happened that fast. Boom, Whisper had control.

"You want to say that to me again," Whisper snarled. "Creeping up on a woman has consequences."

Security rushed over, but her hand rose a few inches from her side, signaling them to stop. Whisper Doherty did not need any help when it came to lecherous guys taking a chance.

"I didn't—I—"

The bead of blood at the point of Whisper's knife grew larger. The woman was tiny but didn't let that stop her. Perched half on the stool, the beauty knew how to stand up for herself. Dohertys, like McDades, learned that early.

"What do you say to my friend?" Whisper asked. "Speak!"

As more people noticed the scene, they stopped to gawp. Being transfixed herself, she couldn't blame them.

"S—sorry?" the guy stuttered.

Renewed pressure on the blade brought more blood. "Was that a question?"

"No. No! I'm sorry!"

Biggs appeared on the other side of the bar. Whisper nodded at him, so he grabbed the guy's arm to hold him in place while Whisper dismounted like a pro and sheathed the knife under her dress against her thigh.

Whisper smiled, even as she turned back to address the assailant…? Victim? Predator? Which was he? "And you're welcome by the way, jerkoff," the Doherty said as security hauled him up. "If my husband was here, you'd never walk again." She winced. "Or have children." Whisper whirled to face her. "Let's go upstairs, High Class. You see what happens when you mix with the masses?"

Whisper came over to loop their arms together and start across the room.

"My colleague—"

"Will be taken care of."

That was a daunting, and somewhat terrifying, prospect. "You don't mean… McDade taken care of… do you?"

"No," Whisper scoffed. "I'm a Doherty."

The guys guarding the stairs moved without blinking, allowing them to pass. Okay, so she was with Whisper. Anyone who'd seen, or heard, what just happened in the club likely wouldn't get in her way. God knew what else the woman had done since her arrival in town.

Whisper led her into the office like it was no big deal. Oh, it was a big deal. For her.

Their arms broke apart as the Doherty ventured toward the desk. "He's a bear," Whisper called back from the decanter in the corner. "Your guy."

"I don't have a guy," she murmured, absorbing mental flashes of memory assaulting her from every direction.

They'd had sex on the desk, against the McDade emblem on the wall, right there in the middle of the rug too. Connel shot a guy not far from where she stood for interrupting their intimacy. He'd watched her with Dasha and Darla on that couch. Touched her—

"Ire will like that you don't have another guy," Whisper said, turning and raising her glass before drinking. "No, actually, maybe not. He's on a violent spree. Maybe he'd like tossing some of your love interests in the mix, just to keep things interesting." With a sort of exhaled laugh, she beckoned her over. "Shit, come in. I didn't think you'd need an invitation."

"I shouldn't be up here," she said. "I'm not supposed to—"

"Look, you're here and it's not for him... apparently." Did Whisper think otherwise? "Come, sit down, we should talk."

Curiosity drew her forward. "About?"

"The family," Whisper said. "You haven't switched allegiance, have you?"

"No!" she said, offended, then faltered. "Connel doesn't want me involved."

Whisper finished the whiskey and put the glass back on the table in the far corner. "Maybe, maybe not." She crossed to sit on the couch. "But I think we can help each other out."

Yes, she was intrigued, no denying that. By what? Connel? Her interest in the family? The investigative nature of her job? Any or all those reasons may be guilty of luring her to sit on the couch by Whisper.

"Help each other with what?"

"Ire's on a kick."

"You said that already."

"He wants the city. McDades have taken over ninety percent of Gambatto territory. And this Harvest deal, what he's got going on at City Hall, it's gone to his head. This isn't going to keep the peace. He won't stop at Harvest; he wants to keep going. To push deeper into Manzani territory."

"Does Evander know that?" she asked, turning on Whisper's suspicion. "I mean…" She slipped off her shoes to tuck her feet under her. "If Evander Manzani wants his own cut, if he wants to cut his father out, at some point, he intends to take over Manzani territory."

Whisper relaxed. "Which puts him at odds with Ire." Sersha shrugged in agreement. "I don't think Vex is stable."

Vex was what they called the youngest Manzani son, Evander, on the street.

"I know he's not," she said.

"He's obsessed with you? That's what I heard."

"It comes and goes. Sometimes he's everywhere, then he'll get distracted by something else. He loops back eventually… or he used to."

"Maybe his arrangement with Ire changed that? You think our boy nixed it?"

"I don't think anyone has that power over Evander. He's challenging his own father, for goodness' sake."

"True dat," Whisper said, head bobbing in a nod. "A guy without limits is… dangerous." A phone on the desk buzzed. "Damnit." Whisper got up to go check it and groaned. "God, people are idiots…" She marched toward the door. "Stay here. I'll be back." The moment she opened the door, some guy tumbled in, like he'd been leaning against it. Unimpressed, Whisper looked at her, blank. "Idiots. We're surrounded by idiots."

Whisper stepped over the guy and went out. It took him a minute to get back to his feet. It was funny. Stupid funny. Until the guy closed the door with him still on the inside. Okay, so she was being watched? It wasn't like she wanted to hang out in Connel's office alone. Someone obviously didn't believe that. Was it a trick? Was Whisper setting her up to see what she'd do? Except her memory was just fine. Even without the guy's presence, she'd have been vigilant of being recorded.

Tossing her purse on the other end of the couch, she got up.

"Stay on the couch," the guy said.

She blinked at him. "Excuse me?"

"I told you to sit your ass down," he said, marching closer.

"I don't think so." She knew better than to be in the corner against a guy like that. "All I want is a drink."

She got two steps when he grabbed her arm to throw her down on the couch.

She'd never been afraid in that room and wasn't about to break the trend. Getting to her feet, she didn't care if he read her defiance as a challenge.

"You think I've never met a bully before?" she asked. "If a woman says she wants a drink, it's polite to let her get it… or you could fetch it for me."

"I'm not your bitch," he snarled, getting in her face.

Her smile mocked him. "No, you're Ire's."

She swerved around him and was quick enough to get further than before. Ha! Next time he snatched her arm, she was ready and braced enough to struggle.

"Let go of me!"

"You heard her."

The Irish lilt in that American voice froze the moment. For a beat, she waited, then the thug turned toward it, showing her its origin.

Ire.

FOUR

CONNEL MCDADE.

"Get out of the city. Tonight," he growled. "I hear you're here at sunrise, you'll never see the moon again."

The thug glanced at her, and she arched a brow. Okay, maybe she hadn't expected Connel to be so blunt, but... No, actually, blunt was exactly his style.

The fingers loosened from her arm and the jerk stalked off, leaving fast. Smart. Connel wasn't always so charitable. He slammed the door behind the guy. The asshole should be thrilled he got out clean.

A mercy she wasn't granted.

The flutter of her heart lightened. Her breathing slowed, but her heart wouldn't still. They hadn't been alone since...

"What do you need?" he asked, his voice little more than a growl.

What did she need? Was that why she'd come? What he thought? That she'd show up and use him for her selfish desire?

Why that word? Why did her stupid mind conjure that word?

The same reason she was reassessing her own motives. Why had she come there? For Tulip? For Steeple?

Not if the stirring low in her belly was an indication. It dipped lower, warming her pussy, exactly what shouldn't be happening.

"Conn," she whispered.

She hadn't meant to. Not like that.

The darkness in his eye glinted the moment the breathy word hit him.

His feet moved while hers were frozen, locked to the red stag head in the middle of the otherwise black rug beneath her.

He stopped, less than a foot in front of her. Them. Together. Alone. Forbidden.

"What do you need?" he asked again.

The bass of his tone rippled through her. The unstable earth lurched beneath her feet. She wobbled, swaying forward until her face rested on his chest. Her eyes sank shut. Taking liberties wasn't usually her style but it was Connel. Restrictions didn't exist between them, or they hadn't not so long ago.

The weight of his hand on the back of her head anchored her. For the first time in weeks, she felt focused, safe, valued. With him, in that minute, her existence made sense. This was it. The reason she walked the world was to be touched by him.

One palm was joined by the other and they arced down to cradle the sides of her head. The pads of his thumbs pressured beneath the slope of her jaw, tipping her head back.

She didn't fight it or open her eyes; the press of his mouth gave her salvation.

It was a dream. Like every dream she'd had since

they'd last been together.

The circle of tension slung low on her hips weighted the arousal tickling her intimate corners.

Using his hold on her head, he directed her body while slanting her mouth, walking her backward until she hit the desk. Their desk. Boosting up onto it, she moaned around the mass of his tongue plundering deeper, harder, demanding her surrender.

His name was in her throat, but she couldn't free it, not while her need for him throbbed throughout her. Sliding her shins up his legs, she coiled them around his hips, using him to pull their bodies together, forcing the solid evidence of his own need against her as the angle between her spine and the desk narrowed. Had he struggled as bad as her? Missed her? Could she believe it?

Seeking his shirt buttons, she unfastened them, desperate to feel him, to lay her hands on him—

"Ire—"

His hand moved, somehow, she anticipated it and slapped the lid of the cigar box shut before he could draw the weapon within.

Their eyes met.

Connel.

Shit.

He cursed and thrust away from her to spin on the guy who'd come in. "What the fuck do you want?"

Whisper appeared behind the stuttering guy. "Cops are here," she said, shoving the guy aside. "A lot of them."

Connel turned to her as she sat up on the desk. "Cops?"

"And her brother's at the head of the pack."

Niall's voice she recognized, but she couldn't take her eyes from Connel's.

"Upstairs," he said.

"He can't—"

"He won't," Connel said, buttoning his shirt. "Go."

She ran past him to grab her purse from the couch and turned on her heels to hurry through the curtain onto the stairs. Already there was movement in the office.

"Ire…" Lachlan said on the other side of her fabric shield. "You having a party in here?"

"Everyone out," Connel commanded.

More movement and the office door closed. She'd sat there before. On those stairs. Listening to Connel talk with her brother.

"What do you want?" Connel asked.

"To look around… That's not a problem, right?"

"No," Connel said. "Providing you have a warrant."

"A warrant? Thought you were open to the public."

"If you and your people want to enjoy Stag as patrons, you'll be extended every courtesy. First drink's on the house."

"That's not what I call good customer service," Lachlan said. "We want the full tour. To experience Stag behind the scenes. Nice shoes. What are they? A five-inch heel?" Her attention dropped to her bare feet. Shit. Her shoes were out there. How did she forget that? "Missing one of your diamonds."

There were rhinestones on the back seam of the shoe. Apparently one less than there should be.

"That what you're looking for, McLeod?" Connel asked. "Shoes?"

"No. Not shoes."

"You ask to search a place, usually means you're looking for something… or are you targeting me for a different reason?"

"Like what?"

"You tell me."

Her heart raced. Part of her wanted to knock their heads together, another part desperately wanted it to be over. Walk out the door, Lachlan. Leave. Don't push it. If he did, he could end up finding something he wouldn't want to find at all: his sister.

"What do you think we—"

Her phone buzzed. Shit. No way they hadn't heard the sound. Despite being on silent, the vibration was way louder than she'd ever heard it. Adrenaline shook her whole body.

"What are you hiding, McDade?" her brother asked, more intrigued than before. "Got anything you want to share?"

"Only the way out, Detective."

"You know, we could be allies."

"You know, we could," Connel said, surprising her. No doubt her brother too. "If you chose a different profession."

She almost rolled her eyes. He didn't need to be antagonistic. Though Lachlan had shown up unannounced to ambush him… maybe antagonistic wasn't so out of line.

"You're—" This time a phone rang from the other side of the curtain. "Excuse me." Lachlan's, obviously, but he didn't go anywhere. "Henry…" Her head rose, that was her grandfather's name. The men in her family often used each other's first names. Henry, Ronald, Lachlan, she wasn't part of that club. "Yeah, that's right…" her brother said. "Understood."

"Wrong address?" Connel asked, a smirk in his tone.

"Family business."

"If I can be of any help…"

She smiled at Connel's offer. Yeah, it sounded

sort of insincere, but she knew different.

"Yeah, right. You care about my family? Did you care when my sister was left for dead for your family?" Her hand flattened on the wall as her butt rose a few inches from the stair. Damn. Did Lachlan have to take it there? "I asked you a question."

It wasn't like her brother to be hostile or for Connel not to have an immediate comeback.

"I did," he said through audibly gritted teeth. "And I made sure it would never happen again."

"Really? 'Cause what I saw was her getting hurt on your watch in your neighborhood. Who runs things around these parts? If I find out you were behind it…"

She bit her lip. If they came to blows… Lachlan never started the fight, he was always calm and levelheaded. Connel she'd expect to be more volatile, more aggressive.

"As I said, it will never happen again."

"My sister doesn't always think things through. Sometimes I forget how smart she is… Then she goes and cuts ties with all things McDade and I remember why she excelled at college."

Her lips moved in silent murmuring of her brother's name. He had to stop or she'd be the one losing her cool. Maybe listening in wasn't such a good idea.

"She is smart," Connel said. The swagger in his intonation set her on edge. "And beautiful."

She sat back on an exhale. Great. This was going just swell.

Lachlan was snide enough to laugh. "You fucking wish, asshole."

"McLeod," a third voice.

About damn time. There was movement and mumbles.

"Guess we'll see you next time," her brother said a few seconds later.

"We're not going anywhere," Connel said.

Footsteps and then the office door closed.

FIVE

SERSHA DIDN'T MOVE. If Connel wanted her to join him in the office, he'd call for her. He'd done that before. If he needed a minute or was pissed at her, rushing him wouldn't help. There was always the chance he'd throw her out. That he didn't want to see her.

If enough cops joined Lachlan's venture, it would take time to put space between them and the club. She wouldn't overlook the chance they'd loiter nearby and watch the place for a while. Not that Connel would be dumb enough to immediately trot out whatever evidence they'd been looking for. Leaving too quickly could walk her straight into their ranks. Explaining her solitary presence to Lachlan could prove difficult.

As she rolled her lips into her mouth, the curtain moved and there he was, in the shadow at the foot of the stairs.

"You know that was gonna happen?" Connel asked. She shook her head. "They'll hang around outside; you'll have to stay a while."

Laying a steadying hand on the wall, she rose to her feet. "How about the night?"

They'd put an end to them. They were no more… Except… their tongues had twined like they hadn't missed a beat. Their bodies hadn't feasted themselves full before her brother showed up and interrupted. They had unfinished business. Unsated need.

"You remember where you are?" he asked, stony-faced. "Who I am?" She frowned. "Don't expect me to be a good guy. I'm no gentleman. If I want it, I'll take it. I'll use you. Any time I get the opportunity. And I'll still walk away."

Did he want her to walk away? No. If he didn't want her there, he'd get one of his guys to toss her out. He wasn't trying to scare her off, he was giving her a chance to retreat.

Rather than take the safe, sensible path, she slid down the zipper beneath her arm and shimmied out of her dress.

For too long, she'd craved him. The opportunity to be with him again was too tempting to ignore.

His jaw grew tight, his scowl darkened. The shadow of the lower hall enhanced his menace. But she wasn't afraid. Not when she'd seen behind the tough veneer.

Reaching behind to unhook her bra, she wasn't shy about letting it fall. He could look, admire, recall when her body was his playground. If he needed the visual reminder, she'd provide it.

Without a word of question or permission, she turned around to stroll up the stairs. At the top, she pushed her panties from her hips, freeing herself from all fabric constraints as she headed for the bed.

He could stay away, avoid her and refuse the obvious invitation. No one had a gun to his head.

Being in the office had been unsettling, but that was nothing to being in his bedroom again. Standing at the foot of the bed, the spirit of each of their previous unions enveloped her.

As her eyes closed, his lips touched the side of her neck. He hadn't walked away, he was there, behind her, his hands sliding onto her hips. They kept on going, up, over her breasts, squeezing her, fondling, his lips tracing old paths.

"Conn…" his name seeped out on her next breath.

She wanted to be on the bed with him inside her but couldn't break contact.

Her weight eased back, finding support in his strength. The comfort of him was home, the heat of his skin on hers, the tenderness in his demanding touch. Somehow, he managed to be everything she needed, to balance desire with consideration. He'd shown her so much, given her so much. The liberty he entrusted to her freed her to explore in ways she never had.

Easing a hand around her back between them, she curled her fingers around his desire and tightened them, squeezing him hard. His lips paused just at the pressure point above her collarbone. A growl escaped him and he pushed deeper into her hand's embrace.

That reaction, any reaction, inspired her confidence again. Before she could tease anymore, he thrust her onto the bed, pushing her hips forward as his knees parted hers. She hadn't even planted her hands on the bed and he was in her, pushing hard, forcing her pussy to take him. A spear of pleasure pulsed through her, tightening her muscles around him so hard her body created a barrier. He spanked her ass, hard, and she yelped, but it turned into a glorious laugh.

"Fuck, McDade," she said on a moan, pushing back as he thrust deep. "I need this."

He spanked her again, then tightened his grip on her hips, fucking her deep as his fingers emblazoned his prints on her skin, bruising her with their strength.

He drove in, hitting her deep every time and bent over her, locking one forearm around her as his other hand sought her clit. It wasn't fair that he could torment her from within and with that tantalizing touch. Her next sound was more of a whine, a mew, a desperate pleading for more of his promise.

"Conn," she whimpered, writhing against his stimulation.

"Everything you need..." he growled, his lips touching her spine, "everything you want... right here."

"Yes," she panted, struggling to remember how she'd lived anywhere but in his bed. "Baby..."

"Aye," he grumbled, drawing out the word. "You ready to beg?"

"Yes," she snapped fast. "Oh, God, yes..." The pressure of his digits, the satisfaction of fullness provided by his engorged cock throbbing inside her, it was gluttony. Sin at its peak. Pleasure was ready to burst, building behind the dam he teased her with breaking. "Connel... Fuck, Conn! Please, baby! Please!"

The gruff heat of his laugh clouded her spine as he kissed it again. His fingertips moved in slow circles and sped, slowed and sped, as he bobbed his cock back and forth an inch within her. The tip of his tongue trailed up and down, adding nimble sprites of buoyant arousal in tiny spirals that darted beneath her skin.

"You enjoy torturing me," she wailed. "Oh, fuck, I forgot how—"

"And this is your reminder," he said, pressing, hurling her through the dam in a torrent so wild, she drowned in the mire of pleasure.

She screamed, loud, his name, for more, for mercy, for forever. Her body was still pulsing, quaking, trying to recover when he returned to thrusting hard and fast, yanking her hips back to meet his pelvis with every advance, forcing her away with every retreat.

Her body didn't want to lose his. Orgasm came again and she clamped tight, her whole body locked in a spasm that he forced his way through, driving himself over the edge into his own completion.

He let her go and she fell forward onto her face, her arms curled beneath her. Her heart was pounding so hard, she could feel it in her skull, all over her body in a constant, frantic pulse.

"Fuck," she gasped, her eyes closed. "Why did we stop seeing each other again?"

His voice came from somewhere near the bathroom. "It wasn't 'cause the sex blew."

"No," she said, a laugh joining her exhale. "It definitely wasn't that."

When the bed moved, she raised her head just enough to see him rest against the pillows propped on the headboard. Wriggling to ascend, her head found the pillow that had been hers… for a short time.

Shifting his weight to the hip nearest her, his fingertips met her spine. "Plan this?"

"No," she said, tossing her hair from her face before settling again. "You use a rubber?" His attention left her body to find her eyes. "Sorry, I don't know why I asked that."

Or why the idea was so unsettling.

Clearing her throat, she started to rise, but his hand flattened on her back, holding her down. "You said the night."

"Can you afford it?" she asked and the question in his eye curled her lips. "Not like that." She laughed. "I haven't descended quite that far. I meant time. You were dealing with something before I showed up."

"It's done," he said, trailing his touch up and down.

The contact drove her nuts. Every atom in her

body shimmered wherever his fingers met.

"Whisper said you've been on a kick. You want to expand beyond Harvest? That was never the…" The twitch of his brows reminded her things weren't like they once were. Before she could apologize or backtrack, she remembered what brought her there, rather who. "Shit. Tulip!"

"The woman you came with? She was put in a cab home; told we did the same with you."

"How did you know I came with someone?"

"Niall and I have known each other our whole lives," he said. "He has a lousy poker face."

"I didn't see him," she said, tucking herself a little closer. "When we arrived."

"You saw Hock. My guys report to Niall."

"He was with you?" she asked. The minute move of his eyelid was confirmation enough. "Is that why you came back?" Biting her lip was supposed to be playful, but sincerity existed in the question too. "To see me?"

"Didn't know you brought the cops."

"I didn't," she said. "I didn't even want to come." His head tilted. Had she offended him? "I said out loud that I didn't…" Her words became wistful as her own fingers found the ridges of his abs. "Tulip asked and… Steeple did too. He said if anything happened to her, it would be on me." Drawing in a breath, she held it a second before sighing. "I was scared to come here."

"Where are you always safe?"

Her smile peeked. "With you." Her eyes slunk up to his. "If I got in."

"You'll always get in here," he said. "The only time you weren't allowed was…" The night of her assault. "I won't let that happen again."

"That wasn't your fault," she said, and this time when she rose, he didn't prevent her. But she wasn't getting up, just sliding a leg across his lap to sit on him.

His back was still against the pillows, though he sat up, he was in a semi-slouch, not upright. "I like to think of that as before this… Before you knew you could trust me."

As they rose, the back of his hands guided her hair away, allowing him to cup her jaw. "I shouldn't trust you."

Another smile. "Ditto."

"You will always have access to me. Whatever you need is here."

Swaying forward, her mouth was on route to his when they were interrupted again.

"Boss?"

"Fucking…" Connel hissed and his hands moved, but she redirected them to her breasts. "Get the fuck outta here!"

There was a bang, a curse, and then the hurry of footsteps. Whoever that was, he'd left fast.

"You have too many new people," she whispered, leaning in to kiss him.

"We're expanding."

"I heard," she said, stroking his torso. "If only empire did it for me…"

"You never cared about the empire," he said and her head shook slightly, her lips brushing his. "You cared about cock."

She laughed, laying her hands on his chest to sit a little straighter. "You gave it to me better than any other man ever did… You ruined me, remember?"

"Aye," he said, the need of his touch growing when his hands skimmed around to squeeze her ass. "Helps that your brother lives with you." Her simple smile came as she relaxed her head in silent question. "You won't hear me denying it."

"You've been watching me?" she asked. "Or has Evander been reporting back? You share personnel now?"

"I underestimated what…"

"What?" she asked, scooping up his jaw to marry their eyes again. "You underestimated what?"

For a few seconds, he searched her. What was he hiding? Too much. Because there was still a line between them, a barrier that meant their time together was limited.

Capturing her in his arms, he flipped her onto her back, coming down on top of her. "I don't want you to leave this room, this bed, tonight, you understand me?"

She nodded. "As long as you're with me, I'll stay."

"And forget sleep, that won't be happening."

With joy, she freed her arms from between them to coil them around his neck. "You're a bad influence, Mr. McDade."

"Aye," he said. "Anything you want in this bed, you get."

If that were true, she'd never leave it and wouldn't let him either. Returning to Stag wasn't meant to lead to this. If she was honest with herself, this was the fantasy. He was the fantasy. Once again, he was bringing it to life for her. It was fleeting. It wouldn't last. But she would relish every second while it did.

SIX

HER BODY ACHED everywhere. Her mind was heavy, tired, soaked in the endorphins of the night. She didn't care that she probably wouldn't walk straight for a week, not while she lay there on her side, head in the pillow, facing the man cradling her cheeks, pressing light, thorough kisses to her lips.

"Conn," she whispered, losing herself in the intoxication of him.

Light intruded from the broad square arch to the living room beyond the bathroom. There were no windows in the bedroom itself, but that entry heralded the day she cursed. Even spending hours with him, having sex, talking, enjoying each other, it wasn't enough.

His phone rang. Again. Somewhere on the floor near the room's threshold, his clothes were scattered with hers, discarded, unnecessary, an unwelcome symbol of their responsibilities beyond that bed.

"Ignore it," he said, licking her lower lip.

Wasn't like they didn't have experience shutting themselves away for days. If that was his plan, she wouldn't resist. She could never resist him.

"They're worried about you," she murmured between kisses.

"They know where I am."

She smiled. "Maybe I'm corrupting you."

He pulled back to meet her eye. "I'm the corruptor."

And that poured ice-water over the warmth of their bond. He sat up, disconnecting completely.

"Conn—"

"Stay as long as you want." He got out of bed before she could make contact with him again. "We're taking our business across town. Some of your things are in the closet."

"Don't walk out on me," she said, stopping him just before he entered the closet. "Will I see you again?"

He turned, something like pity coloring his expression. "This was a one-night deal, I told you that."

"I know." Because it could be nothing else. They'd tried doing the half-measure thing and it didn't work. "So leave me like it will be the last time."

He could've laughed in her face. Could've spurned the request. He could've been cold and cruel; he'd played it that way in the past.

Instead, he came back to sit on the edge of the bed and she wriggled closer. "Use my name any time you need to," he said. Her frown questioned him. "It's pissed me off since I left yours, I never told you to…."

"Use your name any time I need to," she said, folding his pillow under her head.

"Aye."

She sighed. "Now he tells me."

"I'll be there if you need me."

"If I get in trouble?"

"You will get in trouble," he said. "Trouble follows you around."

"Maybe it's my line of work."

"Yeah, and getting involved with Helios Manzani…"

He clenched his teeth and inhaled like he was restraining himself.

"I can tell why you don't want to be with me."

"You were never with me," he said, sinking his fingers into her hair. "If you were with me, things would've worked out a helluva lot differently."

Before she could ask what that meant, he bowed to kiss her and disappeared into the closet.

She could follow him, question him, but what would that achieve? Their one-night deal was over.

***

"YOU COULD'VE CALLED when you got home last night, or this morning," Steeple said as they both sat at his desk. "I was worried."

"You know better than to worry about me."

"Tulip left you at the bar and didn't see you again."

"She wasn't worried. She texted me."

The buzz on Conn's stairs, that her brother would've heard, was Tulip's text. Her colleague called the evening a clusterfuck and said they'd talk the next day, that day.

"You were at Stag. Anything can happen there."

"Yeah," she said, wondering if he'd heard about the cops showing up. "But I've been there a hundred times and I'm still here."

She took her hands off the arms of her chair, showing him a hopeful smile. Was he buying it?

"They tell you anything about Ire?"

Tulip hurried in. "Sersha! You're okay?"

"Yeah, I'm okay," she said, turning back to

Steeple. "She didn't worry until you told her to worry."

"It was amazing!" Tulip exclaimed. "We have to go back tonight!"

"Wait, what?" she asked, her attention pinged between them. "No! We can't."

"They have to know we're serious. Right? We show up, we show them we're not afraid."

"Them who?"

"The McDades," Tulip said, dropping into the seat next to hers. "There's a reason we were singled out to be escorted off the property."

"A reason? What reason?"

"You tell me." Tulip slid deeper into her chair. "We were escorted inside, past the line of people, the VIP way. And that bartender knew your drink."

"I used to drink there a lot."

"Yeah, and then they kicked us out. Either you pissed someone off or gave them a secret signal."

"A secret…" Her focus went to Steeple. "This is not serious; she is not serious."

The door opened again. This time as she began to turn something beyond the bullpen stopped her attention dead. Damn Steeple for his half-glass walls. Lach…

"I said no interruptions," Steeple said to whoever had come in.

"This one you have to take. Sersha has to take."

Colleagues stood gawping at the spectacle that included her father and a phalanx of cops. Lach. She fixated on her sibling there between the bullpen and the reception desk.

Her sinuses tingled as a chill swept around her. They were too solemn. Too serious. Something had happened and there was only one person missing from that squad. The eldest McLeod. Her grandfather.

Rising, she didn't think about anyone but her

brother. What had happened? People talked, watched, whispered. Her father's voice did reach her ears before she got to them, but it was Lachlan she walked right up on.

"Heart attack?" she asked, resenting the heat building in her eyes.

"Why don't you come with us?" someone else said.

Lachlan's hand drifted down her cheek. "Murder."

A short, sharp inhale stalled her breathing. How had she known this wasn't…? The next time she sucked in air, a long yelp came with it. Her hand flew to her mouth, but Lachlan hooked the back of her head and pulled her against his chest, giving her cover for the tears and the terror.

Murder.

How could…? Her grandfather was an alderman, respected, protected… Though apparently not that well. Murder. She couldn't process. Her family dwindled; the three men were the only blood left in her life. Two. Now there were only two.

SEVEN

THE REST OF THE DAY was a blur. Words were said. Condolences given. Somehow, she got back to her apartment with Lachlan, her father, and members of his faceless entourage.

"When did you last speak with him?"

Her hands were wrapped around a hot cup. Coffee? Maybe. She couldn't focus.

"Leave her alone," her father sniped. "She's in shock."

"We need her statement."

"What happened?" Discarding the cup on the breakfast bar, she pushed through the two men crowding her to get to her brother at the dining table. "Lach, what happened to him?"

Other men, strangers, lay things out on the surface, papers and pictures.

"We don't know yet," Lach said. "That's what we're going to figure out."

Figure out. Right. There had to be an investigation. But that was her, wasn't she an investigator?

A knock on the door silenced conversation.

"No more reporters," her father said when a man she didn't know went to answer the door.

Her door. Wasn't this her apartment?

He got little chance to address whoever was there because the woman rushed in with full entitlement. Imogen. She rushed through everyone to grab Lachlan into her arms.

"Do you know how difficult it is to find you when you keep moving around?" Imogen asked, sadness in her censure. "Oh, why didn't you call me?"

"Where's Jagg?"

"Forget about that, would you?" she asked, grabbing the collar of his shirt. "What happened?"

"That's what I want to know," Sersha said.

It was funny her father said no reporters because that was exactly what Imogen was. Just like her. They worked at the same paper.

"We don't know," Lachlan said, addressing them both. "We don't know who's responsible."

"That wasn't the question," she said. "What happened?

"How was he killed?" Imogen asked. "When was he found? When was he last seen?"

Yes, yes, and yes, Imogen got it. Just because they couldn't say who didn't mean there was no information.

"We're still piecing that together," her father said.

"Why does that sound canned?" she asked and went back into her kitchen. "Like a line you'd feed a reporter?" Ignoring whatever was in the mug, she took a bottle of whiskey from the top shelf and poured herself a measure. Gulping it down, she ignored the sounds of disapproval coming from her father's direction. "Okay."

"Where are you going?" Lachlan asked when she

grabbed her purse from the counter.

"To do my job," she said and stopped in front of Imogen. "You in?"

"Oh, yeah, absolutely."

"Immie," Lachlan appealed to her, but she stayed at her flank. "You shouldn't—"

"We don't need official help," Imogen said. "We'll figure it out on our own." Leaving the apartment, they got out onto the street and into a cab. "What's your plan? Where do we start?"

"The same place I always start when I need information from the street," she said and gave the cab driver an address Imogen would recognize. Once they were on the way, she got her phone from her purse. Ninety-six missed calls. A hundred and forty-three text messages. She closed her eyes and centered her strength. "Can I talk to Jagg?"

"Yeah," Imogen said. "I can call him, or we can go over there."

"How are things between him and Strat?"

Imogen squirmed. "Better now Ford's on board."

"If this is uncomfortable—"

"No! You helped me out, I'm going to help you. What about Tulip? She could help too. Weren't you working with her? I heard you got kicked out of Stag."

"Yeah," she said, fixating on the windshield beyond the driver. "Last night."

Were any of those missed calls or texts from Connel? She couldn't see him now. Couldn't go to him. It was still too raw for them both. Maybe if they hadn't so recently fallen back into old habits, asking for his comfort would be a possibility.

They'd been so good, keeping their distance, since their breakup. Why had she gone back to Stag and undone all that progress? If she called now, he'd think she was a crazy stalker or a nutty bunny boiler. Even if he didn't, it wouldn't be fair to lean on him while their association was a secret.

Hadn't she been thinking the previous night how she didn't want to use him for his connections? This would be the antithesis of that. She'd figured out plenty before getting involved with Connel McDade. Her burden wasn't his. Her drive was overwhelming. She needed to see this through. That meant not dealing with the complication of her heartache and sex drive at the same time.

Her head must've returned to the fog zone because they were suddenly there, stopped, the driver asking for a fare. Imogen took care of it, and they went up into the building where she hoped to find some real support.

She knocked, but Imogen caught up and opened the door to go straight inside without waiting for an answer.

Strat was already partway down the hall. "Im—" he started, then noticed her.

"I know I'm supposed to call first."

"Fuck that, Scamp," he said, putting an arm around Imogen as he passed, hooking her into the embrace he snatched her into as well.

Being there, in their three-way hug, offered a chance to sag. To sink into the grief.

Before it could drag her under, she pulled away. "I'm okay."

"Have you called—" Strat paused to look at his daughter.

"Jagg?" Imogen asked, assuming her father's question was meant for her. "You can say his name. You've known it his whole life."

"You could call your brother."

"Yeah, I could," Imogen said, striding into the

living room, dumping her purse on the counter on the way past. "Or I could call my boyfriend."

"So that's it?" Strat asked.

"That's it what?" Imogen asked. "Are we together? Yes, we're together. Which should make you happier than if he'd just fucked me for fun."

Strat held up a hand. "Okay, we're not talking about this."

"That's your answer to everything," Imogen said, appealing to the heavens. "Why won't these idiots talk to each other?"

"What the fuck you want us to talk about?" Strat asked. "How he's a traitorous, lying sonofa—"

"What did he lie about? Huh?"

"Maybe that all those years I thought you were safe with him, he was looking for ways to bone my little girl?"

"No, Daddy," Imogen said, spitting the word. "He didn't know this existed any more than I did. We didn't plan it." But she showed her father a hand and turned her back. "We're going in circles. It's always the same thing." She whirled back around. "Why can't you accept he makes me happy? Why can't you appreciate he loves me?"

"The cop loved you too."

"And you loved to make your little jibes about him as well," Imogen said and thrust out an arm. "Today isn't about us and our messes."

Strat turned to her at the mouth of the hallway. "I'm sorry, Scamp."

"It's okay," she said. "Love is messy. Family, romantic, sexual, in whatever form, it's rarely straightforward."

"Yeah, but we shouldn't be talking about our crap."

"The only support I can give is of the corny

kind," she said. "Appreciate each other while you have the chance."

"She's right." Imogen sighed. "I've seen too much loss recently. People can lose those they love in a heartbeat. We shouldn't take it for granted."

"Do you know what happened?" Strat asked.

She smiled at Imogen. "Not yet. But I will and I'm hoping you can help."

"Anything."

She nodded. "Call the people you call." He nodded, and she switched to Imogen. "I doubt you have chips at the precinct these days."

"Not many," Imogen said. "But I can try…"

"I know a couple of people who'll talk to me too," she said. "If you don't mind asking Jagg to call anyone who might know what's going on out there."

"Yeah."

"You think this was related to… something else?"

"Maybe," she said, licking her dry lips. "What I do know is this wasn't random. My grandfather was protected whenever he was anywhere."

"News is reporting he was found at home," Imogen said. "Steeple's calling in favors. He texted me."

"Home is a good start," she said. "A limited number of people could get past security. Either it was someone he was happy to let in or we're talking a real professional job. Top of the stack level."

"Scamp, you're the closest to—"

"I know," she said. "The families in this city…"

They kept just looking at each other.

Imogen obviously sensed the unsaid and backed off. "I'll go into the bedroom and start making calls."

The moment they were alone, Strat closed in on her. "The Manzanis and McDades—"

"I can't even remember the last time I called

Evander," she said, retrieving her phone from her purse, which she put next to Imogen's. "But he'll meet me."

"We both know that," Strat said. "Sure it'll be uncomfortable, but you have to call Ire too. Ask for his help."

"I don't need to," she said, scrolling through the names in her contacts until she found Evander's.

"Why not? Whatever happened between you, he—"

"—is already on it," she said, raising her phone to her ear. "I don't need to ask for his help. Without talking to him, I know he's doing everything he can."

If he didn't want to help her, he wouldn't help her. Talking to him wouldn't change that. Knowing him like she did, it was obvious he'd be decisive. Going there, talking to him, it would be too easy to give into grief if he was there to hold her up. He'd offer oblivion. Safety. Sex. And she couldn't surrender to that until she had the truth.

EIGHT

"I CAN WAIT outside," Strat said when he turned off the engine after parking much later that night.

"Don't be so ridiculous," Imogen said. "Both of your children live here."

"Yeah?" Strat said. "So does the guy you're sleeping with."

"Uh huh, he owns the building. Where else should he sleep?"

"Anywhere but next to you."

Imogen twisted to look over the shoulder of her chair. "Jagg's inside, my brother too. We'll be fine."

"I'm not afraid of Evander Manzani," she said, freeing her seatbelt. "If you want to stay out here, Strat, stay out here… Though if whoever's out there is taking potshots at patriarchs…"

"Shit," Strat muttered, loosening his seatbelt.

"You'll come in for your sake, but not for mine?" Imogen wasn't amused. "Want me to ask Jagg to protect you?"

"No," Strat said and got out to yank open the

back door for her. "You might want to protect him from me."

"Again," Imogen said, righting the strap of her purse on her shoulder. "You already punched him in the face."

"No one said I was done."

Strat put an arm around her, pulling her close as they crossed the black tarmac that made up the backlot of Jagg's Autos. Jagg owned the place and lived there with his best friend James Stratford, also known as Ford, Strat's son, Imogen's brother.

Jagg and Imogen getting together had been a surprise to everyone. Lachlan took it hard too. He didn't say that, but she knew her brother. Love came in the strangest, sometimes most unexpected, packages. She didn't like to see her brother hurt but couldn't blame Imogen for falling in love with her brother's best friend.

Strat took it so bad because he raised Jagg like another son. She didn't know the latter's family situation, but Jagg lived with Strat growing up, so it couldn't have been great. That elder loved the boy as though he was his own.

Imogen opened the side door and led them into an office, behind the counter and through another door into a hallway.

She heard a TV before she saw what was in the next room. A living room, breakroom maybe, a large space with a kitchen in the corner, couches and armchairs in the opposite one, a pool table by the door.

The two seated guys stood up. Imogen went to Jagg and put an arm around him as he cupped her face. The other was Ford. She knew him. But even if she hadn't, the resemblance to Strat would've made the ID easy.

"I'm sorry about the alderman," Ford said. "About your loss."

"Thanks," she said, having lost count of how many times she'd heard those words that day.

"Strat," Jagg said, holding Imogen against his side.

"We're not okay," Strat was quite firm in that. "But you keep my little girl safe."

"Always."

"It's on you now, Dunn. All on you."

"I get it."

"He's always looked out for me," Imogen said and something of a saucy smile curved her lips. "Gone to all kinds of lengths to keep me, and my virtue, safe."

Jagg's hand dropped from her shoulder; it looked suspiciously like it landed on her ass. "You think that's helping?" he asked, crouching to kiss the top of her head.

"I think I want to go to a club this Friday."

"We've got our own private club."

The couple shared a smile that hid few secrets. Transfixed, it was something to see love right there, in front of her, playing out in real time. Imogen was a good person. She didn't love Lachlan like he wanted her to love him. Someday, her brother would find the love he deserved. There was more hope for him than her.

"This better be worth it," Strat said, directing her toward a stool at the kitchen island.

"It's a crapshoot with Evander," she mumbled, keeping their conversation discreet.

"The guy's not the most serious person in the world. You think he'll take this serious?"

"I think he'll like me asking for help."

"And if he brings up Ire?"

She swallowed, sliding onto the stool, dumping her purse. "Then we're all fucked, aren't we?"

"Do you know what happened?" Ford asked. "You got any details?"

Jagg and Imogen were already sharing the couch

under the TV, though they could've shared the smallest armchair for all the space they left between them.

"That's what we're trying to find out," Strat said to his son, probably blocking out the couple behind him. "We know his housekeeper found him midday."

"Why so late?" Ford asked, sitting in the armchair perpendicular to Jagg and Imogen. "When was he last seen?"

"I know he talked to my brother late last night," she said. "I don't know who else might have seen him."

Ford leaned forward, resting his elbows on his knees. "That's usually the first thing the police zero in on."

"Yeah," she said, leaning back to put an arm around Strat's waist.

He rested his arm over her shoulders. It was nice to have someone to lean on. A strong support who didn't doubt or deny her.

"We're not doing this by the book," Strat said.

Ford scoffed out a laugh. "Your dad's Superintendent, he doesn't have answers?"

"Maybe he does, but he won't give them to me."

"And your brother—"

"I won't put him in that position," she said, having thought about calling Lachlan on and off since they'd left her place. "Someone knows something."

"They say the devil's in the details," Jagg said. "The more you know about what was going on in his life—"

"This came from the top. It didn't happen on the street. He didn't stop a mugging or step out in front of a car." She braced for Imogen's reaction, but her friend offered an encouraging smile. Friend? Were they friends? "It happened in his home. He has an alarm. A security man who stays in the building all night. But he wasn't found until lunchtime. That means no one heard anything. Nothing was off." She glanced up at Strat. "There's a lot of push and pull in the council these days."

"He was suspicious."

"He was," she said.

Evander wanted rid of his father. And his father wanted rid of her. Or he had. Don Silvio Manzani had ordered the attack on her. Appealing to the Manzanis for information was dangerous. Evander was working with Connel in the shadows, feeding him information. While Manzani Senior was trying to blow up the Harvest deal that would see McDade territory expand right on Manzani's border.

No one had paid off her grandfather. At least, Connel hadn't… not the last time they'd talked about it anyway. Maybe things had changed since. Except her grandfather had been suspicious and asking questions.

Had asking those questions got him killed?

For one glimmer of a second, she'd speculated her father may have been aware of the planned attack on her. But she'd shrugged that off, incapable of believing a man so duty bound would do something so heinous.

But others were on the take. Others she'd seen with Connel. Divides were prominent, lines drawn. For those in on it, this was a tale of two sides. Manzani and McDade. For those not in on it, for the decent, honest people unwilling to take a bribe, there were two sides too. Right and wrong. Her grandfather was an advocate for the first. Every time. Maybe getting too close, passing judgment, finally caused his demise.

An abrupt buzzer startled her.

Ford got to his feet. "I'll get him."

"You should wait next door," Jagg said, squeezing Imogen as he kissed her head.

"Why?" she asked, getting up as Jagg did. "No! I thought this was my home."

"It is your home, Genny. Which is why I want

you safe here."

"He's right," Strat said, though it sounded like it pained him. "Evander Manzani is an asshole."

"I've met him before, Dad," Imogen sneered.

Fury lit Strat as his attention flew to Jagg. "What the fuck are you doing letting her around pissheads like that fucker?"

"I make my own choices," Imogen said. "I don't see either of you trying to chase Sersha out of here."

"He's obsessed with her," Jagg and Strat said in unison.

"Shouldn't that be more reason to—"

The door opened and the debate ceased. Evander came strolling in, smiling, absorbing the scene.

Ford appeared behind him and closed the door. "He's got three guys in the hall."

"Which means nothing to Dunn," Evander said, coming her way. "He's faced rougher odds." He picked up her hand to kiss her knuckles. "I'm sorry for your loss, Princess."

Her instinct was always to pull away from Evander when he made physical contact. This time, she had to resist the urge. If she needed his help, she had to tolerate his advances… to a point.

"I want to know who did it," she said, plain as day, just like that.

Beating around the bush got no one anywhere fast.

As Evander straightened, he checked every other face in the room. "And you came to me," he said. "I'm honored."

"I'm exploring a lot of avenues. You're one of them."

"And if I come up with the goods?"

"You don't seem shocked," Imogen said. "That he's dead or that Sersha's asking."

"Sersha and me go way back," he said, turning to peruse Imogen's figure. "Every time you're stunning."

"Focus, Evander," Sersha snapped, trying to save Imogen from the leering she knew only too well. "What do you know?"

"You've got nothing to be jealous about," Evander said, coming in closer, putting himself between her and Strat. "You know I'm all yours. Just say the word."

"What do you know, Evander?"

He inhaled. "Not much. But I can find out… After we talk." That piqued her interest, especially when she read the gravity in his. "Alone. Outside."

"Not outside," Strat said. "In here. We'll give you the room."

Outside could lead to kidnap and torture and God knew what. Did she think Evander would do that to her? No. But she would be the first to admit she didn't always make the best choices.

None of the others argued; they filtered out while Strat held the door for them. They made eye contact. He'd be right outside. Strat wouldn't let anything happen to her. He cared about her… And knew more about her relationship with Connel than anyone else.

"What do you want, Evander?" she asked.

"I'd think that was obvious by now," he said, his hands sliding onto her hips. "You."

NINE

"NO," she said, silencing the voice in her head that screamed déjà vu. "Forget it."

"Don't blow me off," he said, putting a hand on the counter to block her escape route. "Think about this. Your grandfather's killer. I can deliver him to you."

"If you know who it is and are withholding, why would I want to be with a man who'd manipulate me like that?"

"I don't know now, but I will," he said, leaning in. "For you, Princess."

"We've known each other a long time," she said, appealing to his humanity. Now was the time to prove he had some. "There's no reason we can't be friends. Why does it always have to be about sex with you?"

Alone with him, with so many other things hanging in the balance, she couldn't reject him outright. It had always been like that. Balancing his ego with her own revulsion. Evander was attractive, in his own way. Yet he loomed with expectation, as though their being intimate was a foregone conclusion, and it turned her off completely.

One look from Connel filled her with need and contentment. In contrast, just the thought of being intimate with Evander was a nauseating nightmare. In a lot of circles, the two men would be lumped in together like they were the same. They never would be to her. One was defiantly essential to her taking every breath; though he shouldn't be, not with them apart. The other could walk off the end of the earth and she wouldn't care unless someone told her to fake it.

"He couldn't please you…" Evander said, obviously thinking of the man in her mind. "I won't make that mistake…" He stroked her hair. "We're destined to be together. On the inside, with me, we can take this city. The whole city."

"I just lost a man I was close to, I can't think about this now."

Was he playing on her assumed vulnerability? Just when he couldn't get any lower, he dug deeper into depravity.

"I understand. I just need to hear you say what it will mean to you if I take care of this."

"The police are working on the case. Me and my colleagues… I want as many people on this as possible to get to the truth. Keeping up the pressure on the perp from every angle helps flush him out. I'm asking for your help, for your friendship. If you don't want to be a part of this, I understand. I won't be extorted."

His desire only brightened. "Nothing gets to you," he murmured. "You won't give in… What did he have on you? How did he control you?"

"He didn't," she said, showing her defiance. "Why do you think I walked away from him?"

"You play with men like us, you have no idea what we're capable of."

She'd been in the room when Connel killed the

man who hurt her. He had no limits when it came to her safety.

"I'm not playing. I am looking for whoever hurt my grandfather."

"We'll find him and then things will change."

"No—"

"They will," he said, straightening. "'Cause I'm done waiting."

He turned to stalk out and she exhaled. Done waiting? That problem would have to take a ticket. Evander was done waiting. Did that mean more trouble on the horizon?

Strat came back in with the others close behind as her phone rang. Taking it from its slot inside her purse, she braced when she read her brother's name.

She answered. "Lach?"

"Where are you?"

"Why?"

"I need you to come home."

"It's crowded, there's too many people—"

"There are reporters crowded outside Dad's. We can't work there."

"And there's something wrong with the precinct?"

"We're not supposed to be part of the official investigation," Lachlan said. "Working here gives us the illusion of separation."

"Illusion is right." Because cops and officials would tell her father, the superintendent, anything. "I can't be talked down to right now." If anyone tried it, she wouldn't be responsible for her actions. "It's best if I—"

"Dad's gone. He's staying in a hotel tonight. I think he needed some time on his own." She could understand that. "Come home and we'll talk this out. We should be doing this together. You have every right to know everything I do."

Her brother she trusted. She couldn't pass up his offer. "I'm on my way."

TEN

WARY AS SHE ENTERED her apartment, she didn't want to think her brother would set her up, but an ambush wouldn't be beyond her father.

Lachlan was seated at the dining table that was covered with papers.

"You can breathe out," he said. "It's just me."

"Where is everyone else?"

"Home. Gone. We decided to pick it up again tomorrow… Autopsy might be done then."

"Grandpapa gets bumped to the top of the pile?" she said, putting her things on the counter before going to the fridge.

One good thing about her brother living with her, there was always beer in the fridge. She opened two and took one to him.

"When an alderman is murdered, we have to assume it's an attack on the city. So, yeah, he gets bumped up the list. Could still take a couple of days… We'll wait longer for toxicology and DNA results."

Pulling another chair from the table, she sat

facing him. "Grandpapa's dead." Her brother's brows rose as he gently nodded. "Murdered. How?"

"We're waiting for the Med—"

"Goddamnit, Lach, don't give me the—"

"If you'll let me finish," he said, calm though he raised his voice. She pursed her lips and gestured for him to continue. "We won't know everything until the Medical Examiner's report is complete. What we do know? From lividity and rigor, they're putting the time of death between two and three a.m." That was late for her grandfather to be working. Though he was a workaholic, so it wasn't unheard of. "There was no sign of a disturbance in the house. No broken windows, no forced entry. Henry went up to his suite around nine. Made some calls. Did some paperwork. There's evidence he wasn't finished."

"If it was such a peaceful scene, why do you think it's murder?"

"There's blood. He was shot."

"Wasn't security at the house?"

"In the basement," he said. "No one reports hearing a gunshot."

"They used a silencer? Then it has to be murder."

Suicide didn't even register as a possibility. Her grandfather wasn't built that way. Many people might say the same about folks they knew, but Grandpapa certainly wouldn't have left work unfinished before ending himself. An odd, yet significant, factor.

Lachlan's shoulders dropped. "We can't draw too many conclusions while they're still processing the evidence."

"Was anything missing?" she asked. "Any witnesses on the street?"

Her grandfather lived in a townhouse in a quiet neighborhood. People wouldn't necessarily be wandering by, but if strangers were around, they might be noticed. Then again, it was a mature and employed cohort of neighbors. At such an early hour, most, if not all, would be sleeping.

"They're still gathering statements."

"At this time?"

"Not tonight," he said. "Most people were out at work when he was found. We're still tracking neighbors down—they're still tracking neighbors down."

"What was he wearing?" she asked, lowering Lachlan's brow again. "Did it look like he was ready for bed?"

"He was in his pajamas."

"Suggests he wasn't expecting to receive anyone."

"Yet someone was there."

"Maybe someone with a key or lockpicking skills." Which probably covered half the city. "Can't you head this?" she asked, sliding to the edge of her chair to reach for his hand. "Is there no way? There's no one I trust more than you to get this right."

"I'm too close to it. I couldn't be objective. My leading the investigation could jeopardize any prosecution."

She sighed. "You like to think you can do anything for the people you love. Then when they need us most..."

"We can still help. Do some legwork." He paused. "We'll have to think about arrangements too."

"Arrangements for—shit..." Letting go of his hand, she sank back in her chair, her fingers going through her hair. "A funeral."

"The body won't be released for a few weeks... What do you think about a memorial service next week?"

"And then do something quiet for the cremation later?" He shrugged. "What does Dad say?"

"We haven't talked about it yet. There's a lot of

politicking. Who would he endorse for Henry's seat?"

"Oh, God…" Revulsion contorted her expression. "Seriously? Already?"

"The city goes on, right?"

"But so soon? How can Dad be thinking about that?"

"Switching into work mode is good cover," he said. "He doesn't have to grieve if he stays busy."

"That what you're doing?"

"I don't know," he said. "You're doing a good job of it yourself."

Okay, so none of them were the best at confronting and dealing with their feelings.

"A memorial service is a good idea." And there she was, ignoring her feelings again. "Let them have their circus so we can lay him to rest in private when the time is right."

"I'll talk to Dad about it tomorrow."

"He won't care," she said. "He will, but I'll handle it. We just have to tell him when to show up."

"You're probably right."

"You can handle your investigation while I handle the service, but I have people on it too. I'm not giving up on this."

"I wouldn't either. Remember this is a marathon, we won't get instant answers."

"Instant means less than accurate. We need to get this right."

"We will. We trained for this. We've got it. We won't let Henry down."

ELEVEN

THE NEXT FOUR DAYS were beyond busy. The ME's report was delayed, and her father had to release a statement to the press asking them to back off. During that, for the first time ever, his façade of professionalism slipped just a fraction when the reporters bombarded him with questions. She'd almost thought she or Lachlan would have to step in, but he pulled it back. Superintendent McLeod could handle anything, even in the face of losing his father.

In the days, and into the nights, people came and went from her apartment. Blinds were opened, closed, food was delivered, coffee was drunk, and probably the same amount of liquor. One hour ran into the next, over and over, time did its thing.

What was she doing?

Activity kept her mind occupied, so she didn't have to think too deeply about her own feelings. Memorial service details were easier to organize than accepting what they'd lost. Who they'd lost.

As usual that night, the bustle served as a

distraction. When her front door opened, she expected it would be another of her father's underlings.

Instead, Strat took one step in and stopped. Her breathing paused as everything in her zeroed in on him. While she'd been planning the memorial at her apartment, Strat was her eyes and ears on the street.

Why was he there? What had he discovered?

Before her brother or father could ask questions, she erased the space between her and her friend.

"What? What is it?"

"Come on."

Swooping an arm around her, Strat scooped her out of that apartment and down the hallway.

"Where are we going?" she asked.

Somewhere he didn't want her father and brother to know about? They descended the stairs, her none the wiser either. Rain spattered, just a lazy shower barely staining the streets as he rushed her across the sidewalk into the passenger side of his car.

She put on her seatbelt. "Are we running away together?" she asked when he got in.

Rather than start the engine, he adjusted his position until he faced her. "How you doing, kid?"

"Great." Confused. Why were they just sitting there? "Fine."

"I don't think so."

Her eyes widened. "You don't think so?"

She laughed, but he wasn't amused at all. Is that what it was? An intervention?

"You're letting all this shit pile on, Scamp. No one can handle the pressure forever."

"What pressure? There's no pressure. Steeple isn't asking for secrets or expecting me to work. He's called every day, just checking in, not to bully me."

"I'd like to see the guy who'd try that these days." Strat held a stern air that wasn't only concern. "You'll go off the rails, Scamp." This time, instead of a straight laugh, she curled her lips around her teeth trying to hold it back. "I don't wanna see that."

Leaning over, she patted his hand. "Don't worry, old man. I'll try not to get any on you."

"The fact you're making this a joke proves my point. Your granddaddy was murdered four nights ago."

"I am aware, thanks." Folding her arms, this was getting less entertaining by the second. "You think I didn't notice the crime scene photos and witness reports swirling around, under the radar, in my own apartment?" A moment, tense and uncertain, clouded the air for a score of seconds. "What is going on, Strat?"

"It started with him," he said. "Since him you're… You won't even talk about him."

"Why should I?" The last thing she'd do was insult Strat's intelligence by playing dumb. "What is there to talk about? It's done. Over."

"Is it? 'Bout two months ago you were laid up in a hospital bed. You remember that? The pain, your arm, the bruises have hardly fucking faded—"

"I don't have time for this."

When she reached for the door handle, the locks snapped shut.

"You're gonna make time."

Damn the fucking asshole. Strat put up with everything from her, like she would for him. He was her rock, the person she could always rely on. At least, he used to be. That fondness was dwindling by the second.

"Strat—"

"You got outta the hospital and took up with one of the most dangerous men in the city. I don't know what happened there. It's not my business, cool. But something went down between the two of you. It happened. Something happened."

Like murder? Yeah, Conn had killed for her, with

her. That connection, the memory of it…

Pushing her shoulders back, she took a deep breath. "Don't ask me—"

"I'm not asking. This is a fucking list." He curled a forefinger around his thumb and continued counting as he moved down his fingers. "The attack outside Stag, you and Ire's shit, Helios, Silvio, Vex—"

"Evander has always been a part of my life." Unfortunately. "My adult life."

"The Carlyle fire, Marseille—"

"I'm dealing with that."

"That's my fucking point," he said. "You've ran around these last few months taking shit from every fucking angle. You jumped on to my little girl's cause and took all the heat yourself. Now your grandaddy's lost and you're not talking to anyone, not handling it, you're bottling it up, shutting down."

"No, I am staying busy. Lach and I talked about it. I'll deal with the memorial, the service—"

"You don't deal with your father cutting you out, condescending you, dismissing you."

"What do you expect me to do? Go up there and confront him? Uh huh, yeah, it's the perfect time for that."

"It's a parent's job to put their child first."

"He lost his father."

"You lost your grandfather. Your brother lost him. Instead of coming together as a family, you're getting bogged down in the legal shit and filling your apartment with grunts so no one can talk about anything."

"Believe me, it's for the better."

"You talk to anyone after the attack? A therapist or—"

"I don't need a therapist."

"I've seen it happen. The best of people, the

strongest of people, they take on too much and it swallows them whole. You know there's nothing you could fucking say to me that would change what I feel about you."

"You expect me to cry on your shoulder? That's such a guy thing, to think a woman can't keep it together."

"You are keeping it together. And if you had something for you in this. If you had a touchstone, a support structure, I wouldn't worry so much. You're not getting it from your dad and the cop is running around trying to save the world. No one is taking care of you."

Her focus drifted to the raindrops running together on the windshield, lit by the streetlight beyond.

No one was taking care of her.

Where was she always safe?

Connel had said he'd take care of her. He had taken care of her. No man had ever taken better care of her and then snap, she was alone again. In him, the meaning of support changed hue. If he was there, with her, at her side, nothing would be missed, no part of her would be left hollow.

Every day she got up pushing the grief to the back of her mind, to the back of her heart. Losing her granddaddy was something she'd have to learn to live with, nothing would change it.

In contrast, the grief of losing Connel…? How could it be that they were alive in the same city and yet she kept waking up lonely?

"I don't know any other way to be," she whispered. "I have to keep going. What's the alternative?"

She didn't expect an answer or even look right at him. When the car started moving, she couldn't bring herself to care about their destination. Strat had been working overtime and they still needed answers.

Maybe he had a source who wanted to see the family in order to cooperate. That was as much as she could come up with. Either that or he was driving her to a sanitorium. Right then, that sounded like a tropical vacation.

"Scamp. Scamp!"

"Mm?" she asked, snapping out of her funk. In the last four nights, she'd only caught glimpses of sleep; fading from reality was becoming a regular occurrence. "Sorry, my head is…" She swallowed. "I get why you're worried about me. Thank you."

"You say you need me with you."

"I do."

"I watch your back. I'll always watch your back. Whether you like it or not."

Gratitude didn't cover it. She owed so much to Strat. If it wasn't for him, she'd be overwhelmed and probably lost in a hole somewhere.

"Where are we going?"

His visit to her apartment, after dark, was unexpected. How long had they been driving?

"Somewhere safe… Safe for you, maybe not for others," Strat said. "Your place is a zoo; you need shit to stop for a minute."

And her mind went on safari again. "Is cake a normal thing for a memorial?" she asked, frowning. "The caterer wanted to know if we needed a cake. It's not a wedding, it's a wake, why—somewhere safe? Do you have a new source? Someone who knows something about the murder?"

"No."

"I thought you made a breakthrough, that someone or something—take me home, Strat. I don't want to play tonight. I'm not in the mood for games."

"Which is why I checked," Strat said. "He's in New York."

"Who's in New York?" When the car came to a stop, for the first time, she observed their environment. Dread froze in her heated gut. Stag's back lot. Darkness. The exclusive rear entrance used only by those with blood thick allegiance. Stag. "No."

"You've been walking around blind for days," Strat said, putting the car in park to turn to her. "He's in New York. Niall's in New York. As far as everyone is concerned, this never happened."

TWELVE

HER CAR DOOR opened and… Daly. Her head of security, when she'd been a McDade.

"Bluebell."

"I can't be here," she said. Strat freed her seatbelt. With a sure grip on her arm, Daly helped her out of the vehicle. "I didn't want—if he knew what—"

"You need this," Strat said, coming around the car. "Stag's your security. Isn't that what you said at the loft? You feel safer here than anywhere else."

"This is out of bounds. When he finds out—"

"He won't," Daly said, guiding her toward the building. "It's not a lie if we just don't mention it." They stopped by the slightly ajar door. "Whatever you need, you get. He's made that clear."

"We're not together," she confessed. "I shouldn't invade his private space."

"It's as much his as yours," Daly said, shoving open the door to pull her inside.

The dark corridor ran along next to the club. Bass shook the walls; music covered their footsteps as they descended a level. At the end, they went up again, from the basement and boom into the club. The humid throb of music and dancing instantly fogged her skin.

When they reached the spiral staircase, Daly boosted her onto the first step.

Over her shoulder, her eyes met Strat's. "Take as long as you need."

The ascent was daunting and not because she feared what was up there. What if she didn't want to leave? What if he came back unexpectedly and…?

The biggest secret? The guilty truth? Her Stag security was him. Because of him. Before they'd met, his home gave her cover. After the cocoon closed around them, nothing could touch her. Nothing but him.

Crossing the balcony to the threshold of his space, freedom assaulted her the moment she went inside.

His name almost came to her lips. Closing her eyes, she breathed. Her identity there, what she could be, what she once had been…

"This is my kingdom," she whispered.

It wasn't true, not anymore, but she'd embodied it once.

Stepping out of her shoes, she shed her clothes on the walk to his bedroom. Just as she had before, for him, when they were alone.

This was hers.

Maybe that was the root of clenched hope and clarity in her gut. Her father, her brother, they had no idea of her connection to Stag. From the foundations to the rafters, her Stag life was secret. The only person who'd shared it all with her was him.

She crawled onto the bed whispering his name. "Conn…"

Though detergent scented the sheets, there was enough of him in the air that she could close her eyes and make believe he was with her.

"How do I do it?"

Swallowing bitter grief from her parched throat, she pulled back the covers to stretch out, extending her arms until they disappeared beneath the pillows. How many times had they lay there, together, talking, learning each other? Strat was right. An anchor gave her the safety to face her truth. Everything was spiraling.

Since him? Yes, but not for the reason Strat thought. Her grip wasn't slipping because Conn corrupted her. His acceptance had ignited her confidence, giving her silent permission to push boundaries and be more her than at any time in the past.

Connel McDade provided cover and acceptance. He'd never asked her for anything, nothing personal, and had no expectations of her. Not because he didn't think she was capable, but because anything went in his house. Rules didn't exist there.

Resisting the urge to close her eyes and sleep, she slunk out of bed to go into the closet. She snagged his shirt and buttoned it over her chest. Something, somewhere, in some alternate version of reality, they were together. Completely. Open. Public. Allowed.

There would never be acceptance. Her life and his were incompatible. Sense didn't get it. Her body and soul wanted to exist with him.

Going to the bar, she poured two fingers of whiskey, downed them, then poured another two.

What she wouldn't give… Bottle and glass in hand, her wander back to the bedroom came with a weight of admission. Connel McDade changed the course of her life. Had she known one person could be so completely…

Emptying the glass into her throat, she let it drop from her fingers, ignoring the sound of glass splintering on the floor.

Inside, she was afraid. Why? How? What did life want from her? Surrender?

Light glimpsed on the mirror in the bathroom, reflecting off the bottle from somewhere else. Stopping there, the full-length reflection gave her a target. Her mind was lost. Her heart hurt. Or did it? Was it pumping for life or just out of routine?

And that's what it was. Since him. Since losing him, she'd pursued it, pursued emotion, feeling, sensation.

Nothing.

That's what she felt.

Absolutely nothing.

The reflection disgusted her; she disgusted her. Soundbites told people to love themselves, to accept themselves as a complete person. That just wasn't possible, not for her. Raising the bottle to her lips, she watched herself gulp the intoxicating liquid.

What was at the bottom of that bottle? Was it happiness? It couldn't be. There was no happiness without him. Chasing a high that would never come, that's what she'd been doing. Imogen's cause, the fire, all she craved was feeling.

God, she repulsed herself. Who would want to be with her? Connel McDade was more of a man than so many others she'd met, so what? He was the one people feared and reviled. Fuck, she wanted him.

Her lips pressed closer as her nose tingled. No, she wouldn't cry for him. Connel McDade expected more of his woman. Closing her eyes, her head went back. She wasn't his and never would be. Why couldn't she let go?

How could she process losing her grandfather when the real crime happened right there? Not in that room. That wasn't where they'd said goodbye. Grief hung heavy, pulling at her, clawing, tearing at every ounce of consciousness.

If she concentrated hard, she could imagine his lips on hers. Could imagine how it was in his shower when he washed her hair and told her he'd take care of her. Without him, life was harder. She was harder.

What do I have left to lose? Those were the words she'd said to Strat not so long ago. *To fight for your life, you first have to value it.*

Life without Conn was pointless. What did she live for? People expected her to grieve and go on living? That wasn't how it worked in her heart. Shit, why couldn't she pull it together and just get over it?

Because he'd shown her the truth of freedom and it looked nothing like her life without him.

As her chin descended, her eyes opened. Anger. Frustration. Rage. A torrent of negativity swelled within her. Gritting her teeth, her lips curled. Why would he want to be with her?

Connel McDade deserved better.

Her grandfather deserved better.

All of them did.

Her father wasn't wrong to be disappointed. She disappointed herself.

Sucking air through her nose, she filled her lungs and held her breath as long as she could. It came out on a long scream that tore her throat. God, she wanted to hurt. Wanted to burst. Wanted to rip the life from her own skin.

The bottle flew from her hand, shattering the offending mirror in an explosion of liquid and light. She was losing it. Going crazy. Unable to keep a lid on the nothingness inside her hollow heart.

Was she even alive? Did the world exist? This could be a nightmare, her nightmare. Maybe she'd never wake up.

Screaming again, she whirled around to the

closet, pulling her things from their hangers, opening drawers to yank out what was inside. The world was a mess. Her sense of self, her need, nothing made sense, and she couldn't fight her way out of it.

Pain wasn't salved with a potion. She didn't feel; she couldn't live. Her aching throat had another scream in it, so loud and harsh that it disappeared into the abyss of silence.

Thank God for the club below.

Falling to her knees on the mess, she drove her fingers into her hair, pulling hard, too hard maybe, except no ache registered.

She was a mess.

Life was out of control.

Loss was the only thing left. The only out. How long could she keep fighting alone?

THIRTEEN

SHE MADE A MESS. That was what she told Daly on her departure. She'd slept some in the closet and was just too tired to even try to clean up. Daly said they'd take care of it. And there she went, making life more difficult for everyone as usual.

In her kitchen the next night, she drank coffee, giving liquor a wide berth. People sat around the dining table. Her brother and father were discussing something about the geography of the city.

The witness statement on the counter caught her eye.

David Sneddon. The security guy on duty the night her grandfather died. Nothing out of the ordinary. Yeah, she'd read that part before, but two words piqued her interest. Access log. Hmm, she hadn't seen that. Why was Sneddon referencing it?

Access logs showed her grandfather, their shift change, who else was on it? Her grandfather wouldn't write down the time he entered his own home in any kind of logbook. Shit. Was it digitized?

"You want pizza?"

Lachlan was putting on his jacket, coming closer.

"Pizza? No," she said, screwing up her face. "It's eleven at night."

"And no one's eaten since lunchtime. Given you hardly eat lunch, I'll guess it's been longer for you."

"I live on coffee," she said, but poured the rest down the sink. "I'm going to try to sleep."

"That's a good idea. I'll tell everyone to keep it down."

"You don't have to go out for pizza, just FYI. They have these things called deliveries."

Her brother smirked. "Hilarious, little sister. I need to get out into the air." They could all do with a little space and needed to grab the chance when they could. He kissed her cheek. "Try to sleep."

He departed and she exhaled on her way to the bedroom. Sleep might be a pipedream; the place was still bustling when she lay down in bed. She put her phone on the nightstand and sought the end of the charger to juice it up.

A few minutes. She'd close her eyes for a few minutes and try to clear her head. It was best to avoid her father as much as possible, especially without Lach around to referee. Her father didn't want her help. Why should he? Police Superintendent McLeod already knew everything… except what really mattered.

When her eyes opened, it was dark. Quiet. Unsettling. Something didn't feel right. She turned over and stared into nothing for a few seconds before launching herself toward the nightstand to grab her phone. The charging cable fell to the floor. Shit. That wasn't good. Usually, she had to pull it out.

When she tried to wake the device, all she got was a black screen in return. Damn. It was dead.

She stretched as she got up. Even that didn't

shake the tension from her muscles.

People had places to be, things to do, so the silence in her living room was fine. Normal. Right? Yeah, her place had somehow become a hub for the unofficial investigation, but people went home eventually. It was night. Time for bed.

Except when she tiptoed over to the couch, it was still a couch. Unoccupied. Not pulled out.

Where was Lachlan?

She got the remote from the end table and turned on the news channel to look for the time. Two sixteen in the morning. Damn—

"…arrest made in connection with the alderman's murder." The TV was talking and flashed up a picture of her grandfather. "In this troubled metropolis, it's likely no surprise that the perpetrator was one of the city's most notorious crime bosses, Ire McDade."

When his picture came on the screen, she stopped listening. Oh, shit. She couldn't even fathom it. Couldn't think… Shit. Shit. Shit. Where was Lachlan? It was late, he should be home. And she couldn't call him from her dead phone.

"Damnit," she said, rushing into the room to grab her shoes.

***

"NO, I NEED to speak to the detective in charge now," Sersha argued with the precinct desk clerk.

Her brother and father could sail right by. She wasn't so lucky.

"He's in the middle of interrogating a suspect."

"I know and I have information pertinent to his case." The guy wasn't moving fast enough for her liking. "Do you know who I am? Is my dad here?"

That broke through and the guy picked up the phone on a grumble. "Hey," he said to whoever was at the other end. "McLeod's sister is here."

Not the superintendent's daughter or the victim's granddaughter. No, she was Lachlan's sister. And just like that, all was forgiven. She smiled at the clerk, apparently unnerving him.

In under thirty seconds, a door at the other end of the room buzzed and popped open. The moment she saw Lachlan, she hurried to him.

"Sersh," Lachlan said. "What's going on? Are you okay?"

"I need to talk to the detective in charge."

"He's in—"

"The middle of an interrogation, I know," she said, restraining her groan. "This is important."

He put an arm around her to draw her into a corridor with doors along it. Interrogation rooms? Maybe. Interview rooms, that could be a better term. What was PC these days? Rooms that had seen the worst of the worst no doubt.

Her brother took her into one at the end with a couch and a fake plant. Maybe it was meant for victim interviews or a relative's room where people's worlds were shattered by irrevocable news.

"Wait here," Lachlan said and paused by the door. "You need anything?"

She shook her head. "No, I'm good."

Her brother left and the door clicked shut. Probably locked.

Ire McDade.

Even the news hadn't used his real name. Did that piss him off? She'd have to ask, if he ever talked to her again.

Why would he after this? Arrested for her grandfather's murder? Connel? It would be laughable if it wasn't so tragic.

The pale pink walls and functional sectional were the closest to homely she'd seen in a precinct. And she'd been in a lot of precincts through the years.

Breakrooms had vending machines and tables, in addition to practical furniture. And they didn't usually come with fake greenery either. It had to be for some purpose other than the cops just hanging out.

The door opened and she spun around as Lachlan and two other guys entered.

"This better be good," the guy in the middle said.

"Thurrock," Lachlan said, pointing to the guy furthest away, then gesturing at the one between them. "Wanstead."

"You're holding Ire McDade?" No one responded. "Have you charged him?"

"We're about to."

"On what evidence?"

"Listen, honey…" Wanstead started, and her brother flinched when her head ticked to the side. "You run around playing cop as much as you like, but in here, this is the big boy's table. You don't have a damn clue what McDade is capable of." How people loved to tell her that. "We know our job. Know guys like this. And he's guilty."

"No, he's not," she said, folding her arms.

"You don't—"

"Hear her out," Lachlan said. "She's worked with this guy. If we can get insight into his character—"

"She doesn't know this guy," Wanstead sneered. "What? Because she banged out a few words on the Manzanis, she's some kind of expert? Ire's the one for this. I know it."

"He's not," she said, maintaining her calm.

"And how do you figure—"

"Because he wasn't anywhere near my

grandfather at the time he died."

"Oh, yeah? Think you've got it all figured out. No way you can know—"

"I'm his alibi." The men silenced to finally pay attention. "Connel didn't kill my grandfather because I was with him Monday night. All Monday night."

Lachlan was processing, she could tell he was stunned, but she kept her focus on Wanstead in the middle. She couldn't apologize and grovel. This moment had to be about strength.

"He said he was in bed alone."

"He lied," she said. "I was in that bed with him."

FOURTEEN

IF THERE HAD BEEN any doubt before, she'd just eliminated it. No, she wasn't watching him work or beat on people. She'd been in the bed he'd claimed to occupy alone.

"Why would he lie?" Thurrock asked. "Why not just tell us that?"

"Because no one was supposed to know about us. It's supposed to be a secret. We were a secret." She anticipated his next question. "Because I'm the superintendent's daughter."

"Then why tell us now?" Thurrock asked.

"I don't want an innocent man punished for this crime. I want to get the true perpetrator."

"And if he's your secret boyfriend, how do we know you're telling us the truth?"

Now her attention swung to her frowning brother. "Because I was the phantom behind the curtain. That buzz you heard was my phone. It was Tulip saying we'd talk the next day."

"A text," Lachlan murmured.

"And because I heard you answer the call to Henry while you were there." Something they hadn't discussed. "And because…" she took the shoe from the top of her purse and tossed it to Lachlan, "I'm missing one of my diamonds." His gaze shot to her, full of shock and realization. She winced. "I'm sorry. I am."

"You heard our conversation?"

"Yes. I heard you ask to look around while he said it was okay providing you had a warrant. Heard you ask if he cared about our family when he watched me be attacked for his."

"Shit," Lachlan exhaled. "She's telling the truth."

"We can only accept her version if he corroborates it."

"Where is he?" she asked. "I'll talk to him."

Thurrock scoffed. "No can do. We can't trust you won't give contraband or a signal."

"I'm the superintendent's daughter."

"And sleeping with one of the most dangerous men in the city, apparently," Wanstead said. "Give us a minute."

He and Thurrock went out. Another click and she was trapped with her brother.

"I can't believe this," Lachlan said. "How long?"

"It started pretty much when we met," she said. Honesty was the best course. "But we ended it. Remember you showed up at mine and asked who broke my heart? It was him. Well, it was mutual, I guess, but my heart was broken for him."

"I can't believe this," he said again, running his fingers into his hair before leaping closer. "Do you know how dangerous this guy is?"

"I know how dangerous he is."

"You could've been hurt! How can you say you know—"

"He's not dangerous to me. He'd never hurt me."

"Ire used you. Manipulated you. Shit, Sersh, I don't know where to start. I thought you got it. Manzani was into you and you steered clear, you were so smart with him."

"They're not the same," she said, tightening her hold on her purse, grasping the anchor in that turbulent moment. "I didn't want to let you down." A tear slipped from her eye. "I knew if you ever found out… It doesn't make sense, I'm not sure I can make sense of it myself."

Thurrock came back in. "We'll take another swing," he said, side nodding at Lachlan, who went toward him.

She followed, but both men stopped. Lachlan was the only one she saw.

"I have every right to know everything you do."

Those were his words to her.

"I didn't know this."

"As soon as it was relevant you did," she said. "Did I hesitate?"

His nostrils flared as he inhaled, but he relented. "Come on."

Wanstead was in the hall outside a room. She and Lachlan passed to go to the next door. They went into a dark room filled with people. More people than needed to be there she'd bet. At least her father wasn't there.

Light shone from the other side of the tinted window that took up a large portion of one wall. Beyond it, seated at a table, cuffs on his wrists, Connel sat unmoving. Even when Wanstead and Thurrock joined him, he didn't flinch. His focus remained directly ahead.

"Remember anything else?" Wanstead asked. "Anything else you might want to share?"

Connel said nothing.

"Maybe he got his nights mixed up."

"Or it's amnesia."

The cops could mock him as much as they liked,

he wouldn't react. Even if he was seething on the inside, he'd keep it there, hidden. It was about power. Pride. Stepping closer, her hand rose toward the glass, but she paused. She couldn't reach him. Not from there.

"Maybe we should tell him who's been helping us out."

"Yeah," Wanstead said. "Got some interesting insight from an unexpected source."

"Unexpected but not unwelcome."

"Hell, no, definitely not unwelcome."

"Know who we're talking about?" Thurrock asked.

Still nothing from Connel.

"You know McLeod's kid sister, right?" Wanstead got no response. "Followed you around for a while. Did the article on your friends the Manzanis." They were no friends of his and he wouldn't appreciate it being said, still, silence. "Seems to think she knows something about who's responsible for this murder."

"Can you think what she had to add?" Thurrock asked and got nothing. "What she might have told us?"

"What we know about the McDades now…" Wanstead said like it was a big deal. Asshole. They weren't asking him to corroborate anything. They were making it seem like she'd rolled on him somehow. "She sure got deep with you, didn't she? Bet it's tough for a guy to hold his wad around a woman like that."

"Attractive."

"Oh, fuck, yeah, would be something to remember, getting a fit babe like that on her back."

She cringed. Her brother stood behind her. Others in the room had to feel his tension, she sure did. Though some of it could've been coming from the silent man in the room they watched.

"Something only guys like us can dream about," Thurrock said. "But we've got more of a chance than this asshole. What you think, Ire? Think her brother would let scum like you near her?"

"Nothing?" Wanstead. "That your answer, Ire? That's what you are to this, a big, fat nothing?" They waited another few seconds. "That's your chance."

As the detectives pushed their chairs back, her hand leaped up on instinct. "Do rún."

The desperation of her voice echoed through the speaker, stalling everyone. Except Lachlan who snatched her hand from the intercom.

Connel's head turned, his eyes heavy and dark, somehow seeking hers through the one-way glass.

"Tell the truth," she whispered to the man who couldn't hear her.

"What's that?" Wanstead asked, furious. "Some kind of signal? Why the fuck did we let her in there?"

His glare was on the glass too, in her peripheral vision. Connel still fixated on her. Was it anger? Was he mad? She hadn't thought about revealing the secret and what it might mean for either of them. It was instinct. He was in trouble and didn't need to be. She held the key to his prison, why wouldn't she use it?

As his eyes closed, his head turned to the detectives. "What do you want to know?"

"What did she tell us?" Thurrock asked.

"The truth," she said under her breath again, praying he'd feel her somehow.

"That she was in the club Monday night," Connel said.

"That it?"

"She was in my office when your pigs showed up."

"Not a crime," Thurrock said.

"She didn't commit a crime."

"What was she doing in your office?"

"I didn't ask," he said.

"You'd think that would be important," Wanstead said. "Daughter of the superintendent shows up in your office, that would make some guys nervous."

Connel said nothing.

"She show up in your office a lot?"

"Not recently."

"But she was in your office on Monday night? Why?" Still nothing from Connel. Wanstead dropped a hand onto the table. "You don't give us something, you're calling her a liar."

"She's no liar," Connel said. "Whatever she said is true."

He was holding back. Because he didn't know what she'd said, or he still wanted to keep them a secret?

"And what was that?" Thurrock asked. "What did she tell us?"

His eyes flicked toward her for just a glimmer of a second. "My bed wasn't empty Monday night," he said. "I wasn't alone."

Yes, and she'd never thought relief would be the prevailing emotion when that became public knowledge.

"Why didn't you tell us this before?" Thurrock asked.

"She's the superintendent's daughter," Connel said. "You want to be the one to tell him?"

Fear and anxiety seeped out of her, loosening her muscles. On an exhale, she turned to make eye contact with Lachlan, then went back out into the corridor.

Just a couple of steps later, Lachlan's voice rose behind her. "You don't want to hear the end of this?"

"I was there," she called without turning around. "Your people can feed on the details." She paused to look back at him. "I really am sorry, Lach. I didn't want you to find out like this."

But he had, and by morning, the whole world would know.

FIFTEEN

SHE FELL FACE FIRST onto her bed. Her mind was so busy, she couldn't even focus on a single thought. Was she just tired? Exhausted? Sunk by emotional overload? Yeah, definitely that last one.

What would change?

Everything. Everything would change.

Some amount of time passed. Might have been ten minutes. Maybe ten hours. The solid thump on her front door jolted her awareness to the present.

"Sersha!" Her father. Of course her dad would be the first to get to her door. "Open this door!"

Rather than comply, she slithered off the bed and crawled across to lock the bedroom door. If her father was there, Lachlan wouldn't be far behind. Someone had to break the news to him. Ire McDade wasn't their culprit, not for Henry McLeod's murder. For sullying his little girl on the other hand…

It was laughable.

Her father could be outraged. And he would be. No one did indignant better than her father. All her life she'd been aware of disappointing him. How she wasn't what he wanted in a child. Nothing she did was good enough. Nothing met his standard.

But it was only there, in the freedom of admitting her connection to Connel, that she found herself at peace with it. If she would never be good enough, why waste time trying?

Forcing herself onto her feet, she went into the bathroom to get ready for bed. She washed her face, brushed her teeth, and stared at herself trying to figure out what was different. Something was different. A weight lifted with honest words. Why hadn't she given them their power earlier?

She jumped when the pounding on the bedroom door started. Her father wanted to lose it. She'd talk to him. Eventually. But what would she get for it now? He'd shout, she wouldn't get a word in edgeways.

Funny then that as she departed the bathroom, she heard her brother on the other side of the door with their father.

"You need to calm down," Lachlan said. "She won't talk to you like this."

"Won't talk to me?" her father blustered. "She owes us an explanation! How could she do this to our family? How could she debase herself—"

"This isn't helping."

No, it wasn't and thank God Lachlan was there to say that. Debase herself? She was offended. Connel had shady connections, he was in a dangerous line of work, but he wasn't scum. No surprise that her father saw Connel as beneath him; he thought everyone was beneath him.

"She needs to come out of there."

"And she will. Maybe in the morning, we can—"

"The morning? No! It is the damn morning! The

rest of my people are on their way. We need to deal with this tonight. We've lost ground with the investigation and need to redouble our efforts. And we have to get our evidence out of here. God only knows what she's told him about the investigation."

"This is Sersha," Lachlan said. "She wants to find Henry's killer as bad as we do."

"No," her father said. "Clearly not if she's fraternizing with suspects."

"Sersh has been here with us for days. Have you seen Ire?"

"They could be talking on the phone or by video. They do that now. The video."

"Yeah, but why would Ire give a shit? If he was with Sersh when it happened, he's not our guy."

"Just because he didn't pull the trigger himself doesn't mean he didn't order one of his people to do it."

Great. Maybe admitting to being with Connel wasn't the saving grace she thought it would be. Her father only seemed more determined to tar him after learning about their affair.

She pushed the cord into the bottom of her phone. It would charge overnight. Her purse and laptop were in there with her, but how could she work?

People arrived and her father barked orders at them. Everyone was going to feel his wrath while this plagued him. What could she say that would make him feel better? Nothing. Whatever she said would only upset him.

She changed into her dark gray, cami nightdress and folded back the covers of her bed. With all the activity, would she be able to sleep? She'd slept before. By accident.

Sitting down, she tucked her feet under the covers, but wrapped her arms around her pulled up knees. Lachlan was hurt. And he didn't deserve her betrayal on top of everything else. Maybe under normal circumstances, he'd understand someone falling for an unexpected partner. But he'd just dealt with his ex falling for an unexpected guy, they'd lost their grandfather, her father was having a meltdown, and it was on her brother's head.

Resting her temple on her knees, she wanted to switch off. If it was her choice, she'd talk to her brother. Apologize again. Try to make him see she hadn't meant to hurt him; she hadn't wanted to hurt him.

Did intentions matter?

Lachlan hadn't factored much in her decision making when Connel was kissing her. Her family. She hadn't wanted the video out there because her and Connel's intimacy could hurt their careers. What had changed? Nothing. Yet she hadn't hesitated to walk into the precinct and blow up all their lives.

"No!" Her father's shout was so abrupt, she lifted her head. "No! You people out of here! None of you are welcome here!"

"McLeod."

That calm lilt, that knowing… that accent.

Shit.

Leaping off the bed, she ran to the door and threw it open so fast it almost ricocheted back on her. It stopped on her flat hand with the same thud she felt when Connel's eyes met hers.

"None of you were invited!"

"They're always invited," she said to her father, her eyes still locked on Connel.

"No! This is ridiculous," her father exclaimed, his people crowding around him.

Connel's people were behind him too. At the front door, Niall, Daly, Strat, even Hock and Snuff made the trip. And shit if Razer McDade wasn't right there too. Her two lives couldn't co-exist like this.

Why had he come? Why was…?

Ignoring her father, Connel passed him by. Those loyal to the McDades got in the way, working crowd control when her dad tried to follow.

Why was she nervous? Her throat shook with every determined step Connel took toward her. There was purpose, resolve, in his marching gait.

When he got to her, she inhaled, swaying back just a little as his hands rose to her jaw. "Cushla Machree," he murmured, descending to plant his mouth on hers.

The slick heat of his devouring kiss gave her the needed reprieve. Losing herself in the motion, she let him angle her head, to push closer, to comb his fingers into her hair around the back of her head, holding her there, surrendered to him.

She could've stayed there, in that union, until the end of time. As usual, it was Connel who led. When he broke their kiss, she could only breathe into the air he'd left her lips hanging in. He kissed her again, just a brief touch of acknowledgment. Somehow, he was loathed to leave the moment too.

When he turned toward the others, his stance was as bold as if he were in his own office.

"Have you made progress?" he asked, scanning the corner where their investigation information was spread out and pinned up.

"That what you're here for?" Lachlan asked. "To take over? I don't think so, McDade."

"We are not on opposite sides of this," Connel said. "Pride is the only reason to shut me out."

Pride again. Shit. Maybe the McLeods weren't that different from the McDades.

"How do we know you weren't involved?" her father demanded. "Maybe you orchestrated this whole thing."

"To what end?" Connel asked. "Why would I hurt a man important to Sersha?"

"You may have drawn my daughter in with your lies, but you won't manipulate me."

"Okay," Connel said. "That's an interesting take, Superintendent." His focus switched to her brother. "Tomorrow. In the club at noon. Whoever wants to solve this should be there."

Lachlan grew discerning. "We won't share information with you."

"I shouldn't be surprised," Connel said. "None of you trusted Sersha enough to involve her in the first place. Doesn't matter. She has her own team, people loyal to her who will make this their life until it's solved. I'll see to it."

"You're full of shit," her father spat.

Lachlan faltered. "He's not lying. Imogen's on it."

"Jagger Dunn, Strat's son," Connel said. "She even has the ear of the Manzanis. Something none of you can claim… in public." She caught his hand when he muttered those last words. He linked their fingers but didn't turn around. "This can be adversarial, or we accept where we are and deal with each other."

"Accept where we are?" Lachlan asked. "Where is that?"

"Yes!" Her father stormed over to his son's side. "Where are we? The way I look at it, nothing has changed since this morning. Except we now know you took callous advantage of a weak woman."

She didn't want to look at the audience gawping at the scene, and couldn't see Connel's face from behind him, so she was as startled as anyone when he laughed.

"A weak woman…" His laugh died on a rough, "mm" that vibrated in the back of his throat. "Sersha McLeod…" The way he drew out her name was peculiar.

Was he talking to her or about her? "She is not a weak woman. Anyone who thinks that is an idiot. Sersha's strength gets her through every day. And I can see she didn't get that quality from you."

"You think you can come in here and insult us?"

"You think I'll stand here quiet while you insult her?"

"Okay," she said, leaping around Connel to quell the ire before it rose any further. "It's late, everyone is tired. No one should say anything they might regret tomorrow." Connel's chest was hard, warm. Her hand was up there, all on its own, stroking him. Connel was in her apartment with her dad and brother. The others didn't matter. But he was there. He'd come to her. "Why did you come?" Her words escaped on a breath. "Why did you come here tonight? You knew I wouldn't be alone."

"Aye," he said, his gaze searching hers.

"You came here for me," she whispered.

"You sacrificed your honor for my liberty."

"You don't owe me anything. I couldn't let you sacrifice your liberty for my honor. You could've gone to prison. For life. And all you needed to do when they asked for your alibi was say my name. I wouldn't have lied."

"Your wishes were clear."

"And now?" she asked.

Her wish to keep them a secret might have been clear and the reason they ended their affair, but that was no more.

"The only barrier to this that existed has gone," he said, laying a hand on hers to guide it up, under the edge of his shirt to his skin beneath. "Put another obstacle in front of me and I'll obliterate it, Macushla. You declared it to the world tonight. You're all in. Mine. No going back now."

Curling her fingers, her nails dug into the ink beneath them, his stag head tattoo. "I'm a McDade."

"Aye."

"This is too—"

"If you're not family by blood or allegiance, you don't need to be here," Connel declared, addressing those in the far corner.

The front door opened.

"You can't excuse my people," her father said. "Who do you think you are?"

"You like family business aired in public?" Connel asked.

When she turned to check her father's reaction, it wasn't a surprise to see his people shuffling out. Razer McDade held the door. The office lackeys and admin grunts wouldn't want to face off with men like him and the others at his side. When they were gone, Razer swung the door back into its frame.

"That was easy," Daly said. "Never any action when Bluebell's around."

She smiled at him. Compared to other things he did for the McDades, it was cake. Kind of like finding out her coffee order.

"No one wants to start anything tonight," Lachlan said, always the voice of reason. "Maybe we should meet tomorrow. Sit down when everyone's processed this."

"Good idea," Connel drawled without pointing out that had been his suggestion already. "Daly get the car. Make sure those people are off the streets."

Daly saluted with two fingers and went out with Hock and Snuff on his tail.

"You're not staying?" she asked.

He tucked her hair behind her ear. "You want to share a bed with me through the wall from your brother?"

Okay, she pouted, then nodded. "Not even a little."

"We're going to the loft."

"The loft?"

His attention dropped to hers. "You want to stay at the club?"

"No," she said and smiled. "The loft works."

"Go get your shit."

"You are not walking out of this apartment with my daughter," her father said before she even reached the bedroom door.

Connel fixed on Razer; a look passed between them. One happy to end the debate once and for all, whether it meant jail or not.

Lachlan must've seen it too. "It's Sersha's choice," he said. "You can't stop her going with him."

"False imprisonment is a crime," Strat said.

He'd been quiet until then. He looked pissed. Really pissed and Strat rarely got worked up about anything… unless he was punching Jagg in the face.

"You're…"

"Imogen's father," Lachlan said, helping their dad out.

"How are you involved in this?" her dad asked, looking at Lachlan. "Imogen was here. She left with Sersha."

"People care about your daughter," Connel said. "If they didn't have her best interests at heart, they wouldn't be allowed near her. It's as simple as that. I'm not squeamish about doing what's necessary to ensure her safety."

"Conn…"

He remained intent on the others. "Get your shit."

And that was it. Going into the bedroom, she swung Connel's suit jacket, which had been hanging in her closet forever, around her shoulders and stuffed her laptop and phone into her purse.

She returned to him in under half a minute. "Okay, I'm good," she said, threading her fingers between Connel's again.

They crossed the room together.

"You can't go out like that," her father said as she slipped on her heels.

Razer opened the door again. "You think there's a man in the city who'd so much as look while she's with us?"

Connel took her waist to direct her out of the apartment and down the hall. Yeah, okay, her dad kind of had a point that a satin cami didn't offer the best coverage, but she'd be on the sidewalk for seconds at each end of their car ride.

And Razer was right. She could probably walk stark naked down the middle of Main Street without getting hassle. Not now the world knew she had Connel McDade's attention. The only thing was, what did she want to do with it?

SIXTEEN

WHEN THEY GOT OUTSIDE, the Bentley was nowhere in sight. Instead, Daly opened the back door of a long Mercedes. Connel guided her into the rear-facing seat before sitting in front of her. His cousin got in the opposite door, sitting next to him on the other side of the center console.

It was a nice car. Super nice and it smelled new.

"Where's Whisper?" she asked, stroking the soft leather, admiring the red stag head emblem embroidered in discreet locations.

"We don't trust Whisper to control herself," Connel said.

"You put her in a timeout?" she asked, surprised. As she absorbed, she grinned at Razer. "Good chance you'll pay for that, sir?"

"She has a thing about defending women," Razer said. "Gets upset when women are taken advantage of."

"Especially when men take liberties," she said, running her hands up and down the leather. "I know; I have experience with that." Her attention drifted, not to anywhere in particular until she noticed both men were intent on her. "Ignore me."

"Which one of you was touched?" Razer asked, his voice varying baser tones that came from somewhere deep in his chest.

"It was a loser at the club trying his luck," she said, appealing to their cooler heads… if they had them. "He wasn't a threat, he was an asshole."

"Answer him," Connel growled.

"Baby," she murmured on a semi-laugh. "No."

"No one touches a McDade in their own house."

"Okay," she said, slipping her feet from her shoes. "But Whisper took care of it. The woman is amazing."

The men shared a look.

"Your woman goes both ways," Connel said.

"Apparently, so does yours," Razer replied, retrieving his phone from an inside pocket.

And for the first time in maybe her life, she didn't have to be ashamed of her curiosity.

She raised her feet to rest them on Connel's thigh. "He has experience."

Razer crooked a brow at his cousin.

"Dasha," Connel said by way of explanation.

Razer accepted with a nod and returned to his phone.

Connel scooped up her feet and repositioned them to massage the one crossed over the other. "What do you know?"

"They put time of death between two and three," she said. "He was in his pajamas, so apparently ready for bed. Lachlan said he still had paperwork out or the computer on or something. No signs of a disturbance. No broken windows or forced doors. Security didn't hear anything."

"Or they did it," Connel said. "Paying them off

is nothing. Some guys like that just need a word."

"A word," she said, pointing the toes of her lower foot to press them into his groin. "A word from you isn't the same as a word from some street scum."

"This was a professional job," he said, squeezing her foot. "You knew that."

"I did." Because she'd said that to others several times. "It wasn't an accident or random."

"Enemies?"

She shrugged. "Almost too many to list. Anyone who didn't like his politics. Anyone he investigated as a cop. Anyone who wanted his council seat. Anyone who wanted him out. He made decisions that affected people's lives every day. Sometimes his decisions went their way, sometimes they didn't."

"He was asking questions."

The comfort of his massage spurred her on. "About corruption. Who was taking bribes, whose allegiance was where."

"Maybe he asked too many questions."

"You talked to your brother about your father?"

"No. We haven't talked about it at all. I wouldn't even know where to start. How do I tell him our father could be in league with Silvio Manzani?"

The way Razer looked at Connel's profile chilled her.

"No could be, Macushla," Connel said. "He's on the take."

As if she hadn't had enough shocks that week, it wouldn't compute. Wouldn't filter through. Her father… what was he saying?

On the take… how…?

"You can call us liars—"

"I don't think you're liars," she said to Razer, staring into the ether. "It's like… I can't wrap my head around it. I think that's why I blew it off as a possibility…"

The motion of the car and the massage kept her drugged until they stopped. She scrambled to put on her shoes as Connel got out. His hand appeared inside for hers and he kept their link tight as they went upstairs.

On their arrival at the loft, Whisper sprang up from the couch. "Did you get her?" Razer and Connel stepped aside, left and right, revealing her to the woman holding the martini glasses. "I made margaritas!"

She smiled at the gesture. Connel let go of her hand and cupped her head beneath her ear, making brief eye contact, before striding toward the kitchen, cousin in tow.

"I'm surprised you're still up," she said, slipping off her shoes and Connel's jacket.

"Looks like you weren't," Whisper said, though she wasn't wearing much more in a tiny pair of panties and a guy's shirt, Razer's probably. "You just marched right in there."

It took her a second to figure out what she meant. "To the cops? Why does that surprise everyone? Conn is innocent."

"Of this murder? Yeah. Of fucking you…? You didn't want anyone to know, right?"

Whisper put one of the two glasses in her hand. Another two sat by the pitcher on the coffee table.

"Not so much that I'd see an innocent man go to jail."

"So it was civic duty?"

"Don't forget my grandfather is the victim. I don't want the wrong person punished; I want the right person punished." She sipped the drink. "This is good."

Whisper smiled, tucking her feet under her. "I'm a pro. So civic duty?"

She exhaled and curled her legs on the couch too. "It wasn't a conscious decision like that. I turned on the news to check the time and… I reacted. I was there telling the truth before I thought about it. Was he at the club?"

"Yeah, we were all there. The cops busted on in like they owned the joint, totally coming in their pants when the cuffs went on. It happened fast."

It would have to. "Did they get a warrant for the club?"

"No," Whisper said. "Thank God. They had such a hard-on for getting Ire that they couldn't keep it in their pants that long. How did your family take it?"

"My brother's hurt. He's been through a lot. I feel like shit for putting him through more."

"And your dad?"

She exhaled an almost laugh and drank more before answering. "I don't get how he can do something so disgraceful and still spout his righteous bullshit at the same time?"

"Accepting a payoff is a ways away from evil. So he got greedy, he's not alone in that." Whisper leaned closer. "And you're in good company. My father sold me to his enemy. Zay's dad ordered the murder of Ire's and fucked his desperate-to-get-pregnant daughter-in-law all the while aware she was on birth control without her knowledge. Yeah, you don't get the monopoly on righteous, sanctimonious sons of bitches until you've been propositioned by Daddy Burl."

"He'll never get the chance," Connel said, reappearing with Razer.

"Oh, I don't know, we could always visit him in the big house. We could take Nicki, make it a trifecta. Maybe he could get us all pregnant while we're there. Save you boys the trouble."

"No one thinks you're funny," Razer said.

"I think I'm funny," Whisper replied, tipping her head all the way back when the men stopped behind the couch.

"That mouth is better at other things, Peanut," Razer said. "Bedtime."

"And they say romance is dead," Whisper stage whispered her way before tossing back the drink and putting her empty glass on the table.

The hug she was pulled into was unexpected, but not unwelcome.

"Goodnight," she said when Whisper rose and started for the hallway she'd never been down.

She peeked over the back of the couch.

"Front and center," Connel said already heading for the bedroom.

SEVENTEEN

SHE JUMPED UP to follow, driven by an eagerness to please him more than what was promised between his sheets.

But he didn't stop at the bed and continued past toward the closet.

"You switched it around," she said, noting the bed was on the opposite wall from where it had been before.

"Aye," he called back. "Front and center."

Right. He didn't appreciate repeating himself.

She jumped to it and hurried after him. By the time she caught up, the shower was on and he was shirtless.

"Why did you rearrange the bedroom?" she asked as he undressed her.

"In the club, you sleep on the left," he said, squeezing her breasts. "Furthest from the door."

Getting her naked hadn't taken long. "And if I slept on the left here where the bed used to be, I'd be closest to the door."

"Right," he said, his thumbs brushing across her nipples.

"Can we go to bed?" she asked, tucking her fingers into his waistband.

"After I shower off the precinct," he said, sliding back the door to urge her inside.

He didn't need to shower with her, but she was honored he did. He stripped off the rest of his clothes and joined her.

She couldn't help herself and was caressing his chest with eager fingertips when he reached for the shampoo.

"I'm sorry about tonight."

"Wasn't your fault," he said, turning her back to him.

"Why did they suspect you? Did they tell you?"

"They have a witness."

"A mistaken witness," she said, tipping her head back as he worked her hair into a lather. "An enemy of yours?"

"Or someone covering for their crime."

"Whoever it was couldn't have known you had an alibi."

"The circle of people who knew about us was small."

And that circle was getting bigger by the moment. "How are we going to handle this?"

"This?"

"People knowing about us."

With a grip on her arms, he spun her around to meet her eye. Driving a hand up the back of her neck into her wet hair, he gripped it tight, painfully tight, right against her scalp. When she winced, he strengthened his fist until her lips parted.

"You belong to me now, Macushla," he growled, swooping down to bite her lower lip. "You're all mine."

"Do rún," she gasped.

"Not anymore."

The water ran over her forehead into her eyes and down over the knot of his hold. Closing her eyes to the cascade, she barely caught a breath before his tongue rammed into her mouth. Possession had never been like this. He wasn't just holding her, restraining her, he was putting all of himself into her. Not his physical self, the essence of his soul. The dark and dangerous corners he'd hidden from her were plunged into the light.

The danger. The terror. Others felt it. He expected it. And he was showing it to her. Trusting her with it.

Tangled up in pain and grief, she let him kiss her, let him push and pull and tug and tow any way he wanted. Her body was limp, pulled low, putting agonizing pressure on her back, but the pain was nothing to the acceptance of his pledge.

Somehow, her fingers found his cock and curled around it, squeezing him tight, trying to deliver him the guarantee his kiss gave her. His kiss came with a deep inhale, and one hand yanked while the other took her jaw, squeezing it from both sides, deepening his kiss.

She was helpless, powerless in his grasp. Every part of her except the hand she kept around him, constricting it as she stroked and jerked, pleasing him like he'd please himself in her pussy. That was where she wanted him, inside her. Yet the kiss, the desperate bonding, was so devouring, she never wanted it to end.

When he tore his mouth away, he dug his teeth into her jaw, stabbing himself deeper into her fist. Though she tried to bend her knees, he held her in place.

"I want to swallow for you," she panted, speeding her caress. "Please, do rún."

On a growl, he ducked to sweep up one of her legs, planting her foot on the seat as he charged in his crouch, plunging his cock into her. She gasped, grabbing for his shoulders, his frantic motion propelled her from tiptoes into his full control. He hooked a forearm under her thigh, pulling it higher, compelling her to grab for the wall and the top of the stall, seeking balance.

"Macushla," he snarled through gritted teeth, thrusting himself into her one final climactic time, pinning her pelvis to the wall with his.

With her lips closed, she mirrored the deep huff of his nasal breaths. The shower spray cascaded through his hair, running down through her fingers again on his shoulders, splashing in every direction.

She didn't often get to look him straight in the eye, closer to his level, like she was in the support of his arms. He didn't pull out, didn't back off, just let his heart beat against her body.

It wasn't gratitude. Or if it was, it wasn't like any version she'd seen. But there was something there, in the way he assessed her, a scrutiny that sought something in her.

"Baby," she whispered, sweeping her palm from his cheek to his hair, combing her fingers through its dampness.

"Did I hurt you?" he asked in a deep, quiet rumble.

She smiled. "Where am I always safe?" she asked without expecting an answer. "Never apologize for your desire. I want you to want me like that. You could never hurt me. I could never fear you."

"You didn't know."

"Didn't know what?" she asked, her fingers trailing their way down to his chest.

The man was divine in his definition. Cut like glass, without a single fragile quality, there wasn't a flaw in sight. Conflict? That seemed to be written in his DNA.

"I could've turned my back on you. You got me

out of there anyway."

She could've exploded her life and her family's livelihoods without the safety net of his support.

"You've killed for me, do rún. I'd step in front of any bullet for you."

"Gratitude? You think you owed me?"

"I do owe you," she said, writhing as much as his pressure allowed. "For how incredible you make me feel. I'll never be able to thank you for that. Never be able to give you what you give me just by existing… I've lived lonely, do rún. I've lived missing you… Maybe it was selfish." Though she hadn't considered it at the time. "Maybe I needed that push. I'm not sorry, I'm…"

"Liberated."

"Right." And it was mirrored right back in his gaze. "Have I cornered you?"

"I don't cower or apologize, Macushla. This was always a battle you were fighting with yourself."

Was it? Her barriers. Her boundaries.

"To be with you," she said, "I have to be owned by you."

"Protected by me."

"I have to stand proud behind the McDade shield."

"When anyone tries to hurt you, you tell them…?"

"I'm Cushla Machree."

"Beat of My Heart."

That's what it meant? All this time… but he'd been calling her that for…

"Conn…" she whispered, touching his lips. How long had he felt for her? Deeply felt for her…? "I'm sorry it took me so long to see it. That I…" She exhaled, giving every part of herself to him as he moved in her again. "I should've done this sooner. So much sooner."

Because it felt so good to be safe, accepted,

allowed to embrace every part of herself. Every part of him and what they felt for each other was free, no matter which path they went down.

EIGHTEEN

"WHEN HE'S RUNNING the show, he can call the shots." Connel's voice broke through the haze of sleep that held her warm and safe in his sheets. "No extension. A deadline's a deadline... He delivers or he dies..." Despite the light brightening her eyelids, she kept them closed. Being enveloped in the scent of him was too good a heaven to surrender. "Aye. They don't worry about that... I've got the superintendent's daughter exactly where I want her." She smiled, tilting her chin a little in the direction of that arousing voice. Something hit the bed. "I've got business, Macushla."

"With my pussy?"

"Later," he said. "Look at me..."

Rolling to her back, the sheet slipped from her breasts as she opened her eyes. And there he was, standing at the end of the bed, his dark, intense eyes scrutinizing her body.

"Come back to bed," she whispered, using her feet to drag the sheet even lower. "I need my McDade."

"Your McDade's got people to see."

"Are they a better sight than this?" she asked,

arching, wriggling into the twinge of pain he'd left between her thighs. "I want you. Why wake me if you didn't want some?"

"I don't need you awake to take what I want," he said, strolling around to her side. "In my bed, you'll never wake up lonely."

And as he sat on the edge, the sincerity of that sentiment erased every tease. "Conn…" she murmured, losing herself in him as he stroked her hair from her face. "You killed for me." Like it was no big deal, he had no reaction. "I'm sorry I made you wait. That I didn't see the truth." She'd apologized the previous night, but it didn't seem enough. His eyes settled on hers as his hand rested on her throat. "That I let you think for even a second I was ashamed of this."

"Where are you always safe?"

"I'm serious," she said, taking his hand as she sat up. "It was never about shame."

"Macushla, I know how the world works better than any schmuck you've ever been with. I don't need an education. I don't give a shit about the past. The power balance of the city shifted last night. Until it settles, we hold our breath."

"I don't understand," she said, concerned. "What happened? What did I miss? Are you in trouble?"

"You are."

"Why?"

He kissed her. "I'll deal with it," he said and raised his brows in question. "Hmm?" After lingering a few seconds, she nodded. "What do you do if you have a problem?"

"Bring it to you."

"Good girl."

His lips touched hers, but she pulled back. "You've never been faithful to a woman. You do what you want when you want and don't answer to anyone."

"Aye."

And did she want to ask him if that was still true? Something in him almost dared her to, like he expected the question. But that wasn't what worried her. Loyalty was everything to him. He'd referred to her as family, come to her when he could've abandoned her. She only wanted fidelity if it was a choice. Asking for it, demanding it, wouldn't change his desire to be with her and only her. Some things, in this relationship, had to be taken on faith.

Slipping her hand under the open edge of his shirt, she laid her palm over his stag tattoo and got closer. "I am not a slut you have on speed dial." In her certainty, she lit something in him that erased all preconceptions. "You hear me? This is my kingdom. You are my kingdom."

There may have been a whisper of a smile on his lips as he licked them. "Act like it," he breathed against her and pushed his tongue into her mouth in a devouring kiss that curled her fingers into the fabric of his shirt.

Try as she did to pull him down, he only let her get halfway before easing her fists out of his clothes.

"Baby…" she whimpered.

"Strat will bring you to the club."

"At noon."

"In an hour."

He got the chance to stand as she sought the clock on the nightstand. Shit, it was already ten forty-eight.

"Anything I need to know?" she asked, gliding out of bed.

Using him as a pillar of support, she stretched her body on his, straightening her arms above her head and letting them settle around his neck when they descended.

"This is not an easy world to abandon."

Little late for that. "I exist beneath you, under you." And as long as that was true, his protection would be absolute. "My life is yours."

"Aye, but what's your job?"

"To support you."

"Life is about to get interesting for both of us." He cradled the back of her head to guide her hairline to his lips. It wasn't like him to be so gentle. Fuck, could she want this guy more? "I put your clothes for today out in the closet."

In her shock, he was all the way at the other side of the bed before she processed the sentence. "You picked out my clothes?"

"That a problem?"

Only because it heated a quiver of need in the pussy he'd spent all night punishing. It rippled up through her, tightening the muscles that craved his occupation.

"Yes," she said, her palms skimming up to her breasts. "It's not fair to turn me on and leave me wanting."

"Something you'll have to get used to. Get back in bed."

"Baby—"

"Making me repeat myself has consequences." Though his grave tone was heavy, she smiled. "Back in bed, Macushla." On a sigh, she lifted the sheet, but it was whipped away from her fingertips. "Without the sheet."

"Without it? Why without it?"

Sliding a knee onto the bed, she walked on them to the middle and lay down.

"Because I had something installed when the furniture was rearranged."

"What something?"

Retrieving his phone from his inside pocket, he nodded to the ceiling above where the bed had been. A small panel shifted and a black hemisphere descended. The red light at the lowest point clued her in.

"Oh my God! You're obsessed with recording us," she said, laughing, trying to grab for the sheet.

He snatched it away, flinging it to the floor behind himself. "This is live feed only. Accessible by me." He raised his phone and used it to gesture at hers on the nightstand. "And you."

That was a big show of trust. Loosening, she opened her arms on their bed. "I live to serve."

"Aye, you do." He tucked his phone into his pocket and planted a fist on the bed to bow and kiss her. "Make me regret leaving you here alone, Macushla." His whispered words were all the encouragement her fingers needed to float toward her center. "For my eyes only."

"All of me for all of you. My McDade."

He kissed her once more, then was gone, departing their bed, but not the moment. Drawing the soles of her feet up the mattress, she took her sweet time stroking all of herself. He'd need time to access the image and she didn't want him to miss a second.

He'd laid a challenge at her door, no way she'd disappoint.

NINETEEN

"YOU'RE TOO RELAXED," Strat said just a minute into their drive.

As promised, he'd come to the door to pick her up. Only then did she find out Daly, Snuff, and Hock were waiting in the hall between the loft's front door and elevator. How long had they been there?

"Too relaxed for what?" she asked, smoothing the dress Connel had picked out for her.

"For a woman on her way to a meet between her law enforcement family and mob boss boyfriend."

"They've met before."

"Yeah, like this? Everything out in the open? Last night doesn't count. It was put on hiatus until this, until now. Anything you think you avoided then will happen now."

"Everyone's had time to calm down."

"Or work themselves into a lather. I haven't seen Ire today. You didn't want to show together?"

"He had business."

"That I guarantee didn't include feeding orphans

or rescuing puppies," Strat said. "You know it's possible he committed murder… today. It's possible he's on his way from a crime scene right now."

"You think I'm naïve to what he does?"

"I think your brother carries a gun."

"Connel is surrounded by guns," she said. "As he said last night, this doesn't have to be adversarial."

"I have to clue you in on something."

"What? Clue me in on what?"

"You're not the best mediator, Scamp. And there's a battle being fought on too many fronts for any one person to control."

"Conn will control it," she said. "Is Jagg coming?" Strat didn't answer in words; the tightening of his jaw did it for him. "Why do you hate him? For falling in love with Imogen? Your daughter loves a man you helped raise. You should be happy for them."

"What do you care? She broke your brother's heart."

"Yes, she did. I don't know how long it will take Lach to get over that, but I'd rather he be hurt than with someone who didn't love him. Imogen isn't a bad person, it just didn't work out between them. Lachlan will get over that. He'll get there."

"How long will it take him to get over you and Ire together?" he asked, glancing her way and back at the road a couple of times. "That's a whole other kind of kick in the sack."

"I don't know," she said, not sure life was so light anymore. "I didn't want to hurt him. I didn't want to hurt anyone. Conn and I ended it because we thought it was best for everyone. We truly thought that, I truly thought that, but last night…"

"Last night?"

"No man makes me feel like he does, Strat. You warned me, I know you did. You told me if I fell for him

I'd be sucked into a world that would never let me go. The thing is… ending it, cutting each other out, it didn't save me. It didn't free me from that world because… my heart is in that world. So long as he's in that world, my heart will be too."

"Poetic," he said. "Think your dad will see it that way?"

She bristled, her body reacting to the nausea that rooted itself in anger. "He's on the take."

"What?"

"Connel and Razer told me last night. The good and righteous superintendent is as corrupt as the rest of City Hall. All my life I thought he was…" She sighed, though tension made it come out more like a growl. "I walked away from Connel McDade to save my family and all the time my family, my father, was a worse man."

"Worse?"

"At least Connel is honest about what he is." About what he did? Not always so much, but he didn't pretend to shine a halo and defer to any higher power. "My father pastes lie on top of lie."

"Did you call him out?"

"My dad? No," she said. "I haven't seen him since. And I won't call him out because it was told to me in confidence, just like I'm telling it to you."

When he spotted the narrowing of her eyes, he laughed. "Shit, all that moll practice is paying off. Ire tell you to use his name?"

"Any time I want."

His hands slid up to the top of the wheel. "Oh, baby, you are currency now. Just you wait."

Turned out she wasn't the only one waiting. When they turned the corner, a group of men stood by a couple of cars parked on the curb in front of Stag.

"What's going on?"

Her father and brother were a little away from

the group, talking. Strat pulled up a couple of feet behind the closest car.

"Want me to take you inside?"

"No," she said, shaking her head. What the hell were her father and brother doing? "Park and come in round back."

"Yes, mistress."

Hilarious, she tossed him a scowl as she got out, but he was laughing before the door closed at her back.

When Lach noticed her, he raised an arm and her father turned.

"What is it?" she asked, going over to them. "What's going on?"

"We're waiting."

"For what?" she asked.

Her brother tipped his head toward their father. "Ask Dad."

"What are you waiting for?"

"This could be a trap."

"What?"

"We go waltzing into his club, it could be filled with his men, filled with people ready to murder us… just like my father was murdered."

"Here's a good clue it's not," she said, opening her arms. "I'm here. Use me as your shield if you're afraid, Dad."

His back straightened as bluster became stuttering. "I am not afraid. He should be afraid of us. Connel McDade wreaks havoc in this city."

"And if he wanted you dead, standing on the sidewalk wouldn't save you," she said. "Trust me, Conn doesn't make appointments with potential murder victims. Especially not with a dozen witnesses."

"Which you would know," Lachlan said. "If you've been party to a murder."

"What do you want to do? Stand out here and

take potshots at each other all day or go inside?"

"Not sure they want us to stroll up and knock without a warrant," Lachlan said. "Was that Strat driving you?"

"Yeah. Conn trusts him to look after me," she said, distracted by the group of ten or so others a few feet away. "Who are they?" Some of them she recognized from her apartment. "Are they your staff, Dad? You don't want to bring them in here."

"Why not? What'll happen to them?"

"That wasn't a threat," she said, tucking her purse under her arm. "I don't threaten people. I'm the same person I was yesterday."

"And yesterday proved you are not the person I thought you were."

"Okay, you're disappointed," she said, fighting to restrain an urge to scream at his hypocrisy. "This is an initial meeting. In an initial meeting, we want to get an idea of everyone's willingness to cooperate. It's not about a show of strength. You want Conn bringing a dozen of his guys?" Her father's lip moved, but he didn't speak. "If you don't want him to do it, don't do it in return."

"We don't know him, Ser," Lachlan said. "Not as anything but a dangerous criminal."

"And no one's denying he has power or ability, but this is happening here, now, because of me. He's doing this for me, tempering himself and his instincts, to accommodate what's important to me."

"Is he making you pay for it?"

Even her brother wasn't being reasonable.

She glared. "Fine," she said, striding away. "Go. Leave. No one will stop you."

"Sersha," Lachlan called. "Stop!"

Pausing, she spun on the spot equidistant between him and Stag's entrance. "What?"

Something warred within her brother and she got

it, this was a shock. To everyone. These people spent their lives fighting against each other. She was asking them to ignore their natures. Ignore the inversion of their beliefs and cooperate with an enemy.

Lachlan exhaled and looked at their father. "We've gotta give him a chance."

"You can't be serious!"

"What's the alternative?" That they walk away and possibly irreparably harm their relationships with her? "Send your people away. This is one meet. If McDade wanted to take us out, he'd have people do it in secret. This is not in secret."

Her father didn't respond well to orders. Lachlan was giving him the chance to save face and let it appear he'd made this choice himself.

As expected, her father took his time excusing his people and kept three of them with him. Of course. Again, he had to be the one calling the shots.

His posse piled into the cars, some looking more than a little relieved.

"What's their job?" her brother asked, bobbing his chin down the street.

About twenty feet behind her, Daly and Hock stood just watching.

"Me," she said on a smile. "Let's get inside."

As she approached the door, it opened from the inside. The internal hall may be wide, but it was dark, and it took a second for her eyes to adjust. As expected, a couple of guys stood at the bottom of the stairs to the office.

"They just follow you around?" Lachlan asked, closing in at her side.

"They do more than that if someone pisses me off," she said. "Hate on Conn as much as you like, but he's serious about my safety."

"Was he serious about it when you were being

attacked in the street? You want to tell me what went down with that?"

"No," she said, entering the light, cavernous club. "And that's still a raw nerve around here, so don't bring it up."

Like he had at his last meeting with Connel in the club.

A few people already loitered at tables by the large VIP booth that jutted out over the dance floor. Biggs. Snuff. Strat, of course, Ford, Jagg, and Imogen, who smiled and came over to hug her.

"You knew my daughter was coming?" Strat asked.

"Maybe," she said, giving little away.

"Steeple wants a rundown," Imogen said.

"This isn't—"

"We're off the record," Imogen said and glanced at Lachlan. "I know this must be rough for you."

"Which part?" he asked. "My kid sister screwing a mob boss or my ex-girlfriend with her new lover right in front of my face?"

"We only want—"

"I know, Immie," he said on a sigh and took his time about looking around. "Where's the man himself? Couldn't be bothered to show up to his own meeting? Is that how much he cares about you, Ser?"

Daly and Hock had gone to join Biggs and Snuff. The four of them straightened up, garnering such a menacing air that she stepped in front of her brother.

"We're here for a specific purpose," she said, hoping to calm them all. "Everyone has to put aside their grievances for this to work. We're on the same team." Connel wouldn't have put it quite that way. "Ire will be here as soon as he can."

"He is not the only one with a schedule, with responsibilities," her father said. "If he can't put aside other engagements, why should the rest of us? I can only imagine what those engagements might be."

"Is he around?" she asked, looking at Biggs. "Upstairs?"

"No." She was loathed to ask the opposite. If he was downstairs… "He's off-site."

Thank God for that. She could call, but what good would that do? He'd been the one to convene the meeting. He knew the where and when.

"Good, we have time to get everyone a drink."

Biggs stepped away from the group. "Coffee?" Their eyes met. "Irish coffee?"

From the smile that crept to his face, she could tell he read her mind. Aye, it was probably too early for hard Irish liquor.

"Everyone here?"

Thinking of hard Irish conjured something else, someone else. That voice. Her McDade.

TWENTY

AH, CONNEL.

Striding in with Niall and Razer.

Relief. "Where's Whisper?" she asked as the trio joined them.

"Upstairs," Razer answered. "Taking care of business."

In present company, she wouldn't ask for details.

"Will she be joining us?"

"Be careful what you wish for," Razer said, scanning the group with a darkening gaze. "Not all allies in this room."

"We have a common goal. A common enemy," Connel said. "What's said in this room stays in this room. And now everyone's together, I'll make one thing clear. Sersha is not only under McDade protection, she is the primary McDade concern. If you disrespect her, you disrespect me. You disrespect the family. And I don't care who you are, you'll be dealt with."

Okay. Lovely. Great start.

She pounced over to take his hand in both of

hers, pressing herself against his arm. He just kept on sharing that glare with everyone.

"Can I have a second… do rún?"

"Mm," he said and took her over to the bar to put her on a stool. As he moved between her thighs, she slid her arms around him under his jacket. "What's the problem? I won't go easy—"

"I would never ask that." Changing him was not on her to-do list. "I…" She exhaled and lowered her volume. "It feels unfair to ask."

"Write a hit list and we'll eliminate everyone on it. I don't need reasons, just names. Addresses, associates, or employers, if you have them."

She couldn't stop her lips from curling. "You want to murder people for me?"

"Wouldn't be the first time," he said under his breath, sweeping her hair from her face. "You should get some reward for this morning."

"You watched?" she asked, gathering his shirt in her fists at the small of his back.

"Mm, I did."

Pushing her shoulders back, she boosted up as he stooped and cupped her head to marry their mouths. It was impossible not to kiss him. Not to want him. The danger was as potent as ever and they had an audience. But fuck it, Connel McDade was the only spectator to her life she cared about.

"Boss!" someone shouted.

She clenched her fists hard, pulling on his shirt as he ripped his mouth away. "The superintendent's in the room, sweetheart. Probably not a good time to shoot anyone."

"Why do you think I'm unarmed?"

"Does kind of bring me back to my point."

"What's your point?"

"Everything that's going to be shared in this

room is private, right? Probably including the fact everyone's working together." Wouldn't do much for McDade or McLeod street cred to be accused of cooperating with each other. Beyond her scandalous McDade link anyway. "And not-so-subtle threats… It feels unfair to be uncomfortable like this. It's stupid, I shouldn't—"

"Macushla."

Just his warning tone was enough to prompt her on. "Your guys, I trust. McDade men are loyal. They'd go to any lengths for you and know how to keep their mouths shut. Your people—"

"You want rid of your father's grunts? Done."

As he inhaled, probably ready to call out a command, she coiled her leg around his. "No, they make my dad feel safer, fine, whatever."

"Safer?" he asked, wearing a frown. "Everyone is safe. I don't want shit going down in front of you." And, God, her stomach bottomed out in the most rapturous way. Wasn't that exactly what she'd said? "Any shit goes down, you get your ass to our bedroom and wait for me. Understand?"

She nodded. "We don't have to kill my dad's guys. But if we could find out more about them, who they're talking to…" She sighed. "We have to protect you and the family. I don't know these people or trust them not to use what they learn during this against the McDades. Maybe it's paranoia and if I'm being stupid—"

"I'll put tails on them."

Her brows rose, as did her chin. "You will?"

"Aye," he said, peering at her. "Shit, Macushla, you have no idea what I'd do for you."

"If they share something or we find out they're working with—"

"I'll take care of it," he said, his thumb gliding

down her jaw.

Since they were doing so well… "Evander says if he finds my grandfather's killer, he wants me as payment."

His thumb stopped.

A beat passed.

"You agree to that?"

"No," she said.

"You went to him before you came to me."

"I didn't have to come to you," she said, proud of her smile and her guy. "I knew you'd be on it. You don't need my prompt to do what's best for me. You do it automatically." Her hands came back around, this time to undo one of his shirt buttons. "And I'm already yours. We don't need any shady deal to cement that."

"If Vex's proposal is nothing, why tell me about it?"

Okay, so it could come to naught and mean nothing, or not. "It's Evander," she said, insinuating her hand into his shirt to draw a fingernail around his stag tattoo. "I don't want you blindsided. He can be cruel and hears what he wants to hear. I'm not interested in double dealing or causing conflict." Heightening it may be a better description. "If I respect your world, and your position, more likely both will respect me." In the grand scheme of things. "And if you know, you can laugh in his face. If you don't, you might doubt me."

"Never," he said, seizing her jaw to force her head back. "Never, Macushla."

"Hey!" another shout. Her father. "Take your hands off my daughter!"

"Please don't," she whispered in a tease that elevated the corner of his lips. "Will you fuck me on this bar later?"

"I'll fuck you on it right now," he murmured.

On a laugh, she pulled him down for a quick kiss,

then slid off the stool, pouring herself against him.

"Dad," she said, threading her fingers through Connel's, drawing him away from the bar. "Maybe you haven't met, but this is my boyfriend." Her father kept on seething. "You don't know him, I know. Lach already made that clear." She stopped between Niall and Razer. "Obviously, you didn't believe what Conn said, so let me say it. There's nothing he values more than my safety."

"I didn't raise you to be this naïve."

Conn yanked her behind him to put himself in her former place. "Watch your tone when you talk to her."

Her father's shoulders went back as he stormed closer. "You're a scum-sucking, low—"

"Okay!" Lach said, leaping in front of their father to stop him. "Both of you need to sit on your shit or this goes nowhere." Thank God for her brother. "Let's just sit down and take a breath."

As everyone did that, Biggs served drinks. And twenty minutes later, they were sitting in silence, passing around nothing but glares and grumbles.

"Okay," she said because someone had to speak first. "Everyone can acknowledge that there are two sides to this." Her family and her lover's family. "And those two sides have distinct skill sets."

"You're not seriously suggesting we act on each other's intelligence."

"The idea is to share intelligence to get to a conclusion," Strat said, earning himself her appreciative smile.

"We can't trust these people. They could feed us whatever bullshit they want and get us tied up with miscreants."

Her father had never been an anxious person, not that she remembered. And he hid his fear under anger and bluster, but she saw it. If Conn hadn't confirmed it, maybe she wouldn't have noticed, but her dad was definitely unsettled about something more than the murder.

Bouncing to the edge of her seat, she reached back to rest a hand on Connel's thigh. "Okay, then how about we start with your information? Tell us about this witness. The one who pointed at Conn."

"So he can be disappeared?"

"I didn't ask for his name." Though they did now know it was a male. "You can tell us what he said. Did he name Conn, or did he fit a description?"

"No one would be dumb enough to name the boss," Daly said.

Niall had another view. "Unless he had an agenda."

"Should we invite Vex to the party?" Hock asked.

"No," she said, "please, God. Connel in the same room as him is one thing. Add my father to the mix…"

"The asshole prefers you alone," Strat said.

"Something that won't happen again," Connel added.

She looked at him over her shoulder and he wasn't kidding around.

"When he finds out about you and Ire," Lachlan said, "there could be trouble."

On an exhale, she sank back in her seat. "He knows."

"Vex knows—so it was only your family in the dark?"

Now that he mentioned it…

"We'll deal with the Manzanis," Connel said. "Find out what they know."

"And how will you do that?" her brother asked.

"Old man was asking questions around City Hall," Connel said, ignoring Lachlan's query. "Find out who's nervous. Get names or faces. We'll lean on them."

"What the—you can't really expect us to give you names. These are innocent people."

"Not so innocent if they ordered the old man's murder," Strat said.

"Or did it themselves," Daly added.

"We know how to ask nicely," Niall said, earning a few whispers of laughter from the McDade people.

"No one's suggesting hurting anyone," she said, trying to console her brother. Her father wouldn't give first. Her brother, ultimately, wanted the murderer unmasked. "But you can't deny a lot of people won't talk to cops."

"They talk to us, they could get arrested. They talk to McDade's people…" And they could end up dead. Her brother shifted. "Which raises the question…"

"What question?"

"What do you plan to do if you identify the perp first?" Lachlan asked, looking square at Connel. "I won't let you drag my sister down to your level."

"Don't do that," she said. "Don't—"

"Hush," Connel said in his usual unhurried manner. "As I told you before, your sister is a grown woman."

"Yeah, and I didn't know then you were screwing her. Do you have no shame?"

"Do you?" Connel asked. She prayed he didn't stand up. If Conn got to his feet, his people would end this in a heartbeat. "Your sister showed loyalty to my family when she came to the precinct and told the truth. Will you punish her for that integrity?"

"You belong behind bars," her father barked.

"Maybe," Connel said, speeding her heart with his restraint. "But not for this."

And he wasn't the only one playing dirty. That her father could be so brazen in his judgment… Her eyes met Strat's, sure he could sense her conflict.

"He's supposed to be the angry one," Strat muttered as though they were the only two people in the room.

"Sersha has a point," Imogen said. "There are many skill sets in this room. You should play to that."

"Won't be long before the world knows about her relationship with Ire," Ford said.

"If they don't already," Jagg added.

Chances were, word was out there. The precinct was a sieve; keeping a secret there was nigh on impossible. And why would they? They'd released Connel on her assertion of being his alibi. That information had to be shared to justify letting him go.

"Steeple knows," Imogen said. "Which means the other papers do. Ours might not publish it out of respect for you, but—"

"They'll have to follow suit eventually."

The words in print didn't concern her. The Chronicler couldn't show too much restraint on her behalf. Not that it mattered. Steeple was in charge of his department, not the entire paper. Decisions like that were made further up the chain.

"You're currency now," Strat said like he had in the car.

"Increases her profile," Imogen said. "You should get security."

"She has security," Daly said, perhaps offended his ability was being called into question.

"Didn't make any difference to my grandfather," she said. "He had security and they still got to him."

"I'm betting he didn't sleep next to a mob boss at night."

Ford had a point. It would be difficult to take her off the board when Connel was so quick on the trigger.

"What do we have on motive?" Niall asked.

"You have your theories, Detective?"

"All the standard theories have to be eliminated first."

"Sex or money," she said, recalling what Connel said about motives.

"Power. Revenge. Pride. Envy."

"Can't go wrong with the deadly sins," Niall said to Lachlan. "We're Catholic, Mr. McLeod. We're familiar."

She smiled, holding back her laugh, and cleared her throat when Lachlan turned back.

"Was the old man screwing anyone?"

Daly's question hitched Lachlan's chin just a little as his eyes rose.

"Yes," she said, reading her brother's reaction.

His attention leaped to her. "He told you?"

"My father wasn't in any relationship," her father said.

"No one said nothing about a relationship," Niall said. "Anyone he's fucking is a suspect."

"The police eliminated her from suspicion," Lachlan murmured.

"I can't believe this!"

Her father's surprise was as potent as hers, but she held the latter back.

"If the police are done with her, no reason we can't ask a few questions," Daly said, eyes locked on Niall. "There's no interfering with a whatever if they've cut her loose."

They'd cut Connel loose too. Somehow, she doubted that was the last time he'd be hauled in by the cops.

"She might prefer to talk to a woman," she said, hoping Lachlan would let more slip. "I can talk to her if—"

"No, I'll do it," Lachlan said. "She knows me."

"Might make her more comfortable," Strat said and sucked in a breath. "Next on the list is debts."

Daly was on the ball. "Everyone has those."

"My father's credit is exemplary," her father insisted.

"Not all debts are financial," Niall said. "Wanna see Ire's ledger?"

"Yeah, actually," Lachlan said, his brows rising. "I'll look at anything you show me."

And that flash drive came to mind. Shit. What had Strat done with it?

"No one is poking around in each other's business here. We're not investigating each other."

Though, she'd asked Connel to investigate her father's people. Having them watching set her uneasy. They weren't active participants or invested. Why did they have to bear audience to this clandestine meeting?

"And if we think someone here might be involved?" Imogen asked. "What do we do then?"

TWENTY-ONE

SILENCE.

Her eyes narrowed on Strat, but he offered the slightest head shake. He hadn't exactly had time to clue his daughter in on what they knew about the superintendent.

"Bring it to me," she said when no one else spoke. "Does anyone here suspect me?" No response. "Can everyone agree I wasn't the shooter?"

"Aye," Niall said first, to her surprise.

Or she would've been surprised, except his boss and oldest friend was her alibi.

"You don't have an investigative mind," her father said.

"Funny, 'cause that's only what I do all day," she said, trying her best not to let her anger out. Snark didn't count; that was too small to pull back. "But I didn't mean I'd solve the mystery all on my lonesome. I meant if anyone has worries, concerns, suspicions, bring them to me, I can help expand or eliminate them."

Her father wouldn't come to her in a million

years. In a billion years. Under normal circumstances, he might go to Lachlan, but they couldn't forget her dad's hands were dirty in this. That was one thing they already knew for sure.

Taking Connel's arm, she rested his hand on her thigh, so his fingertips relaxed at the hem of her skirt. Something about the skin-to-skin contact comforted her, and that was as much as she could get in that minute.

"We'll hunt down the debtors," Niall said.

"Shouldn't be too hard for the likes of you." The second the words were out, Imogen panicked and tried to pull them back. "I mean people must tell you things. If his debts weren't of the official variety, they were the unofficial kind and that's more your wheelhouse."

"Good save," Ford said insincerely. "Jagg and me will ask around the City Hall folks."

"My people can do that," McLeod Snr. said.

"Yeah, but they won't tell the family anything incriminating," Imogen said. "My dad can help."

"Can I?"

"Yes," Imogen drawled. Her attempt to force Strat and Jagg together wasn't exactly veiled. "They'll feel more comfortable with you around. A lot of them are older folk."

"Funny," Strat said, deadpan, but more than a few other faces enjoyed the daughter's tease. "You gotta ask the boss; I'm supposed to be keeping bossette alive."

Bossette? Now there was a joke.

Connel just looked at Niall. "Two hours this afternoon," the lieutenant said. "Update us after."

How did Connel do that? Communicate with such little effort? He did it with her too and they weren't lifelong friends.

"I can stick with Bluebell today," Daly said. "Our asking's better done in the dark."

"I'm only going to work, I don't need—" Conn

squeezed her thigh and that was enough to silence her on the subject. "Anything else?"

"Reconvene tomorrow," Niall said.

Some rose. Not her or her brother. "Uh, we can't… the memorial service is tomorrow."

"We'll do it after."

"You expect us to say goodbye to our grandfather and then come here for a meet?"

"It's okay," she said, intervening before tensions could rise. "Anything pressing, you can tell me. I'm sure I'll be around. I can let the others know. We could meet here the day after, Wednesday… if that works?"

"Aye."

With that agreement, everyone stood to split off.

"Ser," Lachlan said before she was completely up.

When he nodded her over, she joined him. "You okay?"

Her dad stayed close too.

"We want to do dinner tonight," Lachlan said. "At your place. Eight thirty. Just family."

Okay. Ominous. But with everything that had happened in the last couple of days, necessary.

"Lach?" Imogen called from her place with her father, brother, and boyfriend.

Lachlan went to join them, and her father huddled with his own people.

"Macushla."

The call wasn't loud, it didn't need to be. Snapping out of the moment, she about-faced to go over to Connel, Niall, and Daly.

"Sorry," she said. "My family isn't always…" Except they kind of were.

Connel's head jerked right, sending his boys trotting off. Not that they were delicate or graceful in any way.

"That was a stone-cold bluff," Connel said, almost impressed.

"What?"

"You didn't know the old man was fucking anyone."

"No," she said, sliding a hand up his chest. "But from the look on Lachlan's face, it was obvious. If he felt like he had to protect a confidence, he might not—"

"You're good at the game," Connel said. "Your father doesn't see it. I see it."

"You've seen me since the beginning, somehow. And I care more about you than him," she purred, pressing herself against him. "We're having dinner tonight."

"We?"

"Lachlan, my dad, and me. It's at my place. Will you come?"

"They don't want me there, baby."

"He said just family. Isn't family important to you?" she teased, knowing the answer. "You don't have to be there, just know you're invited."

"You belong to me, Macushla. Wherever you are, I'm invited."

Did that work both ways? Maybe. But he'd put such a premium on protecting her that it was possible he didn't want her around while they worked.

The McDades did have a specific skill set. She'd never be refused by a potential source again.

"High Class!" Another call, this one drew everyone's attention. Whisper stood on the apartment balcony, looking down over the club. More specifically, at her. "Your next appointment's right here."

Someone like Whisper Doherty-McDade got what they wanted, regardless of what else was happening.

Still, she looked to Connel to get the nod before heading over. Whisper disappeared back inside while she ascended the spiral stairs. In the apartment, the beauty was mixing drinks behind the bar.

"Hey," she said. "You okay? We missed you downstairs."

"I'm not so good with an audience. Zay says I act out."

Yet that didn't seem to bother her. "Your input is valuable. To me."

"I'm not from around here."

"But your name still means something on the street."

"You want me to kick ass? I'm there. But you don't want my theories."

"I do."

After a little side-eye, Whisper exhaled. "From everything we know, it's obvious. Someone killed your grandfather to shut him up. Though that could be my life experience talking. All it takes is one right question to the wrong person and people get nervous."

But who? "Conn says my grandfather never took a pay-off."

"From the McDades. But we're not the only party in town, sugar."

No. True. Who else was in play? And was this anything to do with the Harvest deal? If her grandfather wasn't under McDade influence, could it be someone else learned that and didn't like it?

"Does seem more likely than a scorned lover. Though a lover could get into his bedroom easily."

"Maybe it was more than one person. Was the lover a genuine lover or a mole?"

Oh, now that possibility would fester. She hadn't known there was a lover until Lachlan gave it away. Finding out more about the woman jumped up a couple of places on her mental to-do list.

"Debts. Family. Any feuds we should know

about?"

"All families argue."

"No judgment here. Fights at the Doherty house growing up always got bloody."

"Sometimes that's better than staying quiet and keeping the peace."

"The McLeods aren't that different to the McDades or the Dohertys. We're just more… direct."

"Yeah. What's it like being married to your blood enemy?"

"You asking as a McDade or a reporter?"

"I'd never print anything that could hurt the McDades."

"Then we're on the same page, even if your guy does have a stick up his ass," Whisper said and raised a shoulder in a half shrug, while still working. "Much as I hate to admit it, he's right. I call it uptight, he calls it smart. I like to stir the pot, but I'm impressed actually. He's smarter than a lot of other guys at the top. My father got himself killed; my father-in-law is in prison. Didn't work out so well for them." The McDade wife made eye contact. "You know that's how this ends, right? Your guy gets dead or goes up the river. As long as your guy's in it, that's the only way out."

"Are you warning me off?"

"No! God, no." Whisper poured the margarita and handed her a glass. "Their relationships with their fathers are difficult. Zay kept quiet during the trial, yes, but he hasn't had love for his father for a long time. Taking him down, it changed things. Now the Doherty crews run with the McDades and with the Gambatto family imploding, there's a lot of opportunity. Ire's done good seizing those opportunities."

"Are you and Razer staying to have his back?"

"I'm saying your ass is valuable. And as the McDades gain more power, you become more valuable."

"Meaning…?"

"And Ire? Well, he's in demand and seriously protected."

"I'm not getting it. Conn makes sure I'm protected. If you think I should be scared—"

The woman turned fast, slamming her back against the wall, landing a blade at her throat.

"You make sure you can protect yourself," Whisper growled against her cheek. "You never go anywhere unarmed."

"A gun?"

Whisper backed up, showed her the blade, then picked something up from the bar to shove it against her. "My daddy always said, 'you pick up a gun, you shoot to kill.'" Mrs. McDade downed her drink in one and dropped the glass in the sink. "Sometimes it's more fun just to scare them. Come on."

A blade, in a sheath on a strap, that's what she'd been given. Whisper was halfway to the stairs.

"Where are we going?"

"Basement," Whisper said, stopping at the top of the stairs. "Forget what you learned in your self-defense classes and daddy's helpful hints. You're going to learn to fight like a Doherty."

"What way is that?"

Satisfied pride spread on Whisper's face. "The best way. Dirty."

TWENTY-TWO

EVERY MUSCLE ACHED, and that was with stretching. Thank God she didn't get jumped on her way to work or she'd have been too stiff to resist. The guys might have snickered, but they didn't jeer her. How long would that last? If she kept sparring with Whisper, she'd have to insist on it being a private affair. And would check Connel had no camera in the gym.

Yes, they had a gym down there. More than one. With weight benches and cardio machines. There was also a boxing ring and sparring mats. The McDades kept in shape.

Daly stayed at her back with Strat not far behind. They didn't say anything in The Chronicler elevator. With the memorial service planned and a dozen people on the investigation, it was time to show her face at work. She'd neglected the office for too long. When the elevator doors opened on her floor, it was a relief the reception desk was absent flowers. Maybe Evander figured she'd take a few more days off.

"Sersha," Lucy said, leaping to her feet. "We

didn't know you were coming in today."

"It's good to see you too."

Lucy scrambled about on the desk. "I've forwarded your messages in email. And I've got these…" she put a stack of letters and a box on the reception hutch. "Other gifts are in there."

"Gifts?" she asked, turning in the direction Lucy nodded. "Flowers and… things."

The interview room by the reception was teeming with flowers. The door was closed, but the panel next to it was glass.

"Shit, where did they come from?"

"Everyone. There are cards. Condolence cards."

Of course. "Collect the cards. I'll thank who I need to thank. Send the flowers over to the hospital or some funeral home or whatever. Give them out to guests."

"You don't want them?"

"What am I going to do with all those?"

"Would Ire get jealous?" Surprise brought her attention around; the young receptionist immediately shrank. "I'm sorry, I shouldn't—"

"Conn has nothing to be jealous of." She squinted. "But they wouldn't go great with his decor."

"It wasn't him, was it? Ire McDade. Is he your secret admirer?"

Subduing a laugh took effort. "No."

Wasn't much secret about him anymore. Man, it was liberating.

She smiled and headed for her desk. People might think her being with Connel changed everything about her, it didn't. Some things? Yes. But not everything. Having him mentioned to her, in relation to her, was a new thing that would take some adjustment. Some part of her still thought of them as a secret. Except they weren't. The world knew about their relationship, she'd have to get used to being probed.

At her desk, papers filled the in-tray. Junk mail. Post-its. Leave the routine for a couple of days and the space becomes a dumping ground.

"Sersha?" Tulip's voice turned her around. "I'm so sorry about your loss."

"Thanks."

"I couldn't believe it, I… I'm so sorry. Do you have any leads?"

Not something she really wanted to talk about. "We're leaving the investigation to the police."

"That must be difficult. As an investigative journalist, this is what we do."

"Yes, there are just more… pressing concerns."

"Right because you're with… Did your family know that before he was arrested? About your sexual relationship with Ire McDade?" Was this woman interrogating her? "Makes sense now why you had me removed from Stag. That was you, wasn't it?" No, it wasn't. "I'd love a quote. I know it doesn't seem like the right time—"

"No, it doesn't."

"I'd just like to fact check a couple of things."

A couple of things and probably a whole lot more. These things snowballed fast.

"I have to see Steeple."

She tried to sidestep, but Tulip got in her way. "It will only take a second."

"I don't want to talk right now," she said, skirting the woman, intending to go to Steeple's office.

"I know about Nicole McDade," Tulip called after her. "About the bounty."

She turned, almost gobsmacked until she saw Daly hurtling toward them.

Racing back to the woman, she caught her cuff and pulled hard, dragging her across the room and tossing Steeple's door out of the way to shut them inside.

"Are you insane?" she hissed at Tulip.

"Sersha?" Steeple said, rising from the desk.

Tulip kept her focus. "Don't ever, ever, say anything that could, in any way, be construed as a threat in front of Conn's guys."

"What's going on?" their boss asked.

"It's one big game of Telephone," she explained to Tulip. "You say something, one guy repeats it to another, and it gets back to Conn's ears."

"Are you afraid of him?"

"No," she said. "But learn you're playing with live ammunition when you wade in with these families. Learn it fast. Don't get caught in the crossfire. And, shit, where did you grow up? I thought the innocent thing was an act."

If this was an act too, the woman had to be careful facing off with "shoot first, ask questions later" McDades.

"I didn't expect you today," Steeple said. "What's happening? What happened?"

"Nothing happened. Tulip's just overeager."

"I don't think it's overeager to report the news. You lied to us. To your people. You didn't say anything about being romantically involved with Ire."

"To you or my family."

"So how do we trust you?"

"Do I care if you trust me? What difference does it make to you?"

"You had valuable information, instrumental to my story, and you didn't even hint at it. Why not just refuse to help? Why come along?"

"I came along because Steeple told me to. And so you wouldn't get hurt."

"The bounty is why Razer is here, isn't it? Why is he protecting his sister-in-law?"

"You'd have to ask him."

"Great," Tulip said, plucking a phone from her pocket. "When? I can fit into his schedule."

"I'm not his social secretary. Jesus, you think Razer McDade does what I say?"

"Tulip, will you give us a minute?" Steeple asked. "Please."

The woman looked at them both and then left, slipping her phone into her pocket.

Steeple gestured at the first chair and sat in his seat again.

"You better not demand I give an interview," she said, dropping into the seat. "I can't. And I can't believe she was so... forward."

"It's her job. One you used to do too. Don't blame people for treating you different. Everyone is shocked."

"About my relationship with Conn? Not my grandfather being murdered?"

"Now that you ask, yes. I'd have put money on the second being more likely. I'd have bet my house on the first never happening." He linked his fingers while pulling in closer to his desk. "Is it real? How did you...? Ire McDade doesn't play around."

He did actually, when it came to women. Though that wasn't Steeple's point.

"He's a serious guy."

"Yeah, and getting mixed up with the McDades like that..." He lowered his volume. "Do you know things? I'm not asking you to tell me, but... does he talk to you?" She said nothing. "You're like... Shit, Sersh."

"No one expected it, I know. Neither did I."

"You're together? What are we talking? Marriage and kids and—"

"Let's not get ahead of ourselves. I know this is a shock and there's a lot going on, but I cannot be The

Chronicler's gal on the inside. That won't happen."

Though for a brief time, she'd considered using sex to get a story. What a delusion. She'd never wanted to manipulate Connel for anything other than sex.

"The attack, when you were attacked. Was that because of this?"

"No." A possibility, a wondering, trickled into her mind, which, for the first time in weeks, was sharp. Now that they had confirmation… "Huh."

"What?"

"Nothing." She leaped to her feet. "Can I go?"

"Uh, yeah," he said, sinking back in his seat. "Just let us know if there's anything you need."

What she needed was a shot of whiskey and a little inspiration. Maybe she'd find the second if she could order her thoughts.

Snagging her phone from her desk, she went into the empty breakroom and closed the door before dialing.

"Macushla?"

"Those guys who, you know, in the alley," she murmured into the phone.

"Attacked you?"

"We know it was the Manzanis, but do we know the order came direct from Silvio Manzani? Might his people have taken initiative on their own?"

If they did it once, maybe they did it again with her grandfather.

"Going after the superintendent's daughter is risky. In McDade territory they could start a war. They'd need permission."

"From Silvio?"

"From someone higher up."

Could that be Evander? Not if he wanted to foil his father's plans to prevent the McDades acquiring the Harvest site. Swerve? Possibly, that guy didn't seem to ask anyone for permission. Though, thus far, they had no evidence Silvio's go-to guy was involved with Harvest at all.

"They wanted to know who you greased. If my grandfather found out who was working with the McDades, could one of your allies have pulled the trigger to protect themselves or the family?"

"No one would act without my consent."

"Unless they were doing it to impress you."

"If anyone on my books was responsible—"

"They're sweating right now," she said, finishing his thought with fewer curse words than he'd use.

Pre- their relationship going public, a McDade ally might expect praise for eliminating a threat. Post… yeah, that person would be a wreck.

"Has to be someone he knew to get into his bedroom," Connel said.

"Whisper said something about that today. She wondered if the girlfriend could be a mole."

"ID the girlfriend and my guys will find out."

"Thanks, baby."

"Any virgin trigger-man will be nervous. We wait to see what Strat turns up and plan from there. No use pulling in my people with the cops watching."

"Okay," she said. "I just wanted to put it out there."

"You at work?"

"Yeah," she said and sighed. "It'll take some time for things to go back to the way they were."

"You're a McDade now, Macushla. Things will never go back to the way they were."

On that note, the line died. The past was gone, the future was all they had. What the hell was that going to look like?

TWENTY-THREE

HER APARTMENT WAS UNLOCKED.

Lachlan was in the kitchen when she went inside, her father at the dinner table.

"Whatever this is about…" she said, dumping her purse on the breakfast bar. "Which, by the way, I don't need three guesses to figure out, I'm really not in the mood to be lectured."

"Is anyone ever in the mood to be lectured?" Lachlan asked, retrieving a glass to pour wine from the open bottle.

"Whatever you're gearing up to say, trust me, I've had the conversation in my own head. Any judgments you want to share I already heard today. I don't think I went five minutes without someone stopping at my desk to chat or interrogate me."

"And that doesn't tell you something?" her father asked. "Being with him is insanity. Who knows the damage that's already been done?"

"Already been done? Oh, I've told him all the

family secrets, given him keys, alarm codes, everything. He's raiding our family gold vault right now."

Her father, Ronald, stood up, but it was Lachlan who spoke.

"Provoking each other won't get us anywhere. Neither will being facetious." Shame, and she did it so well. He planted both hands on the counter. "Have you thought about this? Considered that Ire might be using you?"

Despite her initial urge to respond with offense, she took a breath to calm herself.

"You admitted yourself that you don't know him as anything other than his job. You don't like his job—"

"His job is his life. He is the job."

"Can you say any different?"

"I don't go around torturing and killing people."

"You don't carry a gun every day?" she asked. "You don't protect yourself?"

"I'm protecting the public."

"Not for nothing, but Connel doesn't carry a gun."

"He doesn't need to, his minions do."

Minions? Nice one, Dad. She was unmoved.

"Dad," Lachlan said, presumably reasoning that wasn't helpful.

"Connel is more than just a leader. Keeping his people safe is important. Loyalty is everything to him."

"You think he's been faithful to you?" her father asked with sneering pity. "That man sees you as a tool. An object."

Exhaling, she picked up her wine and sank onto a stool. "Thank God he didn't come. What an introduction to the family."

"You invited him?" her father snapped.

"Wherever I am, he's invited. We're a couple, Dad. Together."

"This is unbelievable. How can you be so stupid?"

"Okay, cool it," Lachlan said. "We're here for dinner, right? Let's just sit down and eat like a regular, happy family."

Now who was delusional? A happy family?

Lachlan had done his best with the spaghetti. Better than she could've. None of them had the time or inclination to cook.

They sat at the table and ate, paying more attention to the food than each other.

Grief should have the power to bring them together, especially still so close to their shared tragedy.

Someone's phone rang. Not hers. Lachlan looked at their dad, who slipped a device out of a pocket.

"I have to take this," he said and rose to head for the front door.

"Uh, Hock and Snuff are in the hall." Both gaped at her, so she aimed for a light smile. "You can use the bedroom."

Unimpressed though her father was, he diverted and answered the call as he went in and closed the door.

"He gonna find anything in there?" Lachlan asked with enough of a smirk to amuse her.

"Like what? Gags? Whips? Chains? Drug stash? Hooker boots?"

"Got experience?"

"Oh, yeah, with all the above. Conn denies me nothing."

Her brother pushed his plate aside. "Does that stretch to intel?"

"He'll share what he knows about Grandpapa—"

"I'm not talking about that. He says he's in on that. I trust he'd tell you, though I'm not sure I'd want him to."

"Why not?"

"Because no one answered my question. What will the McDades do if they find the perp first?" Now it wasn't so funny. "I don't want you party to anything illegal, even something like this. If I find out he's put you in danger or forced you to be a part of his crimes—"

"He doesn't force me to do anything."

"I'll take him down, Sersh. If he dirties you, it will be my life's work to—"

"You know you said in the office that you could be allies. Why can't you see that's true? Look past your prejudice, your preconceived notions about him."

"So tell me something else, Sersha. Tell me something about him that will pull the wool from my eyes."

What could she say? Nothing that would make Connel look weak or vulnerable. It wasn't all about the job. One thing that made him vulnerable who Lachlan would never exploit? Her.

"He values me, Lach," she said, putting her own food aside. "You might think he's playing me. Dad might believe I'm naïve. But neither of you have seen the way he looks at me, heard the things he's said. You don't know the lengths he's gone to for me."

That struck a chord with her discerning brother. "What has he done for you?"

"He protects me." Without missing a beat, she wanted to alleviate his suspicion. "My life. My well-being is the primary McDade priority. Didn't you hear him say that?"

"Words are easy."

"He didn't tell the truth at the precinct to protect me."

"And you're saying he wouldn't expect you to speak up?"

"He didn't arrest himself. He didn't snitch and

push the cops in his own direction. He didn't orchestrate my confession."

"Didn't mean it didn't work for him."

"Oh, yeah? He could've outed me when you were in his office. He could've rubbed our relationship in your face. Not only didn't he do that, but he ordered his men not to mention my name next to his. He was protecting you too because you matter to me."

"You don't get it. Buying time for you to get attached means he guarantees your compliance when he needs it. Men like him are strategic. They think a few moves ahead and know sometimes sacrifices have to be made."

"He's never asked me to spy or give him information." Sure, he'd asked her to run an errand, but that was irrelevant because she hadn't followed through. Connel hadn't tortured her. Ever. Not with anything except her own desire. "He's a good man."

Her brother scoffed. "No, sis, he isn't. And it's terrifying you could believe that."

"Is this what it's going to be? Always? He doesn't talk down about you. He doesn't criticize and mock you. From an outsider's point of view, you're the antagonist here."

"I don't like any of your boyfriends. That's my right as your older brother. But you've never had a boyfriend who could put a bullet in you for forgetting to take out the trash."

Her head shook. "You don't know him. He would never—"

"They call him 'Ire' for a reason." Yep, and her brother wasn't the first person to say that. "The guy has serious anger issues."

"People frustrate him." Especially those who interrupted while they were naked. "And he doesn't... I calm him. I don't know how or why, but when he gets angry, I can dial him down."

"Strange superpower," Lachlan said. "Do you really want to be around when that power runs out?"

"You're determined to think the worst. Any woman could get just as angry with you. An asshole in the street could walk right up and shoot you just for being a cop. Should we talk about that?"

"You're having sex with Ire, right?" he asked. She didn't answer. "That means alone. Sleeping. Naked. Vulnerable. When he gets bored with you, he could send you off anywhere in the world to live in a brothel."

"Only if I asked nicely." He glared at her sass. "Things can go wrong in any relationship. Conn and I are at least aware of our differences. And, yes, we make allowances for those differences, but any relationship requires compromise."

"This is more than compromise."

"You and Imogen were perfect for each other and it didn't work out. I didn't talk about her sending you off to some far-flung place."

"Ire has the means."

"But not the will. Why would he want to get rid of me? If it doesn't work out, then it doesn't work out."

"What if there's someone else? What if you meet someone else?"

"I love Connel," she said, and he blinked in surprise. "I'm not shopping around. I wouldn't cheat on any boyfriend. It's a respect thing. If I'm in a place where I have to go looking elsewhere, then it's time to end the relationship."

"Easy to say when it's not real, when it's just intellectual."

"Beyond my views on the subject," she said. "You think I would do that to another guy, to any guy, set him up as Conn's enemy? Shit, it's hard enough when Evander's around and I couldn't be less interested."

"Because your boyfriend is a lunatic."

"No, he isn't. Evander is the one not getting what he wants. I've made it clear to him."

"Something you've been doing for years and the guy still hasn't got the message. McDade won't stand that for long."

That was a point she couldn't deny. "Connel knows about Evander and his behavior."

"And he's cool with it?"

She wasn't sure that was a phrase she'd ever use to describe Connel. And that was in spite of him being the coolest person she'd ever met.

"He deals with it."

"He doesn't feel threatened?"

Now that was funny. "Why would he feel threatened? My feelings for Conn are real. I tell him everything."

"Everything?"

"There's nothing I'd hide from him."

"You'd tell him everything. Private family business?"

And there wasn't a thing she could say against that when Connel knew things about their family that her brother didn't.

"We don't choose who we fall in love with," she said and immediately regretted it, thinking about Imogen. "Do you feel threatened? He'd never hurt us, Lachlan. He'll go to war for this family if necessary."

"And if he causes that war?"

"Evander was a problem long before I met Connel."

"It's my job to worry about you."

"It's also your job to trust me."

Their father returned as they held eye contact.

"What's going on?" her father asked. "What are you talking about?"

"Tomorrow's a big day," she said, standing up. "I'm going to bed."

The conversation wasn't over. It never would be. Her brother didn't understand, but at least he was reasonable about voicing his issues. The men in her life would take time to adjust to each other. She'd just have to do whatever she could to calm their concerns.

TWENTY-FOUR

TOSSING AND TURNING, the decision to sleep alone became frustrating. Though not frustrating enough that she wanted to get up.

On any normal night, she would, but with the memorial the following day, dark circles were a real concern. Staying up late wouldn't make the event any easier. Where was sleep?

Rolling over, her hand sought her phone on the nightstand. Quickly switching to her recents list, she dialed and closed her eyes, head still in the pillow.

"Macushla," he answered, amped, that much was obvious from his breathing.

An agonizing wail blasted her ear, opening her eyes. "You're working? Sorry, I know it's late."

"Your text said you were staying at your place."

"I am. Do you want to come over?"

Though her brother in the next room was still a factor.

"This could take a while." Another scream and Connel's voice changed direction. "Shut the fuck up!

Interrupt my lady one more time, I'll put a bullet in your balls."

"You're working, I'm sorry, I'll—"

"You are more important than street scum." Just the simplicity of his statement helped her mood. "Dinner didn't go well?"

It would've been better if he'd been there. Better for her anyway, she needed the support. The men may not have enjoyed being forced together. That powder keg could go any time. Probably best it didn't happen the evening before a potent and emotional occasion.

"My dad's disappointed in me."

"He was disappointed in you last week."

Before he knew about her relationship. Good point. Why should it change based on this development? She sure shouldn't be losing sleep over it.

"Lachlan's worried about me."

"That's his job." Exactly what her brother had said. "The day he stops is the day I'll have a problem with him."

Despite her family's negative response to the relationship, Conn was realistic and non-judgmental. People thought her family was good and he was bad news. Yet her lover proved to be more accepting than the outwardly respectable men.

"You know you've made it better," she said on an appreciative sigh.

"That's my job." She smiled. "Want Daly to pick you up? Got plenty of assholes for you to beat on."

A laugh bubbled out. "I'll only get turned on."

"It's my job to take care of that too."

His job. Her job. Their relationship was real. That reality would need an adjustment period too. How could she be with Connel McDade? That might be a question others considered. Her? Now it was out there, she wasn't going back. Living without him once was once too many.

"What did the guy keeping you from my bed do?"

"He owes me money."

Didn't everyone? Money or favors. Pushing the comforter from her chest, her hand rested over her breast.

"If it gets him that kind of attention, I'm swiping your wallet next time I get the chance."

"Stealing gets a whole other kind of punishment."

"Yeah?" she asked, trembling at the gravel in his voice. "You promise?"

"Macushla wants to play."

"Do rún, with you, I always want to play. The time we lost—"

"Time we'll make up, baby."

Licking her lips, she couldn't stop them curling. "It shouldn't turn me on," she whispered. "That you're out there taking care of business."

"Family business."

Was it the McDade part or the violence? Or was it that a man with such power could turn that authority to her advantage with the click of his fingers?

"You said today I didn't know what you would do for me."

"No rules in our house."

"I'd never… your family, the love you have for them and what they stand for—"

"We," he said. The impact of flesh on flesh echoed down the line. "Our family." Another hit and another. Not much response from the recipient. Was he conscious? "What do you need, Cushla Machree?"

"To know that you're with me. I couldn't sleep and just hearing your voice… I swear I'm not one of those crazy, needy women."

"I know what you are."

A shriek in the background of the call and boom, a gunshot startled her. The scream that followed pricked her hair on end.

She sighed. "I'm interrupting."

"It'll do him good to bleed for a while."

"I will never come between you and your work. Do what you need to do. Where will you be tomorrow night?"

"The loft."

"Tomorrow won't be much fun. That it's my grandfather's memorial is one thing, but going alone, while my dad's haughty and lapping up the sympathy… I'll do my best not to provoke him. More for Lachlan's sake than mine."

"Loss brings a family together or tears them apart."

"Strat has his own theories on that too."

A sob behind the screech became a whimper.

"Keep the fucker awake," Connel snarled at someone. "If he passes out, he misses the show."

More crying.

"Go work," she said. "Thank you for picking up."

He said something in his foreign tongue. She didn't understand it, but a smile settled on her lips and her eyes closed.

Connel McDade, the medicine that soothed all her ails.

TWENTY-FIVE

HOW MANY MORE hands to shake? Kisses on the cheek and elongated hugs may look good to onlookers, but they didn't alleviate grief.

The memorial was supposed to be for people who cared about her grandfather. People who cared about the family. So many of them didn't. Still, she'd done her duty alongside her father and brother greeting everyone who appeared.

Yes, this was the McLeod family, car crash in action. Welcome to the shitshow.

"Shall we go in?" the pastor asked, arms open toward the mourners gathered on the stone stairs.

Her father took the lead on going inside and others followed. Lachlan glanced back to check on her, but with the priest at her side, he continued without her.

She didn't even want to look up. Didn't want to catch anyone's eye. The platitudes were too much. It was no one's fault. What could anyone say that would make it right? Nothing.

Voyeuristic, that's what it was. Strangers wanted

to gawk at the grieving family. To see the lustful woman who'd gone against her father and bedded with the enemy. She couldn't think straight. What was the purpose of the day other than to advertise their loss?

The pastor paused, scanning the street. People's heads turned and whispers broke the air.

What caused the stir?

She had to turn to—a fleet of black town cars came to a stop in front of the cathedral. Who was…?

Almost in unison, people emerged. Dressed all in black with just the occasional fleck of red.

"Shit," she whispered under her breath.

As her lips twitched to a slight smile, a tear slipped free.

McDades. A lot of them. And after the massacre of other families on the east coast, they didn't gather in close quarter groups when they didn't have to. Only one man had the authority to allow it.

Whisper, Razer, Niall, Hock, Daly, every McDade in her life.

Strat. Ford. Even Jagger Dunn stood with them. The Manzanis may have something to say about that.

She inhaled. It was such a show of support. She hadn't explicitly invited them, so as not to put Connel in a difficult position. Or had she feared how a refusal would hurt? How could she have doubted him? There he was, her guy at the head of the pack, serious, somber, and completely fixated on her.

Like true soldiers, the group formed into two lines of height order behind him.

The back doors of the two vans at the front and back of the pack opened. A dozen men poured onto the street, spreading out to provide security, she guessed, from the way they dispersed and took posts.

Her eyes closed, freeing another tear. If she didn't take a breath, she'd come undone. How could anyone doubt her guy's love or that he'd always do what was best for her?

How had she existed without him?

As her eyes opened, she smiled at their ranks. Strat winked, infusing her with a strength that could get her through anything.

Conn's eyes stayed on hers; he ascended until he was right there at her side. Without a word, she threaded her fingers between his. The gentle squeeze of his grip released the tension from her body.

He was there. With her. She wasn't alone.

And if people had come to gawp, they sure had something to gawp at now.

Leaning in, his words warmed her ear. "You are never alone," he murmured, brushing away her tear. "Our army will always raise you up."

The pillar of his strength held her firm.

"Father," she said to their priest before she lost her shit, "I don't know if you've met—"

"We're old friends," Connel said. "Aren't we, Father Fitz?"

"Mr. McDade," he said. "It's a pleasure to have you with us."

"We're here for Sersha," he said. That voice, with that intonation, wasn't one to be ignored. "Do your best work."

The Father gulped and no one else said a word. Not one single word.

Conn nodded up the stairs, where the gawkers had their ball. Though the pastor glanced at her, he didn't hesitate to proceed inside.

She went up with her guy's hand secure in hers, his people at their back.

Others seemed tense as they went inside, yet her whole world was lighter.

She glanced back. The McDade gang shuffled

into the back rows on both sides of the aisle.

"Thank you for being here," she whispered, cupping their joined hands in front of her.

"You'll pay for it later," he murmured without caring whispers followed their advance toward the front.

Her impervious man sailed down that aisle, strong and indifferent to speculation. She'd never considered it, but it must've followed him all his life. Scrutiny. Rumor. Judgment. Growing up, her grandfather and father got attention. She'd been invisible. Connel McDade never had and never would be invisible.

"Let's hope there's no mandatory confession," she whispered. "You'd be in the box a while."

"Only if I took you in with me. Show's better than tell."

"Want to make the priest blush?"

"Guy's a masochist in our playroom, baby. We own him."

He didn't mean. Actually mean… Her father noticed before her sibling. Holding her breath, she carried on, taking a seat next to her brother.

Lachlan leaned in. "This a good idea?"

The question wasn't disapproving, just dubious. Progress. At least that's how she chose to interpret it.

Taking her brother's hand too, she held it on his knee. These men were the most important in her life. They gave her stability, certainty, and nothing could make her abandon either of them.

***

NUMB, WHEN LACHLAN leaned in to kiss her cheek, it hit her that it was over. Her grandfather was gone.

The moment her father and brother stood up, others waylaid them. Good. Her head wasn't on straight and didn't need benign conversation. Someone took her hands to pull her onto her feet.

Connel. He laid her hands flat on his chest, but she slid them apart to rest her face against the reassuring beat of his heart.

"Do you want us to stay and pay our respects?"

The line up. Was she supposed to shake hands and accept condolences again?

"Thank you. I can't even… thank you for being here."

"I'm always at your back, Cushla Machree," he said, stroking her back until his hands closed around her jaw to tilt her head back. "You are our strength."

She didn't feel so strong. "If we line up, we have to do it next to my father and Lach. I don't want people touching you," she said, more guarded given all that had happened. "I don't trust any of them."

"And you think I trust them near you? I am the only man permitted to touch you. My hands will be the last your skin ever feels."

Swallowing, his possessiveness blessed her. "Conn…" Sinking forward again, she closed her eyes, nestling herself close. "Am I embarrassing you?"

Cradling her skull, holding it tight, he kissed her crown. "Never."

Using him as a leaning post, a support, was tempting. But what was her job?

"To support you," she whispered. On a deep breath, she stepped back, straightening her spine, finding her starch. "I'm a McDade."

"Keep these people safe," Conn said to someone she couldn't yet see. "All of them."

Niall appeared beside them. "If that means cracking skulls?"

With half the city's LEOs present to bear witness…

"Sacrifices have to be made," Conn said and kissed her head again. "She doesn't leave your side."

Connel strode off with his lieutenant. Turning to watch their departure, she wasn't even surprised to feel Strat there with her.

"How you doing, Scamp?"

"It's over, you know."

At the head of the nave, the McDades didn't gather long. Conn's slight head shift sent them shuffling out in front of him.

"The service?"

"I don't know," she said on a sigh. "Thank you for coming. Why didn't you tell me Conn was bringing everyone?"

"I didn't know. Got a text from Niall to congregate at the club. Bold move, the guy gets style points."

A slight laugh slipped from her lips. "He does," she said, looping her arm through Strat's. Her brother and father were already shaking hands by the door. "No one wants to shake my hand."

"Fuck them, Scamp. Who needs them? You had a fucking platoon show up for you. Got a feeling the boss would line up every person in the city if that's what you wanted."

She sat on the pew again, taking Strat with her. "I'm not offended. I don't want to shake their hands either. It… it's strange. I'm used to being the least important member of my family. These people will shake my hand, they were polite coming in, but people look at me differently now. Like my life is…"

"Public property? This is a first for the McDades in this city. To be so publicly linked to the highest-ranking officials? People wanna know…"

"What do they want to know?"

He stretched his legs out, crossing his ankles.

"How you did it."

Another smile, though she lowered her chin, appreciating the private memory. "I didn't. It was all him."

"You got in there somehow, got close to him. People want to know your story. The news reporter has become the news. They want to know it as much as they're terrified by it."

"Aren't we all."

"Are they coming to the wake? Is it a wake when there's no body?"

"No idea," she said, resting her head on his arm. "There's cake. That's about as much as I know."

"Think you should shake some hands?"

Opening her hand, she scrutinized her palm. "Think maybe they'll wonder where these hands have been?"

Strat groaned. "Thanks, Scamp. Like I needed that visual."

"I didn't mean that!" Her next laugh was loud. Unashamedly. "Though because you mentioned it, I haven't had Conn today. He was working last night."

"Shit, I'm sorry I brought it up." He hadn't, but okay. "Now I need a drink. There a backdoor out this joint?"

TWENTY-SIX

THEY GOT A DRINK at a corner bar and took their time wandering along to the restaurant. What was there to rush for? Everyone would still be there when they arrived. Who would dare miss the harlot's entrance?

The banquet hall teemed with people, though it was probably just her imagination that every eye in the room landed on her the moment she stepped inside. And with an older man, gasp, where was lucifer? Just how many men did she have?

Luckily, her father chose that exact moment to get in her face.

"Where have you been?" he snapped. "Did you disappear with him?"

"I disappeared with Strat," she said. "I'm surprised you noticed I wasn't here."

"You made a farce of a somber event."

"How?" she asked, frowning. "I didn't make a farce of anything. It's only because of me that any of this shit is organized."

He blinked in surprise. "You curse at me?

Today?"

"Dad, aren't you sick of this hostility between us? Live and let live."

"You don't—"

"Can we take today off? Avoid me if you want."

"So you can indulge your betrayal?"

"Emotions are high—"

"For once in your life, think of your family. How does it look? You walking into the service with that man?"

"Me," she said. "I walked in with him. No one asked you to join us. The world knows, Dad. Why shouldn't the man I love support me on this difficult day? Didn't you always say I should be with a strong man? What was it you said I needed?" Her eyes went to their top corners as she searched her recollection. "A real man. Someone with a... clear head? Smarts? Bold?" A fake smile spread across her lips. "Full marks. My guy hits all those markers and then some. Toss another couple at me, I bet he'll pass those too."

"L... love?" he said and shook his head. Trust him to have only heard part of her statement. "This is— it's an insult to everything my father died for."

"What did he die for, Dad? If you know, if you're so sure, tell me. What did Grandpapa die for?"

"It wasn't for this. It wasn't for an abuse of your position in—"

In the same moment he stopped speaking, fingertips trailed down her upper arm. No need to check who could make her shiver like that. She swayed back, resting her weight on his body.

"Go relax, Macushla." Twisting to peek up at him, his cool gaze remained on her father. "I've got this. Strat."

Her friend put an arm around her, and she went with his guidance. If Conn wanted to speak to her father, there was no reason to stop him. Maybe he'd have more luck. She'd been trying for a couple of decades and hadn't yet broken through to him.

"I can't even look." Her elbows landed on the bar as Strat reached over to signal the bartender. "Is it carnage?"

"Something stiff and Irish," Strat said, ordering drinks.

She blew out a laugh. "Maybe if we were alone. But in front of all these people…"

Strat rubbed her back. "They have to face off sometime. Better in a room of people where they should keep their pistols in their holsters. You must've known this would happen."

"I haven't had time to… It didn't occur to me that this would ever happen."

"Are you sorry it did?"

Turning her gaze up to him, she didn't have to think twice. "I don't know how I ever lived without him, Strat."

His scrutiny narrowed like he really wanted to look into her. "How much faith do you have in him? How much do you trust him?"

"Completely."

"Family comes first. His family."

"Yes, and I will never ask him to act in any way that could hurt the family. They're my family too. They're your family. We're family." She took his hand. "Are you sorry? Outing us to them? If you want to walk away—"

"I never would," he said, swiping his thumb across her cheek. "Not sure I'd trust you to play nice with anyone else."

"True. You already know my secrets. No chance I'm opening up to anyone else."

"Do you tell McDade your secrets?"

She straightened when the bartender put two

glasses down. "Some of them." She raised her glass to his. "Sláinte."

They both drank. Strat sipped, she tossed hers back in one and discarded the empty glass on the bar.

"No prizes for guessing what you withheld. If you want to be part of the family, he has to know everything. That's the price of admission. Your business becomes his. Everything. Especially something that could come back to bite you on the ass."

"It will not come back to—"

"The history of people being bitten on the ass by secrets they've said won't be found out doesn't land in your favor, Scamp. The truth will get out eventually; it always does."

"You've told me that before."

"Apparently, you weren't listening. Trust me, Scamp. I can keep you safe from street scum and traitorous assassins. The guy in your bed?" His head shook. "I can't keep you safe from that."

Their gazes locked, but the assessment only lasted a few seconds. Strat nodded behind her and she turned to Connel directing her father through people and past tables toward them.

"Everything okay?" she asked, not convinced by their expressions that the matter was closed.

With a slight jolt, her father stopped, and Conn's hand dropped.

"Sersha..." her father said, and she just stood there waiting. "I... I'm sorry." And her jaw dropped. What the hell was—"What I said was inappropriate, your relationship is none of my business."

"I... what?" She couldn't... Had she hit her head? "What?"

"I'm sorry. I love you..." Glancing at Strat and Conn, she didn't even know how to respond. "I'm proud of you."

"You're… Oh my God." This was Connel, all Connel. She didn't exactly believe her father was sincere, but fuck, it was a wonder to witness. "Thank you."

The astounding shock that almost decked her was watching her father look to Connel for the nod before walking away.

"Whoa," Strat said. "That's a neat trick."

"What did you say to him?" she asked, moving against him. "How did that…?"

Strat handed three fingers of whiskey to both her and Conn. "Threaten him with your enforcers?"

"Didn't have to," Conn said, touching his glass to hers when she raised it. "I'm good at what I do."

"I'll say. Wonder what else you can make him do," Strat said. "Remind me never to cross you."

"I don't think you ever planned to."

"Boss?" Niall's appeal brought them around. "Entertainment's here."

"Entertainment?" she asked as the lieutenant stepped aside. Through the vast windows at the front of the building, trouble brewed. "Oh, shit."

Swerve and Vex got out of a car on the opposite side of the broad street.

"Fuck."

"We've got this," Connel said, handing his glass to Strat.

She caught his arm. "Baby." When he looked at her, she didn't know what to say. She didn't want him to get hurt, to go out there and brawl or… "Remember your audience."

He came to kiss her head before urging her back against Strat. The men made eye contact then Connel was striding away, Niall with him. With a glance at this guy and that, they followed their leader.

Razer, Jagg, Ford, oh shit, if Vex called in his troops…

"Let them be, Scamp," Strat said as the McDade crew walked out onto the road to meet Vex and Swerve in the middle, literally stopping traffic.

Not one horn blared. Cars kept their distance and seemed happy to do so. Locals, obviously.

Conn and Vex, toe to toe. The room held its breath. People weren't even subtle in standing up to watch what they could see and not hear.

"I just got him out of the interrogation room," she murmured, holding her glass to her chest. "I don't want tonight to be bail."

"Welcome to your new life, Scamp. And for what it's worth, I don't think they'd bail him," her friend teased. "Not him."

"Thank you, Strat." She swallowed some more liquor. "That makes me feel so much better."

He laughed. "Come on, you don't laugh about it, you'll go crazy. Your guy's smarter than to rumble with a wraparound audience. And a blue one at that."

"Conn can't use what he knows about Vex in front of Swerve."

"Because Swerve is Silvio's lackey." Silvio being the don and Vex's father. "What does Ire know about Vex?" After a second of eye contact, she drew her eyes away. "Strange to see the two of them together, Vex and Swerve."

"I'm not reading too much into that. It's better that Silvio sent Swerve than came himself."

"You sure? Swerve isn't known for his self-control."

"He doesn't have to be—" Outside, Ford stepped up beside Conn, Jagg not far behind. "Go, Strat. That's your boys."

She took the glass from his hand.

"I can't leave you."

Imogen rushed over. "Dad, get out there. Stop

this!"

"Fuck," Strat said, scooping both women against him to hurry them across the room. "Cop!" Her brother was literally coming out of the restroom, thank God, and hadn't seen the show yet. "Do not fucking leave them."

With that, Strat stormed across the room to go outside.

"What is going on?" Lachlan asked, following everyone's focus. "Shit. Fucking Ire McDade—"

"No, actually," she said, giving Imogen a glass. "He's defusing the situation."

"Since when is he a mediator?"

"Believe it or not, he's an excellent negotiator, and he's aware of the audience."

"Oh, so if it wasn't for the audience—"

"He doesn't need violence to handle Evander Manzani."

"How do you know?"

She smiled, very aware of the intention of her brother's question. "Because he's a professional."

"Oh, a professional? Ire McDade? A professional what? Criminal? Gangster? Thug?"

"He is an entrepreneur; a business owner."

She didn't expect Lachlan's laugh to be so genuine. "By day, maybe."

Nearby, Whisper turned her back on the scene, squeezing her eyes closed.

"Whisper," she called, getting the woman's attention, gesturing her over. "What's wrong?"

"I'm not watching."

"I see that. Why not?"

"Because I—"

"Before, uh, this is my brother," she said, cutting Whisper off. "He's a cop. Vice."

That cooled Whisper's focus.

"Thank you for being so subtle in telling her that,

sister."

"Why are you not watching?" she asked. "Because Raze told you not to go out there?"

"You know, he's not wrong," Whisper said, taking her glass. "Sometimes I just can't help myself."

"Oh, we have movement," Imogen interjected.

Yes, Vex and Swerve returned to their car. The McDade side didn't move, didn't flinch until the car disappeared around the corner. When their boots were back on the sidewalk, traffic started again, moving as if nothing had happened.

What would they have done if Connel and his people hadn't shown up?

Imogen and Whisper both hurried away, presumably to meet their men.

"What does he have on him?" Lachlan asked, though his gaze was set in the distance.

Was he asking or was that rhetorical? "Who have on who? I don't know."

"Stay here. I'm going to talk to Dad."

Great. Yeah, go have fun, that wasn't a conversation she wanted any part of.

"Sure know how to throw a party, McLeod." Tom Rigger. From the paper. Propping up the bar. "We'll fill column inches with this."

"Oh?" she asked, strolling to the bar next to him. "You really think you want to do that? Exploit the death of a respected alderman and your colleague's loss for your own gain? Maybe it's professional progress that interests you. Take a leap. Imagine the progress of what happens to you if you upset me. How does that factor into your career plans?"

"Threatening people now?" he asked, smile on his face.

"You just threatened me! What do you call talking about printing my family's grief? Isn't that a threat?"

"Scamp!"

Strat called from a dozen feet away where the McDades congregated, sitting, spreading themselves out without opposition. And there, at the head of it all, was her guy.

"Enjoy the show," she said to Tom and went to the table.

Strat gave her shoulder a squeeze when she nodded in thanks. Whatever happened, she'd get the skinny later.

Dropping onto the couch by Connel, she exhaled. "God, I wish bad things on that guy. Pain, torture, death. Asshole."

"Which guy?" he asked, his hand sliding up her thigh.

"Tom Rigger." She nodded in his direction. "He works at The Chronicler."

"Niall," Connel called toward his guy.

Why did he…?

Niall approached. "Boss?"

When the next words out of Conn's mouth were in his mother tongue, she sensed trouble.

Wait. "No," she said, twisting to land her hands on her guy. "I didn't mean literally."

"No?" he asked, a twitch of his head.

"No," she said, erasing her worry to smile. "No, baby, it's venting, not a call to arms."

He nodded Niall away with a minute movement and the guy complied.

"Be careful with that tongue, Macushla."

"I'll reserve it for doing this."

Boosting up, she kissed him, quickly slipping her tongue between his lips with a passion probably better reserved for their bedroom.

Yes, she had to watch what she said, but damn if

there wasn't something seductive about a guy who'd do anything for her. He hadn't even asked why, just prepared to fulfill her wish.

"My new favorite hobby, doing that with this audience," she said, her lips still near his. "What did Evander want?" Though the answer was obvious. "How did you get him to go with Swerve watching?"

"You trust me?"

"You know I do."

Tipping her head forward, he kissed her hair. "Then trust me," he murmured against her.

Drinks were poured and passed out, the noise level rose. Strat stood with the expansive group. Like she could read his mind, she sighed. He didn't have to look at her all disapproving like that. Yes, there were things she needed to tell Conn. There just hadn't been... time.

"To Alderman McLeod," Conn said, raising his glass. "Without him, we wouldn't have our Bluebell. Sláinte."

The group reciprocated and drank.

Dropping her weight against his upper arm, she waited until he'd swallowed before speaking. "You know you just thanked my grandfather for having sex."

Without shame, his eyes found hers. "As it's our responsibility to do the same."

"Ire!" someone called and he shifted closer to the voice while sticking next to her.

The same? They were supposed to have sex? No problem there, but... had he just implied they'd have kids? This day could not get any heavier.

TWENTY-SEVEN

"TALK TO ME."

"Hmm?" she asked, eyes closed as she counted the beats of his heart beneath her head.

Satisfied didn't cover it when talking about their sex life. Sated and boneless, it was a wonder she remembered how to breathe.

His fingers tangled in her hair then combed themselves loose. "Your mind's racing."

How did he know that? She could ask, but it didn't matter. Why shouldn't her lover read her thoughts?

"Strat asked if I need therapy. Steeple brought it up too."

"Do you?"

Her smile touched his chest. In bed in the dark, in his loft, she'd been spoiled with his presence that day.

"There are things I haven't… said."

"Talk to me."

"I don't know…" And he just let the silence hang. "Sometimes the suggestion offends me… But when I'm alone, it's like… My mind gets busy and I feel like I'm losing my grip."

"I've got you."

"I trust in that." She didn't need a handle on things because Conn would always steady the wheel. "I think about it sometimes, for no reason… that word I struggle to say."

"Attack," he said without hesitation. He'd been the one to point out her hesitancy first. "You think about the attack."

"I asked Lach not to bring it up at Stag because it was a raw nerve and here I am—"

"Nothing's off-limits between us. Talk to me."

With that permission, the words just started coming. "It's cold, you know? This lingering thing that just—for no reason, I get a shot of, the memory and… I feel exposed, vulnerable, I suppose you could call it." She exhaled. "I replay that night and I… I'm not usually that oblivious, so unaware of…"

"Keep going.

"The way I reacted when I lost Stag. I'd never been so adrift; I honestly didn't know what to do. I guess that's why I just mindlessly walked away. I wasn't thinking about traffic or people; I sank like I'd been sucker punched. Never again was a long time. The thought of never seeing you again… We'd been so amazing, to have that snatched away from me…" The alcohol and hormones combined to loosen her lips and she just kept going. "He picked me up, the first one, his hand closed over my mouth—I didn't know what was happening until my head hit concrete." His grip bunched in her hair. She smoothed a hand down his torso and eased away to rest her head on her own pillow. "It was instinct. I didn't think, I just acted. Smart or not."

"It's adrenaline." Sliding down, he lay with her, his face just a few inches away. "No one knows how they'll handle these situations until they're in them."

"I was mad. Madder than I've ever been. My heart was going so fast, I… I tried to hurt them, to fight. I resented them for—and then I resented myself for being so weak and useless."

"You're neither."

"How do you do it? Live with violence like that hanging over you every day? Are you ever scared?"

"Yes," he said. Despite asking, she hadn't expected such a direct answer. "When I found out it was you." Another surprise. "My life has always been this. I'm aware it could end any time and made my peace with that long ago. But you…"

A man without vulnerability let her in and presented a weak spot to the world. Rather, she had presented it when she marched on into the precinct to free him.

"When did you know? That this wasn't… that I wasn't a slut on speed dial?"

"From the moment I laid eyes on you."

Had she been so blind?

"And the blackmail was…?"

"Never meant to play out the way it did."

Because she was a valuable asset. Or she could've been. Instead they got lost in their attraction.

"Stag has always felt safe. I don't know why I—" She squeezed her eyes shut. What was she doing talking about this shit with Ire McDade? "Sorry, I'm—must be too much liquor."

As she tried to roll away, he caught her face, pulling her back, bringing them closer. "Talk to me."

"You don't want to hear me ramble. I'll figure out my—"

"Our. What's in your head belongs to me. All of you belongs to me."

And what peace that gave her. "You need a

woman strong enough to handle her own shit."

"I need a woman willing to open all of herself to me. Hold back and you're just another extra, not worth my time."

"I give all of myself to you. I'm also aware you deal with real stakes, life and death shit. I want your focus on avoiding prison so I don't wake up lonely every day for the rest of my life." His eyelid twitched, just a fraction, but the question was clear. "Yes, your hands will be the last my skin ever feels, prison or not."

"Life on the lam?"

"The sex is incredible and you can cook. I'm locked in. No going back now."

"You're all in."

Just like he said before, which got her to thinking.

"You want me to share everything, to open all of myself to you." Her statement required no response. "I want to know you like no one else does. I'll take Ire McDade, I want Ire McDade, I need him. He's a part of who you are and I'm crazy about him. But he's not all of you."

"Are you sure?"

"Yes, I am sure. Ire McDade didn't cook for me. He's not the man swearing to take care of me and washing my hair. Ire McDade didn't ask if he had to be careful downstairs or come kiss me in front of my family. I want Connel too." Without a word, he stared into her. "Will you take me one day?"

"Take you where?"

"The island."

"I haven't been back for years."

"It doesn't have to be tomorrow, just… someday."

"After you take care of our unfinished business." Which was? They had unfinished business? "But what?" She didn't get it. "McLeod said nothing in the car, but…

what?"

"I don't know what you mean?"

"Your story, the night you met Vex. You started and didn't finish. Your brother always said you could call no matter what, and he said nothing in the car, but…"

Glimmers of a past conversation tickled the edge of her consciousness. "Oh my God, you…" Shock stunned her. They'd had that discussion two months ago. "How do you remember that?"

"Because when I ask questions, people answer them."

And she hadn't. "I… can't even remember what I was going to say."

"Your brother picked you up from the club. Start there."

"Lach always told me I could call and he wouldn't get angry. We rode the whole way back in silence, but I knew he was disappointed. He didn't have to say it; I'd disappointed him."

Something she'd done again when he learned about her current relationship, of where her heart lay.

Scooping his fingers between hers, he put them on his body. "Now who do you call if you're in trouble?"

"Strat," she teased and laughed when he grabbed her hip to jerk her against him. "You. I'll call you. Except…" She frowned. "What will we do if we find the murderer first?"

"What do you want to do?"

Were they deciding together, or did he expect her to know the right answer?

"I don't know." He gave her time to think. "If it's Silvio related, there are rules, right?"

"Aye, I can't hit him, but I doubt he was the triggerman."

"Was it the triggerman's fault if he was following orders?"

"How'd that work out for Pietro?"

Another good point. "Losing my grandfather is difficult. Losing you would be a whole different kind of hurt."

"Why would you lose me?"

"Because if we find him first and take care of the problem, everyone else will still be looking. What will be the point of us pursuing an assailant we know is already dead? Except when we give up the investigation or lose interest in it, we'll draw attention from the others in our task force, and I don't want that."

"Unless we're kissing in public."

"Well, yeah, that's a different—wait, are you saying you don't want—if you don't want physical contact or for us to acknowledge each other in public, we won't. Shit, I didn't think much about how outing us affects your credibility. I'm sorry."

He jerked her against him again, pressing her down into the mattress when their bodies met, his grip tightening.

"You'll do a helluva lot more than acknowledge me." He'd said the battle was one she fought only with herself. "If I am your kingdom, you better be ready to stake a claim. There are no limits, no boundaries between us, Cushla Machree."

"Strat's scared I'll spiral without an anchor. I told him, in my own way, I didn't value my life. I have been… crazy recently, taken risks and pushed limits. Being without you, lost and alone, maybe I wanted to hurt myself…" She sighed. "Or maybe I wanted your attention, to prove to you I can be strong and worthy of standing at your side."

"Cushla Machree." He kissed her. "You are a warrior and my queen."

TWENTY-EIGHT

OFFICIAL WORD.

Authorization.

Permission.

Access.

Who could travel freely in and out of her grandfather's house?

She wasn't often there, but it still chilled her to be standing outside, looking up at the tall, narrow building. Her grandpapa lost his life there, in those walls. And it was on her not to toe the official line as her brother and father would, but to get to the truth. Unbury the secrets and air out the skeletons. Whatever it took—

"Do you have a key?" Daly lounged against the car he'd just freed her from. "Or is the staring part of your schtick?"

"You're one to talk," she said, looking him up and down. "All you need is a toothpick and you're cliché central." His lips reacted. "You better hope Connel never needs you to sneak up on anyone because they'll see you coming."

"No, Bluebell, what I do requires people to know exactly who I am and who I work for."

And with the ink declaring their relationship still wet, the newspapers weren't done with their scrutiny.

So even if, before her, Daly kept his identity a secret, no one would confuse him now. How many others would be allowed this close to her under Connel's watch?

"I don't have a key, but security should still be in there." She started up the stairs. "Stay here."

"Don't think the boss will like that."

With a hand on the stone rail, she twisted to talk. "I want as little McDade DNA around here as possible. No way I want this pinned on us."

"You and the boss took your time leaving his bedroom this morning." His smirk teased. "I'd say you're packing fresh McDade DNA, right from the source."

Now that he mentioned it…

With Connel on her mind, she ascended to press the bell. It didn't ring inside, not that she heard. Security should be in the basement. Unless they had abandoned their posts. Wasn't much to protect, okay, fair, but they'd still want paychecks.

Looking up and around, a small black half-sphere on the frame above her head must house some type of camera. That would get a view of more than just the door. Surely the cops would've checked the footage. Hmm, how did she get a copy without rousing suspicion?

The black circle a few inches from her forehead was more intrusive. Talk about in your face. A white light came on above it and, with a flash of green, the door clicked open.

Great. Her face was so recognizable, no words were needed to grant her entrance.

Whoever was on security wasn't too vigilant. Hadn't they heard who she associated with?

On a typical visit with her grandfather, she'd sit with him in the living room or the office. This wasn't business as usual. This was stop and look around. The entryway and the staircase up were maybe ten feet apart. Henry's bedroom suite was on the top floor. Someone could easily come in through the front and go straight up without hindrance. Around the walls and coving there were no obvious cameras. Made sense. Who wanted to be filmed while going about their private life in their own home? Though in his position, private meant something different to regular folks.

And the access log. Where was that? No book or scanner anywhere she could see.

Instead of going up, the shiny black door by her shoulder provided access down. Security, and other McDade staff, had their own space in the renovated basement. This was no standard home. Henry McLeod took security seriously, almost to a fault. In hindsight, the man had a point, though the efforts proved futile. Even in his own home he'd been unsafe.

Security was immediately to the left at the bottom of the stairs. The door was marked; she knocked lightly. No use putting people on the defensive with aggression. Nice. Kind. Polite. Back to playing the game.

She heard wheels on a hard floor and then the door opened to reveal a guy still in his desk chair, pushed from the bank of monitors to her position.

"Ms. McLeod."

Easy, slow, no drama, no fear.

"And you are?"

"Horton."

"Hey, Horton." She spread on a wide smile. "Obviously you know who I am, which is good, because I have a few questions."

That registered on his expression. "Cops already asked a bunch of questions."

"I know, but these are of the unofficial variety."

Deliberately dropping her purse at the doorjamb, she wandered in without invitation. Wasn't a big space. A control desk, a few screens and a TV on the left-hand wall. How many security infractions could there be while the guard was watching the game instead of doing their job?

"We're all sorry about Henry; he was a good guy. No one wanted him hurt."

"Someone did." She landed another smile on him. "Were you working that night?"

A question she already knew the answer to, a control question, if you will. A chance for him to tell the truth first.

"No, not me."

"Who was on?"

"Sneddon."

"Is he on today?"

"No, he hasn't been back. A PTSD thing."

She nodded like she understood, but seriously? What had the guy seen that traumatized him? Nothing if she trusted his statement to the police, which she didn't.

"I'm sorry to hear that. Is he okay? Have you spoken to him?"

"Me and him weren't that tight, he seemed kinda…"

Her brows rose, hoping to encourage him. "Kind of what?"

"He hadn't been around long, wasn't sure he was cut out for the gig."

"What makes you say that?" Backing up, she perched herself on the control desk. Sensing his reluctance, she laughed. "You know who I'm seeing, right? Who I sleep next to every night?" Immediately, a flash of panicked fear crossed his face. Leaning over, she rested a reassuring hand on his shoulder. "I keep bigger secrets than your casual opinion on a colleague's character. Sometimes there are things the cops don't need to know. If you made that judgment, I support you. Nothing you say here will get you in trouble with the cops."

"Cocky, without the goods to back it up. Sometimes Sneddon was… flashy, you know, with cash. I don't know his past or anything, but a guy who sits in this chair all night isn't doing it 'cause he likes staying up in the dark."

"Why is he doing it?"

"Because he needs the regular paycheck and he has professional pride, means a lot to me, this job…" He faltered. "Or it did."

"Did Sneddon come from a rich family?"

"I don't know." Horton shrugged. "But he wasn't always flush with cash. Some days he was flashing it around, next day he'd be bumming smokes and sweet-talking Lupe into giving him food."

"Lupe?"

"Housekeeper. She was with Henry a decade or something. This hit her really hard."

"Yeah, I think I remember her."

God, it was disgraceful, how little they knew about each other's day-to-day lives. Did she remember Lupe? Someone served coffee whenever she was over. Would she recognize the person? Was it the same person every time? Shit, she had no idea. The McLeods only ventured into each other's homes for a reason. Any big event, they reserved a table and ate out. Who were her family? They didn't know each other at all. She'd hidden a relationship, her brother lost one with a woman she barely knew, and her father was cavorting with gangsters… Okay, so she could be tarred with that brush too, but her cavorting didn't hurt anyone… not as such.

"She hasn't come back since that first day after.

She was just broken up."

"Were they close?"

Another shrug. "Dunno. We spend most of our time down here. No cameras in Henry's room or in hers."

That raised her chin. "Her room? She has a room here?"

"Yeah, but only stayed in it sometimes. If there was something happening or she had to be around in the night. Henry said he had all this space and nothing to do with it, so... Woman spent more time here than anyone."

Huh.

"What is the setup for going in and out? Do you need to register guests or can just anyone walk in any time?"

"No, definitely, no."

He rolled across to the desk and brought an image of her up on the screen. Her. How did he...?

"That was just now," she said, recognizing the car behind her. "Upstairs."

"Yeah, the camera takes a picture of anyone who rings or beeps in."

"Beeps in?"

"Yeah, it's a scanner too." He flicked the badge on his belt. "Have to beep in and out. Ties into the payroll system as well. Henry never complained about overtime. He was a good boss. Dunno what will happen now."

No, to any of them.

"Is there a way to download the information from that night?"

"Yeah, not that there's anything to see."

"What do you mean?"

"Your grandfather beeped in, and we had a shift change after, but that was hours before... Was a quiet night. No one in or out after eight p.m.”

And time of death wasn’t until the early hours. A suspect would’ve had to lie in wait for a long while, increasing the chance he’d be seen.

“Was Lupe here that night?”

“No. Think she blames herself. Said if she’d been here, it wouldn’t have happened.”

Either the housekeeper was privy to the details of her grandfather’s life, or she thought a lot of herself.

“Where can I get hold of Lupe? Do you have a number?”

Shoving back, he rolled over to a drawer and retrieved a pad and pen to write a number. “Cops have all this.”

“Yeah,” she said, taking the slip of paper he tore off. “Thanks.”

Maybe this Lupe could fill in some blanks. She dipped to pick up her purse.

“Ms. McLeod…”

She glanced back. “Yeah?”

“Whoever did this, the asshole who… Is Ire gonna take care of it?”

Another smile. “No,” she said, much like Niall once upon a time. “I am.”

“If he’s ever looking for guys… I’ll be out of a job soon.”

“We’ll keep you in mind.”

Her grandfather’s death threw a lot of people for a loop. A person’s reach was only truly known after they were gone. He may not be walking the earth anymore, but his presence hung heavy over them all.

TWENTY-NINE

THE FRONT DOOR beeped again to grant her departure at the same time her phone rang.

"Yeah?" she answered the unknown number.

"Not for nothing…" came a female voice, "but I learned something interesting you might like to know."

Daly opened the car's back door for her. "Strat's," she whispered to him on the descent inside. He nodded once, and she went back to her call. "Who is this?"

"Your bar buddy. You know, the colleague who didn't get an invite to the memorial?"

What was…? "Tulip?"

"Glad I made such an impression."

"Did you ever meet my grandfather?"

"That's beside the point…" The woman could be really annoying unless taken in the right way. She hadn't given it much thought, but Tulip was persistent, she had to give her that. Dogged, that was maybe a better word. Harassment with an objective. "So you want to know what I know?"

"Maybe. What'll it cost me?"

"I scratch your back..."

"I've got to know how much the information is worth to me before I decide if I'll pay."

"To you or your boyfriend, I don't care which of you pays the debt."

Bringing up Conn early, hmm? Good sign or bad? "What did I tell you about saying things that could be construed as threats? Always assume someone's listening."

"Is that what you did when you and Ire got together?"

So not a line of conversation she wanted to continue. "What is this information?"

"Your guy's name found its way into Wanstead's ear after a tip from one of his CIs."

"Wanstead's CI?"

"Yep. Long standing relationship. I also heard, don't know if it's true but, this CI might've come into a little cash around the same time."

Now that was interesting. "And the CI's name?"

"Nu uh, I'm not the only one scratching here."

"What do you want?"

"An interview."

A blast of laughter left her. "An interview? With whom?"

"Nicole McDade has a price on her head. Why?"

Wasn't that a question she wanted the answer to as well?

"Okay, I'll see what I can get you," she said. "But, Tulip, seriously, you better trust me to handle this. You start mouthing off or it gets out you have this information and aren't sharing it, there's more than just me interested. Sit on it for a minute. And, Tulip...?" No acknowledgement. "Thank you for bringing this to me."

They might figure it out without going back to

Tulip. Which would work in Tulip's favor. If Conn, or an associate, decided to extract the information from her on their own, it wouldn't be pretty.

"I'm still trying to decide if I can trust you."

"Ditto," she said and hung up only to dial another number.

"High Class! S'up, baby?"

"Hey, Whisper, are you coming to the meeting today?"

"Probably not, but we can spar after, if you want."

"Thanks, I'm still sore from the last session."

"With me or your guy?"

That salacious tone was hilarious. The Doherty was funny. Somehow it had never occurred to her before their introduction.

"Could go either way, I guess," she said.

"And those guys, the ones we're protecting ourselves from, they don't care if you're sore. They don't care if you're tired. They don't care—"

"I get it, you're right…" Funny wasn't Whisper's only attribute. Mrs. Doherty-McDade was savvy too. "I just talked to one of my grandfather's security guys."

"Get anything juicy?"

"A number for his housekeeper and word on the security guy working that night. Something doesn't sit right."

"Trust your gut," Whisper said. "His story doesn't add up?"

"He talked about the access logs in his statement to police. I went to find them, but they're digitized. Guy I spoke to said no one was in or out, but it would be good to know if someone tampered with the logs. Maybe the cops are on it." She'd have to ask Lachlan. "They'd have checked that, right? If only we had full access to their investigation so far. I don't want to go down the wrong road or waste time—"

"I know a guy."

"You know a guy?"

"Who'll check out the logs thing for you."

"I thought you weren't from around here?"

"Don't have to be. Digital is universal. He can hack just the same here as in New York."

"Okay, thanks." She paused. "Where is Nicki?"

"Pretty Nicki? The Grand, how come?"

"Who's on the door?"

"Ask Niall," Whisper said. "He'll have a system. You looking to sneak in there?"

"Maybe."

"I'm game. We can split the pot."

Her lips curled. "Think our guys would like that?"

"We'll be richer; they'll forgive us. And we'll make it up to them, that's what sex is for."

"Except we'd be helping the Byrnes." The Dohertys blood enemy. "They put the price on her head."

"Hmm, good point," Whisper muttered like she was weighing the decision.

"Is she in a suite?"

"Room eight, thirty-two."

"Oh, she won't like that. Just a room?"

"It's for her own protection," Whisper said. "People are less likely to look for her there… and she ain't picking up the tab. Biz closed all her accounts."

Destitute and desperate, yet Nicole still wanted her say.

"You'll call your hacker guy?"

"Yeah."

"Thanks. Think about coming today. I appreciate your input, your experience."

"Did you just call me old?"

On laughter, the line disconnected, and she shook her head. Whisper was an unexpected friend, but not an unwelcome one.

The car stopped. She scrolled to the right contact as she got out and went up the stairs. The call went through to her most secure friendship. Most secure until she told him her plan.

"Scamp."

"Hi! How did you sleep?"

"What did you do?" he asked, deadpan.

"I didn't do anything. Why would you think I…" She sighed. "I need to talk to you."

"You are talking to me."

"I know and I'm just wondering, as a friend, if you're in a good mood because I'm about to land a doozy on you."

"My mood was fine until you called," he said. "I leave you alone for one morning and you hatch some scheme that will probably end with one of us behind bars."

"Or in the morgue," she added into the silence and knocked on reaching the right apartment door. "I'm kidding! Geez, Strat, it's a joke."

Kind of. Keeping the mood light wouldn't lessen the weight of what she intended to suggest.

"Hilarious when you—"

He stopped when he opened his door and there she was, hanging up the phone. "You said I should call first."

In she went and he swung the door back into its frame. "We're meeting in the club in less than an hour."

"I know, but I need to talk to you."

"You said that already."

She sat in the chair by the window. Strat didn't sit. Feet apart, arms folded, he was doing the dad face thing.

"I need a teeny favor. That's all. Just a teeny-weeny little favor."

He wasn't moved. "From me? What's wrong with your boyfriend?"

"My boyfriend…"

Maybe it was the way she trailed off or the way her head turned, but he sucked in a nasal breath.

"You don't lie to Ire McDade. You don't ask me to—"

"It's not lying. It's telling the truth, just… after the fact. He's used the omission isn't a lie thing on me, we have that in our favor."

"What is it you want?" Hmm, was it the time to ask? "Don't ask, don't get."

True. "I need a meet."

"A meet with who? Bet your ass your boyfriend can set up any meet in this city faster than I can."

"I would do it myself, but the guy I want to meet he's sort of… ethereal. I don't know his base, or his number, and I really, really want to go under the radar."

"Under what radar? Any lowlife would hack off his own dick if it pleased the guy you're fucking."

"This isn't a regular lowlife."

"So it's an irregular one? McDade's reach is better than mine."

"Not in this area, not discreet anyway."

"Who is it then? It's not a regular lowlife or a McDade, and—" Struck by some kind of understanding, his brow relaxed. "One of the other families?" Sucking her lips around her teeth, the need to brace couldn't be too overt. "Gambattos are done, Scamp. You have Vex if you need into the Manzanis."

"I don't want to go through him. This is… unrelated to him. He'll turn it into a show and I really need discretion."

"Who you want to talk to? Hell is—"

"Swerve," she said.

Barefaced incredulity slackened his expression. "You've got to be kidding, babe. Swerve? He's a fucking maniac."

"People say the same thing about my guy and Whisper's. We get along fine with them."

"You're sleeping with them. You gonna sleep with Swerve?"

"No," she said, restraining a laugh. "God, no. I need to talk to him."

"Why?"

"Because we say we're trying to solve my grandfather's murder while missing a huge part of the puzzle. If he was asking questions around City Hall and someone got nervous, anyone on Silvio's side, they'd go to the source. If Silvio paid for this hit or sent one of his guys, we have to know."

"And you think Swerve will give you answers? No. Shit, you've heard the stories about him. Silvio's desperate to bring him in, to get his loyalty… He treats Swerve like the son he always wanted, and the guy hardly gives him the time of day. This is a guy with serious issues and nothing to lose."

"Maybe this hurts Silvio and maybe Swerve wants that. There's a lot of resentment between them."

"The guy disappears. Swerve can leave the city, the state, I don't know. He disappears for weeks and months at a time. The guy has no base, no home."

"Then we need to find him. He was in town yesterday, he showed up at the wake with Evander. I want to know how that happened too."

"Vex is already on it, right? He'll find out if his dad—"

"No, he won't. Not from the source anyway. Silvio can't stand him."

"Because he's not Hell or Atlas."

The two elder Manzani sons; Vex's brothers.

"Because he's him."

"Why do you think Swerve will share anything with you? This game, you know how it's played. You want something from him, you have to give him something in return. Tit for tat. Quid pro quo. What do you have that he'll wa…?" After another crash of shock, his head shook slowly. "No, Scamp."

"It might be our only play."

Strat stooped closer, his voice got low. "You saved that woman and now you want to hand her over? They'll kill her. And not quickly."

"I won't really do it."

"You gonna tell him you took her? If you tell Swerve, if you hint, you're the one hiding her… You better be damn sure he'll play nice or he'll snatch you instead. There's payback. You took from the Manzanis."

"Yes. I did."

"You told Immie, my daughter, to lie about her involvement. You took the whole weight on yourself—"

"You're welcome."

"You think I want to see you strung up any more than I want Immie at risk? You tell Swerve this, he could kill you on the spot."

"Then you and Conn are off the hook with the investigation."

"And what do I tell him, huh? Ire? That I knew about Jane Doe all along and didn't tell him?"

"He has enough going on."

"Is that what it is?" he asked. "You're protecting Jane Doe from the Manzanis." They knew her name. Her first name. Select people did anyway. Using the anonymous moniker was just a smart habit. "From Swerve and Silvio… Are you protecting her from the McDades too?"

"Conn doesn't need her. She's nothing to the McDades."

"She's valuable. Have you asked what she knows?"

"No. What she knows is her business. I didn't do what I did to leverage her or what she knows."

"Yet that's exactly what you're talking about doing."

"It's a game," she said. "I ask, he laughs at me, I tease him with what we have, get the information—"

"And then don't pay up? So not only will you have taken from the Manzanis, but you'll double-cross them too? Ire can't protect you from that. That's not you did nothing wrong. That's you failing to pay. Debts have to be settled and the price is her life."

"Or mine." Blinking, her gaze begged him to understand. "Isn't it worth it?"

"No. To find out who killed your grandfather? No, sorry, to *maybe* find out. We don't know if the Manzanis are responsible. They could know nothing about it. Then you lose your life for nothing." He exhaled. "All the manpower Ire puts into keeping you safe from outside threats, he can't protect you from your own stupidity."

"Risks are part of the game. Why shouldn't I up the stakes?"

"Because your grandaddy would kick your fucking ass."

"You don't know him, you didn't know him."

"He's a father, just like me, and I'm telling you, he'd tell you to leave it the fuck alone before trading your life for information that's useless to a corpse."

"It's not useless to Lachlan."

"And what will losing his sister do to him? After losing Imogen, your grandaddy…"

She sighed. "I need you with me."

"Not on this. Your life means more to me than this."

"Fine," she said, surging to her feet. "I'll deal with it myself."

"Scamp," he called after her. She stalked down the hallway. "Stubborn fucking woman!"

Yeah, and that wouldn't change anytime soon. Did she know better than to be careless? Yes. But Strat said it himself: debts have to be settled. That went for the Manzanis, the McDades, and the McLeods as well.

THIRTY

AT STAG, she didn't wait for Daly and got out of the car to go over to her brother outside the main door.

"What's going on?"

"Dad's finishing a call," he said, indicating their father pacing the sidewalk a few yards away, his lackeys beyond.

"Okay."

When her palm landed on the door, Lachlan freed a hand from his pocket to catch her wrist.

"And we were told to wait outside."

"By whom?"

"I haven't learned their names. One sycophant looks just like another." His attention flicked right. "No offense."

"Might take some if I knew what it meant," Daly said from the back of her shoulder.

Good delivery, but he wasn't anywhere close to an idiot. Still, nothing wrong with people underestimating you.

"Why'd you think they asked us to wait out

here?" her brother asked. "They covering something up in there?"

"Am I in there to know the answer to that?"

"I like to think you'd be with a guy where we don't have to make that distinction. There's something in there they don't want us to see."

"They don't want *you* to see," she said, extending her ease. "There is no us here. They asked you to wait. I can see whatever's going on in any McDade space."

"Yeah, she gets to see more McDade than the sycophants," Daly said in jest.

Lachlan didn't react to the tease. "He'd let you walk in on him doing something illegal?"

"He's a business owner. I told you that already. Just business."

Daly backed her up. "Aye. You won't hear me contradicting her."

"He could be in there with another woman."

She faked a horrified gasp. "He could be! Although, except, yeah, he does know how to be in proximity to a woman without his cock leaving his pants."

"Maybe he'd ask you to join them."

She leaned in. "Been there, done that. Anything goes in my guy's world."

What was it about being near Connel that obliterated her inhibitions? He wasn't in her eye line, but he'd be in that building and that was enough.

The door opened from the inside. Dingo. Yeah, she knew him.

"Bluebell," he said, shocked. "Why are you outside? Why are you waiting?"

"Just talking to my brother."

"The boss doesn't want you waiting."

"I wasn't waiting," she said, going inside to head down the entry tunnel. "My choice. You won't get in any trouble."

"Who won't get in trouble?"

That stern voice brought them all around to check the ingress they'd just walked by.

Conn appeared from the office stairway with Niall, Doyle, and a couple of others.

"Everyone here?"

"'Cept you and Strat."

"We shouldn't wait for him. Strat," she said, stroking Conn's chest when he stopped with her.

"Because…?"

"He might not be coming."

"You want him here, we'll get him here."

"No, it's fine." She sighed. "He can come or not come, it's his call."

"You want to push this back? We can do it another time."

"No, everyone's here already. Strat and I will figure it out. We're in a fight… kinda."

"About?" Her head dropped back to show him a smile and his eyes quickly read hers. "Something you don't want to talk about in front of our current audience."

"Why does she have to hide things from your guys?" Lachlan asked. "They tend to go off message?"

"The McDade element isn't the problem."

"She can say anything in front of her family."

"No, she can't."

Connel caught her hand, interlinking their fingers to guide her down the hall into the club.

She came to a stop at the sight within. Two mobile whiteboards, one with pictures of male faces. Hock was writing on the other. Bullet points. Things they knew.

"What is this?" she asked.

"Command Center," Lachlan said, continuing

past them with the others. "This I recognize."

"You want to take it seriously, we take it seriously," Conn said, releasing her hand to slide his onto her lower back. "We will do this every damn day until we find out who's responsible. I'll close the club, close every business we have, spend every cent—"

"Do rún," she whispered, her hands finding his chest. Grief and gratitude dampened her eyes. He narrowed on the reaction. "How do you know when to stop? What's too far?"

"For you? Nothing," he said, almost angry in his assertion. "There is no limit."

"No, I don't mean…" She watched her fingers slide up and down beneath his lapel. "How do I know when to stop? When I've gone too far for the answers?"

"That why you and Strat fought?"

She nodded, skimming her hand higher until it was over where his tattoo would be beneath the fabric. "I don't like being told no."

"You dig your heels in. I've noticed."

"Someone knows the truth. Someone knows who killed Henry."

"You tell me everything. I'll tell you when it's too far."

"Let's get started!" her father declared, marching forth, his people behind him. "I have things to do."

He sailed past them without even attempting to look their way. In the past, her father was happy to share his displeasure. Whatever Connel said to him at the wake worked long distance. Nice.

As she and Connel went to the group to sit down, things got going.

"Henry was sure talking to people around City Hall," Ford said, standing by the whiteboard. "Folks admit it was shaking things up but are reluctant to put any face to the concern."

No Imogen today or Whisper. Raze was off on the periphery. More than a dozen McDade soldiers protected their perimeter. Intimidation or necessity?

"If you've got names, we'll follow up," Daly said. "Old man owed nothing off the grid. No gambling, no drugs, no hookers."

"He didn't share his suspicions with his lady friend," Lachlan said. "Though she admitted he'd been distracted and tense for a few weeks. Could've been just regular council stuff, but it wasn't like him to be stressed."

Look at that. Her brother. Ford. Daly. All factions working together, almost.

"Still don't have anything concrete on who shopped our guy to the cops."

"Uh, I kind of have a lead on that," she said to Hock, also on his feet. "I know who it was, I just don't know who it was." She frowned at the contradiction. "We're haggling over payment."

"We've got money," Niall said.

"No, this isn't about money," she said. "They want something else."

"Something what?" Connel asked, gripping her thigh. "Something I'll tan the guy for?"

She pressed her hand on his. "It's a woman, actually." Not that gender made anything prohibitive. "And I won't sell your virtue. I'll figure something out."

"They want me?"

"Let's talk about this later," she said to her guy, bouncing her hand on his.

"You can just tell us who," her brother said. "We know the source. We can tell you if the info matches up."

"I'm a journalist, Lach. We don't give up sources."

"Did this someone approach you?"

"This is a McDade problem," she said. The

shock that impacted her brother rebounded to her. Had she really…? "One we need to solve, I mean. The price will have to be paid by the McDades, if we decide it's worth it. I don't want to compromise your professional integrity any more than I want to compromise mine."

"What do you think this person will give you?" her brother asked, a little harsher than before. "Even if you find the witness, what do you expect to learn?"

"It's a lead," Daly said. "A good cop should know to follow those up."

"If someone recounted what they saw, that account won't change from what they told us."

"If they really saw it." Which they hadn't because Connel couldn't be in two places at once. "If they didn't, their motivation could be key."

"Some people won't talk to cops," Niall said, reiterating what had been highlighted at their last meeting. "We can be more persuasive."

"And if I hear something happened to this witness—"

"Things happen to people every day. You want to blame us for every assault this city sees?"

"Odd that you went straight to assault."

"No one ever got arrested for asking nicely."

Oh, damn, typical. Just as she thought things were going well, everything went to shit.

Her brother's position wasn't enviable. "I can't claim not to know there was a threat to this person."

"Who threatened him?" Hock asked.

"You think I don't know what persuasive means?"

"If someone's coming for us, we have a right to defend ourselves."

One voice rose over another. This was fast becoming a—

"Hold," Connel's voice boomed above them all

and everyone silenced. "Watch your tongues around Macushla." Oh, she'd heard worse, but didn't mind being Connel's diffuser. "One at a time."

"We don't ignore leads."

"I'm not saying you should," Lachlan said, a tad calmer.

Her father was just sitting there. Barely looking at anyone, his attention fixed straight ahead, while the surrounding grunts took notes. This was his father they were fighting for. Did he resent not being in charge?

"Are you gonna join us?"

Ford's question brought everyone's focus around to see what he was seeing.

Strat leaning against the hallway wall, arms folded. His eyes stuck on hers and he turned his head, rolling his shoulder on the wall to disappear back into the darkness of the tunnel.

Jumping up, she hurried across the room to meet him in the shadows.

"Tomorrow," he said in a low murmur.

"Thank you. Where?"

He shook his head. "Not for you. For me."

Wariness grew acute. "You? I don't get—"

"If you're so sure dangling her in front of—"

"You don't even know where she is."

"I don't have to know. Your plan isn't to give her up, is it?"

"You can't walk into the firing line like that. You can't… No."

"No?"

"No, I won't let you. I won't let you risk—"

"You were happy to risk it. Makes more sense coming from me. People know we're connected now. This isn't a leap."

"But you weren't there. You didn't find her—"

"You did, yeah. How many people know you

snuck her out of the hospital?" Oh, she didn't like this. Didn't like it one bit. "That's a question, Scamp. I need to know who knows."

"Me and you, that's it."

"Me and you?" he asked. She didn't like how he peered into her like he questioned her honesty. "I'm the only one who knows where she is."

"Ire?"

"No," she said, shaking her head. Rising to her tiptoes, she clasped his folded arms. "I won't let you do it. I can't, Strat. You have a family. You—"

"You have your whole life laid out."

"Not much more than you." They joked about Strat being old, but he was only in his forties, not over it yet. "This was my play, my decision."

"I won't let you do it, I can't. The meet's already set, it's done."

"No," she said, her mouth watering as her sinuses tingled. "It is not. And I will—"

"It's done," he said, raising his arms, freeing them from her hold. "You want to know who killed your granddaddy—"

"And if they don't know? If Silvio and Swerve are not the ones responsible? You're putting yourself in the path of a bullet." If he was lucky. "Don't do this."

"How the fuck is it different?" he hissed. "This is what you wanted."

"I didn't," she said, her lips drying. "Please, Strat, I can't let—how will I look your little girl in the eye?"

"Same way you'd have me look at her if I put you on this course."

"But you didn't! I did it myself. I did all of this myself!" Tears fell, but she swiped them away fast. "I do not want you putting yourself between me and this bullet. I'll take the hit! I want to take the hit!"

"Turnabout is fair play, kid. You protected

Imogen. Now I protect you both."

Turning his back, he walked away.

"Strat," she said again, but he didn't react. "Strat! This isn't what I wanted! Strat!"

He walked out the front door, disappearing into the light. What did she do? How did she undo it?

On a surge of adrenaline, she rushed back to the club to lock on Ford. "Do not let him out of your sight."

"What?" he asked, smacked with her urgency.

"Go after him! Do not let your father out of your sight!" Ford was already halfway across the room when Jagg leaped up too. "Yes! Go! Both of you. Do not let him out of your sight. Not for a second!"

"What the fuck is—"

"Just go!" she screamed, gesturing them out.

As they retreated, she exhaled, and fell back against the club wall, eyes closing. What the fuck had she done?

THIRTY-ONE

"WHAT'S GOING ON?" Lachlan asked. "What happened?"

Rather than her brother, she sought Connel. "I fucked up."

"I'll fix it," he said with a glance at Niall that quickly transferred to three McDade guys.

They sped out in Ford and Jagg's wake.

Could she really trust the Swerve meet was tomorrow? Even if it was, Strat could bring it forward if he feared she'd act on her own to circumvent him. More McDade manpower decreased the likelihood of Strat walking into trouble. If it came to it, they could hold him down.

"You're guarding Strat now?" Lachlan asked.

"And you can't tell Imogen," she said. "It'll complicate things. She'll worry and end up in the line of fire."

"What the hell's going on? Is this about your source?"

"No," she said, her forefingers finding her temples. "This is about a decision I made that Strat is taking ownership over.”

"And you're scared he'll get hurt?" her brother asked.

"He *will* get hurt, but that's not the point." Though it was in the moment. "This was all me. Others shouldn't face the consequences."

"Doing the right thing never starts with doing the wrong thing."

Oh, Lachlan, it was almost laughable. "We are so far beyond that point. Like super, light years away from that line, brother. And it started off the other way around. I did the right thing. What people would think is the right thing and… I fucked up."

"And whose fault was that?"

Maybe she was supposed to say Connel, but it wasn't on him. The McDades weren't a part of this calamity.

Confusion reigned over most expressions. Before she could look at Connel, her father's not so smug smile jabbed at her. He wasn't looking at her. No, he wouldn't be that direct with Connel in the room. It made her sick, nauseous, to lay eyes on him.

"I want you to leave," she murmured, almost under her breath, fixated on her father. Her subconscious finally freed itself. "You hear me, Ronald?" That snarl got her father's attention. "Get up out of that chair, walk out of here, and never come back."

"Sersha," her brother exclaimed. "What are you—"

"Get out of here!"

When she thrust away from the wall, every McDade stood up. Her father, on the other hand, stayed put.

"You have no right to—"

"This is her kingdom," Connel said and issued a command in his foreign tongue.

Every man in the room converged around her father's group.

"Wait a fucking minute," Lachlan said, rising. "What is going on?"

"Strat's on a suicide mission, saving me from myself. That's what love is. What a father's love is. How do you look at yourself in the mirror, Dad? What do you have to be proud of? Was your father proud of you? Did he know the truth of who you are, of how you treated your children? Of how you ignored and belittled us?"

"This is not the place for—"

"Get out!" she roared, striding another few steps. "I don't want to fucking talk to you! I don't want to hear you or have you anywhere near me!"

"This is because of him—because of—"

"Because I have finally found my voice in this darkness. You bring nothing to the table. You're useless and I will not open this forum to you so you can squirrel away information that does not belong to you. Every other person here wants to solve this. We want answers. We want to know who killed a man we cared about. Why are you here? You haven't offered one word of support or intelligence. It's like you've given up the investigation before it even started. You have no interest whatsoever and sit there like you don't give a shit who—" And with a thud of unwelcome clarity, her eyes cut to Connel. That stern expression, the certain stance, her guy was on the same page. "Oh my God."

What will be the point of us pursuing an assailant we know is already dead? Those were the words she'd said to Connel the previous night. People would notice if they lost interest, and she'd noticed her father's complete lack of it.

"It's time to leave, Superintendent." Still her guy only had eyes for her. "Now."

"What are you going to do? Beat me? Hurt me?

Drag me out? Put your hands—"

"I won't touch you," Connel said, whipping around on him. "No McDade hands will touch you."

"Then I don't see how you can—"

"We'll call the cops," Niall said, reading his superior.

"You'll…" her father spat in disgust. "Do you know who I am? I run the police! I am the police!"

"Be embarrassing for you if we have to call them to report your trespass," Niall said.

"Especially if we ensure there are plenty of cameras outside," Daly followed up. "We have access to make that happen. From the broadsheets to every kid with a blog and a smartphone."

"The superintendent arrested for harassment and trespass."

"They wouldn't arrest me."

"Whether they do or not, makes a great picture."

As the McDades enjoyed that, Lachlan stepped up. "Why are you doing this, Sersh?" he asked. "Why now? Why turn on us?"

"You're welcome here," she said. "I love you and you've always supported me. You want to solve this. We need you. We don't need dead weight."

"Couldn't have said it better," Niall agreed.

All focus tracked to Connel. "You are charged with upholding the law, Superintendent. Shouldn't you also obey it?" he asked. "Want to go quietly or make a dramatic exit the city won't soon forget?"

Whatever his decision, she'd said her piece. Life was so exhausting. If she didn't walk away, she'd end up screaming the place down. Connel would handle her father; he'd done it before and wouldn't shy from doing it again.

Walking away, she wanted to just be for a minute.

"Sersha?" Lachlan's call stopped her at the

bottom of the spiral staircase. "We're your family."

"You're my family, Lach," she said before turning around. "Strat is my family. Conn is my family. The McDades, even the Doherty. That man…" She nodded toward their father. "To be family, you have to understand it. You have to care and love it more than you love yourself. Strat knows what it is to love a daughter. That guy…" She nodded toward Ronald without looking at him. "He loves only himself."

"You'll regret this."

"I do regret it," she said. "I regret not doing it sooner."

Going up the stairs, her pulse slowed. Strat could get himself killed. The only completely innocent party on their side, Strat didn't deserve to pay for her decisions.

She got a drink and went to the bedroom, though it was the bathroom she ended up in. Past the shower, staring into the pristine mirror, the only remnant of her meltdown was her own memory.

She didn't hear him, but he was there. "Sorry about the mirror."

Moving closer, his reflection joined hers. "Was easily replaced," he said, bowing over her to kiss her collarbone.

When her head turned that way, he lifted just a little. "You knew," she said. "Motion activated cameras?"

Nudging her head aside, he kissed her again. "Aye."

Closing her eyes, she couldn't believe she'd fallen for it. "Your men don't hide things from you."

"This place is as much yours as mine." Daly had said that too. "Stag's doors will never be closed to you."

"This isn't Stag, this is your private space."

"And yours."

"Is he gone?"

"Aye. Talk to me."

Spinning around, she tossed back the drink and put the glass on the vanity. "After."

She pushed him to the wall, but he flipped them around, forcing the air from her lungs. The confinement, the trap of him holding her there with his body, eased her every ache.

"Beat of My Heart," he growled, slamming his mouth onto hers.

That was it. His way of telling her, showing her, that nothing was beyond his limit. Whatever she'd done, he didn't even need to hear it to know he'd support her.

An almost sob dammed in her throat as she struggled for breath. He came lower, capturing her wrists to hold them on the wall above her head.

The prison wasn't needed; she wasn't going anywhere. Captivity wasn't its purpose. Holding her still, crouching to push himself against her hips, holding them fast, was a gift. His way of showing her she was under his control, his protection. His way of taking care of her.

A kiss wasn't enough, she whined, the sound vibrated in the union of their mouths. If she could fall to her knees and beg, she would.

God, she needed him. Not sex. Yes, she wanted it, but he steadied her. Balanced her world. Anchored her cause.

When his mouth left hers, a desperate gasp strained her throat. He didn't let her go, thank God. His forehead landed on hers, pressing into her almost painfully to fix her in place.

"You are never alone."

Such a simple whisper, yet it reached into her, cradled her, kept her, treasured her while arousing her.

"Mo Grá." He withdrew, searching her gaze. "It's the only one I looked up."

He'd told her he was no longer do rún, but he

would always be her love.

His lips touched her hairline. "Cushla Machree…"

That she heard, the words that followed were a mystery. "That's not fair."

Ignoring her tease, he scooped both hands around her jaw to tip her head back and kiss her again. A slow, much more intimate kiss that did nothing to help her already tender, sentimental heart.

His jacket hit the floor before he picked her up. She worked on ridding him of his shirt. The quicker they could get to—landing on the bed was like finding her safety net. Her guy above, the stability below. She was terrified, no other way to put it. Strat thundered on to protect her and he'd find a way, unless his boys could stop him. Her friend, her best friend, was in danger because of her. Conn was her only hope of surviving the guilt, surviving the fear.

Fulfillment became all about him when his cock bedded itself deep within her. That need to be full, to have him occupying her, all she could do was be.

"Conn…"

His name tasted so good on her lips.

He replied, in a low rumble, words she couldn't translate. His eyes, the determination in them, she saw beyond a man looking for carnal climax.

She didn't care if it was complicated. Where they were, was where they were supposed to be.

THIRTY-TWO

SOMEHOW, SHE ENDED up on top. After the second time? Maybe it was the third. Sex rehab was her kind of therapy.

As she collapsed against his torso, movement was difficult. "I'm staying here," she said, eyes closed, head on his chest.

"Okay." He pushed her hair away from her cheek and temple. "I've got nowhere to be."

That was probably a lie, but she wanted it to be true so accepted it.

Rocking her hips just a little, she reminded him he was still inside her. "Right here."

"Soon as I'm hard, I'll have what I want."

"Good."

"Won't care if you're asleep."

She kissed the skin beneath her cheek before settling again. "I consent. Now and always. Sleep or not, I want it… from you. Only you."

"What'd I say about other guys?" His fingers rested in her hair. "Talk to me." This again? "Enough distraction."

Just what she feared him saying. There was no getting out of it.

"I dragged Strat into this, doesn't feel right doing the same to you."

"There's no 'you.' Talk, Macushla."

Exhaling, confession time dawned. "I took from the Manzanis," she admitted, unable to look him in the eye. "Strat knew, I knew, it would be trouble. I'm not stupid." Though the opposite could be argued simply because she did it. "And now, I thought… we don't know if Silvio is involved, if he…" Another truth was unavoidable. "My dad knows, doesn't he? He knows who killed my grandfather."

"Maybe not the shooter, but aye, he knows more than he's telling us."

"More than he's telling Lachlan and the police. I could understand him not telling me; he doesn't trust me. But Lachlan…"

"If your brother knew, he'd tell the cops, and the perp would be locked up. What did you take from the Manzanis?"

He'd looped right back to the conversation she didn't want to have. The truth could endanger the man, the family, she valued more than any other.

"I thought I was doing the right thing. A good deed. A necessary deed… I had no idea that it would lead to this."

"What's this?"

"We need to know if Silvio is responsible for Grandpapa's death."

"You want to trade," he said. "What they know for what you stole?"

"Stole is a strong word, but… I thought if we could talk to someone from the Manzani side, not Vex 'cause he's useless and hasn't come up with anything, someone useful. What happened with him at the wake?"

"Doesn't matter. Did you reach out to Vex?"

"No, I… I went to Strat because that's what I do, and I didn't want to put you in the middle."

"I'm not in the middle, I'm at your side. We stand together."

"I know, but if you ask, if you get—it's not discreet."

"You think I can't be discreet?"

"I think pushing the McDade button could be nuclear."

"They know we're involved."

How could he be so calm when everything in her was fraught?

Rising to sit, her legs stayed astride him. "Yeah, and they've possibly already murdered one man I love, I can't—shit."

Getting up, she went into the closet. Except she needed a shower, she couldn't—something snagged her wrist. Someone.

"You get defensive with me, I'll use a different tack."

"I went to Strat; I asked him to set me up a meet because I thought if I could ask—if I could look into the eyes of… It doesn't matter. He was against it."

"Good. He should've told you to come to me."

"He did. More than once."

"Then he gets to live."

She sighed, yanking her wrist. "Conn."

His grip clamped tighter, jerking her hard against him. "You bring everything to me, Sersha McLeod."

"I was so lost, I… I can't be strong like you. I fake it in front of other people, but I can't with you. You see right through me."

"My strength belongs to you. Your fire gives you all the guts you need to be with me."

"And if I disappoint you? I don't want to…"

And that was… What was to stop the same thing happening with Conn? She'd told Strat and he'd put himself in the firing line. Would Conn do the same thing?

"Sersh…" He grabbed her jaw to pull her face closer to his. "Nothing you say, nothing you've done, will change us. Can I trust you?"

Connel's people told him everything. There were no secrets because loyalty was absolute. That was his world, and she needed to be part of it. That might mean accepting less than savory practices.

"Do you trade in women?"

"Do I…?"

"Exploit women for profit?"

"No."

Could she believe that? "Do you pimp women out?"

His frown deepened. "No."

"You don't make money from prostitution?"

"No," he said. "I make money from rent."

That was unexpected. "Rent? I don't—"

"We provide safe premises for women to work. They pay to rent a room and keep every cent they earn. With their rent comes security."

Like someone might rent a chair in a salon to make their money freelance.

"Do you sell them drugs?"

"No drugs allowed on site."

"How do you—"

"We have rules. Anyone causes trouble, they're out."

Yeah, that was the McDades call, because there was no national body monitoring non-existent regulations. The McDades could make up whatever rules they liked and enforce them any way they pleased.

"But the women here, for the party—"

"We pay them to appear."

"And take their money?"

"No, they keep everything they earn. Trade with the john is between those two parties, no one else. Everyone draws their own lines."

"And if a john tries to take more than that or refuses to pay—"

"The McDades look after their people."

Something he was proud of, something he deserved to be proud of.

"What about porn?" Curious, his hold loosened. "Is there any industry the McDades avoid?"

"Pharmaceuticals.   Prescription   and recreational."

"Because?"

"Dealers end up using the product. Makes them unreliable, easily influenced. People need to put the family first. Addicts always prioritize their addiction."

Like he did with her.

"And your prostitutes aren't drug addicts?"

"They're not my hookers and what they do off-site is up to them. How would you cope? Spending every hour of the day and night, playing with the cock of some incel paying you to act like he's the hottest fuck you ever had?" What a futile and heart sickening way to live. "It's not their fault, most of the time. Unstable and desperate fucks a lot of folks. A lot of families."

"What other industries do we play in?"

"Money lending, construction, protection, rentals… we pick up stock where we can, pass it along." Code for theft, she'd guess. "Gambling, to a certain extent. Clubs, we look after our people."

"Do you harass those who don't pay for protection?"

"No," he said. "We offer payback for those who do. We don't just protect, we stand up for our own.

Paying the McDades means protection, not extortion… We're not shy 'bout that in the right field." Yeah, like her experience. "Game the stock market when we get the chance."

"Insider trading?"

"What has this got to do with the Manzani trade?"

"I took from the Manzanis. I can't trust Vex."

"Who's the meet with? Silvio?"

"Swerve."

His head almost fell back, in its tilt, she could hear him groan.

"Macushla."

"I know! Don't get mad."

He hissed out a breath. "Give me whatever it is. I'll do the trade."

She cringed. "This is where your disappointment comes in."

His chin dropped as he frowned. "You lost it?" She shook her head. "Destroyed it?" Shake again. "Sold it?"

"I never intended to hand it over."

His hands fell to his sides, bewildered, like he couldn't comprehend it. Shock wasn't a typical emotion for this man.

"It's about pride," he stated.

"I know that."

"There's a way the game is played."

"Strat told me that too."

"You carry the McDade name now," he said. "Your reputation is our reputation. To insult the family name—"

"I get it. I know. I'm sorry. It was an impulse; an idea born in the midst of desperation. This is why I say these things out loud to Strat before I do them. His reaction is a barometer of my craziness."

"He shouldn't let you do anything dangerous."

"Wish granted." Sinking forward, her face came to rest against him. "He arranged the meet… for him, not for me. He's going to screw the Manzanis so I can't."

A hand curved around the back of her head. "What do you want?"

One simple question.

Her simple answer. "Strat safe."

"Anything you want, I can make it happen."

"Will you protect my friend?"

"Aye. Have the Manzanis called in their chit?"

"They don't know I have it. As far as I know, they don't know." He followed one hand with the other until his thumbs pressed into her jaw to tip her head back. "They know it's gone. They don't know I'm the one hiding it."

"Why would you do that? Take that kind of risk without the McDade shield?"

"I don't know," she admitted. "It's pathetic."

"Talk to me," he beseeched. "Macushla, I need to trust you more than any other person alive." Given the longevity of some people in his life, that was quite an ask. "Where are you always safe?"

"With you."

His hold strengthened. "Trust me," he said through gritted teeth. "Come on, baby. Trust me."

THIRTY-THREE

"I'LL SHOW YOU. My phone's on the bar."

Conn let her go through to the living room to open her purse and take out her phone. As she loaded up an app, he sauntered up beside her.

The picture cleared and she handed him the device.

"What is…?"

"Live stream. We call her Jane Doe," she said, peeking around the device to see the woman sleeping in bed. "Her first name's Marseille. That's all I know about her."

"You took from them? You took her from them? From the Manzanis? You saved her."

On a nod, she shrugged. "Like I said, it started with the right thing. I took her to the hospital. She wouldn't talk to cops, which worked out, because… if she talked about the Manzanis…"

"They'd kill her."

"Right. I went back to the hospital, asked if she had support, if she could keep herself safe. She doesn't have a clue how deep she's in but knows if the Manzanis find her, they'll kill her. This woman is a loose end. I don't want her dead but…"

"You planned to tell Swerve you have her. To ask what they know about your grandfather's murder in exchange for this Jane Doe." Disgrace coiled around her. "Strat said no. That was the fight. And when he showed up here…"

"He's got a meet with Swerve, tomorrow, he's going to do the dangling."

"It's her life—"

"No," she said, touching him. "Strat doesn't know where she is and didn't ask. He couldn't hand her over even if he wanted to. It's not in him to endanger or jeopardize any woman. He won't do it. No matter the cost."

"He'll make the deal then renege."

"They'll kill him."

"Aye," he said, turning the phone to her. "Where is this?"

"Lach's old apartment. It was just lying there empty. He's moved to mine and Imogen's with Jagg. Imogen gave me her keys after her stuff was out, asked me to pass them onto Lach." Which she hadn't. "It's quiet. No one's looking for her there. I started bouncing around hotels, keeping her moving. Wasn't easy when I didn't know if Evander was watching me. This place feels safer."

Providing Lachlan never went back.

"And your plan, long term?"

"I didn't have one. I don't have one. She's innocent, Mo Grá. If she'd done something wrong, I'd understand it, but she hasn't. They want to dispose of her like she's trash and she doesn't know why."

"Because she's seen too much."

"Maybe. I didn't ask. The more I know, the

greater the chance the Manzanis want rid of me too."

He put the phone down by her purse. "That won't happen."

"Not if you or Evander get a say. Remember Silvio isn't my biggest fan. I could contact Hell, but that's the long way round. I don't think we have time for that."

"What do you do if you have a problem?"

"Bring it to you."

"Thought you understood that when you said it before. I am your first call and your last."

"I want to know who killed my grandfather, but not at the expense of other lives. Strat's important to me."

"He'll be taken care of."

"If I pit you against another family, you could get hurt."

"You didn't care when Vex found out we're together."

"Because Vex is a bug, an annoying gnat. Being with you liberates me from him. You can handle Vex."

"I can't handle the don?"

"Evander doesn't have Silvio's reach. Silvio plays by the rules." Most of the time. "But Swerve—I'd never forgive myself."

His rough, entitled fingers pushed vertically up her face, curving around into her hair to bring their eyes closer.

"Put another obstacle in front of me, I'll obliterate it. Trust me, Macushla."

"I need help." Breathing out the words was a relief. "I don't know what to do with Marseille. I want her safe. She's looking to me, and I've got nothing."

"Ask."

"Help me."

"It's handled," he said, softening, curling and straightening his fingers against her scalp. "No limits.

There's no limit to what I'd do for you."

"Just remember you're my last line of defense. Without you, I'm vulnerable."

He didn't care about his life whereas she did. A guaranteed way to ensure he took more care of himself was to highlight what losing him would mean for her safety.

"That'll never happen."

With his hands looser, she could lean over to snag her purse without losing contact. "The keys…"

She put them on the bar by her phone.

"You never have to think about it again. It's dealt with."

And that was a weight off. He'd told her he'd protect Strat too and she believed him.

"Thank you, baby."

"You're not gonna do this again. I don't care what shit you're into, you talk to me. There's no line I wouldn't cross for you."

"I want you to be proud of me," she said, accepting the simplicity of her need, "not to bring shame or drama to the family."

"What is your job?"

"To support you."

"Trust me."

"From the first moment you touched me, all I wanted was to belong to you. To be yours."

"You are mine."

And if something happened to her, Conn's position would be stronger with more information.

"Tulip," she said. "At The Chronicler. She called to tell me Wanstead got your name from a CI. A long standing CI who turned up flush around the same time. She doesn't know if the two are related."

"It was a setup."

On an exhale, she nodded within his hold. "That

would be my guess. Wanstead wanted you in the interrogation room."

"Someone did. Why?" he asked, narrowing his gaze, like maybe he wasn't really asking.

Maybe he wasn't.

"Do you have history with Wanstead? He's a jerk."

"Plenty of that going around," he muttered. "Wanstead's background noise."

"If you have no personal beef, he's in someone's pocket."

"In debt or looking for a favor." He snapped back to focus on her. "What's the CI's name?"

"She wouldn't tell me. Not until I scratched." His frown prompted an answer. "She'll scratch our back if we scratch hers. She wants to know why Nicole has a price on her head. Asked for an interview."

"With who?"

"Me, you, Nicki, I don't know, she wants answers."

"We'll take care of her."

"Nicely," she said, moving against him. "The Chronicler are our allies until they're not. And I don't want to lose my job."

"Your job is safe, baby."

Because he'd make sure of that. "Having Tulip on our side could work out for us in the long run."

"You want me to play nice."

"I would never dream of telling you how to do your job." Her smile brought him lower. "Mine will be easier if we don't intimidate my colleagues."

"Wanstead's handler set me up."

And she didn't forget that for a second. "There's a silver lining," she said. "A clue. Whoever it is, they didn't know about us."

"You suspected our people?"

"Vex knew about us. So if it's a Manzani play, at least we can rule out one suspect. Him and his people."

"Never thought it was him, he's too simple."

Funny, she'd said something similar about Vex in another scenario. "I haven't heard from him in a while, makes me nervous."

"Nothing to be nervous about in our kingdom."

"You still working with him?"

"Using him for what I need. He's not my equal."

"No…" Backing up, she hooked her hands onto the lower bar and boosted herself up to sit on it. "He is not." Brushing her heel against his thigh was enough to tempt him between them. "You are my anchor, Mr. McDade."

"Holding you down."

"Keeping me steady. Without you, I'm adrift. It's not that I don't trust you, I always trust you, I just… If I wake up one day without you… I can't be without you, Mo Grá. I can't."

"You won't be. Present or not, I'm at your side."

Did she like that? The ambiguous statement could be interpreted in many ways. She'd never force her guy to say more. Neither of them knew what was around the corner.

Roused, something lacked.

Sliding her hands up his body, her arms relaxed around his neck. "Tell me something." He didn't react. "Confide in me, Mo Grá."

"I protect you."

"I won't act on whatever you tell me. If my burden is yours, then yours is mine. Let me be your sanctuary." He didn't have to open himself to her. Nothing would take her from him, not voluntarily, but if he wanted their worlds to unite, they had to… "Complete the circle." Anything would suffice. She only needed a glimmer. "How are things going with Harvest?

Are we secure yet?"

"Votes lie about equal with two holdouts."

"Undecided?" she asked, her fingers playing in the hair at the back of his head. "You need both of them to secure the win. What happens if they're deadlocked?"

"Bodies start dropping."

One on each side until the rest got the message. One side would have to go further, much further to win. Offing city officials could bring seriously unwanted attention to their business, especially after her grandfather's murder.

"Anyone we know?" she asked.

"Steinham, Blakely."

"Jim Blakely?" After his nod, she smiled. "I dated his son in high school."

"A perfect reason to kill him."

"His son isn't the one holding out," she said, sensing his tease. "Rich of old Jim though, seriously, to be hesitant of a dark path like he's some saint." Maybe he and her dad were related. "If the rumors are true..." The twitch of his brow alerted her to his interest. "Talk about a trying time for the family. Donovan was the year above me. We were together for a couple of years; he dropped out before his senior year. Said the family were moving across town."

"They weren't?"

"Oh, they moved, left the state for a while, but not for Donovan's benefit. The marriage eventually broke down, his mom started drinking heavily, lost everything. Donovan ended up in prison, I think. All because the prestigious principal, Jim Blakely, his dad, got a student pregnant."

"A teenager?"

She shrugged. "That was the rumor."

"Rumor to others, you got it from the source."

"By proxy through Donovan, yeah. Really fucked

with his head. It was all hushed up, of course. The girl was supposed to get an abortion and didn't. Jim denied it was his."

"Did they do a paternity test?"

"No. They paid an obscene amount of money to the family to keep them quiet and, like all scandal, it faded into fable. For the rest of us anyway. The girl left school, but she was already showing. The line was 'troubled teen,' but she was an honor student… Though, I guess if she was fucking teachers, grades could be questionable."

"What was her name?"

"The girl, uh…" She should know the answer. Did she know the answer…? "Louise, I think. Louise Greco, something like that, she was in Donovan's year."

Tucking her head against him, he kissed her crown. "Good girl."

Smiling, she tightened her embrace. "One for you… Now one for me…"

He scooped her up off the counter. "You'll get yours, Macushla."

"I need something a little more… intimidating. A lot more intimidating."

Stopping on the threshold of their room, he scrutinized her with concerned interest. "What do you need?"

"The security guy working the night of my grandfather's death, Sneddon, he's been absent, claiming PTSD. Some things the guy I spoke to said… I want to talk to him. This Sneddon."

"You want the guys to bring him in? The basement's at your disposal. He'll tell you anything you want to know by the time we're through with him."

"No, I… thought I'd ask nicely first. Kinda nicely. Maybe play good cop to one of your bad cops?"

"What department?"

She laughed. "No, I don't need an actual cop. Can I take a couple of your guys with me when I talk to him? Just to be a menacing presence. I would never ask them to do anything."

"Ask? No. The McDades and their allies know to treat every word from your mouth as a direct order from me."

"I don't want to take advantage of you."

"That's exactly what I want to do with you," he said, continuing until she was on her back in their bed. His hands skimmed high on her thighs. "McDade is in you now."

"No," she said, looping her arms around his neck. "But I hope he will be very…" she kissed him, "very," another kiss, "soon, Mo Grá."

Knowing the words was one thing, saying them aloud transformed them. Every minute that passed saw them fall deeper into their addiction. He said there was no line he wouldn't cross for her. Trust him? Hadn't he figured out yet that her dependence on him was almost complete? Together with him, she was invincible.

THIRTY-FOUR

ON WAKING, night still surrounded her, but no lover lay by her side.

Huh. Where did he…?

Voices carried from the living room. Was her guy out there? Someone was, and that someone wasn't alone.

Dragging herself from the comfort of their bed, she donned one of his shirts and wandered through to join the voices.

Yep, her guy sat on his own in the middle of the couch. Other people, men, four of them stood. Two together at the far corner of the coffee table, one paced, one loitered behind the armchair.

"…the balance is my problem," her guy said.

"Ire, we've gotta worry about the—"

On her approach, the others froze, though she didn't care why. Rounding the couch, she slid one knee up the outside of Conn's thigh and slung the other across his lap to sink against him, nuzzling his neck. With him in only sweats, only the fabric she wore kept her skin from his.

Arching her shoulders, she fumbled with one button and another, opening the shirt to rest her flesh on his. God, to be against the beat of his ferocious heart… The one reserved for her.

Kissing his neck, she rubbed herself on him, absorbing a settling peace.

"Worry?" Conn asked, stroking her hair down her back while talking over her. "Do what you're told. That's all you've gotta worry about."

"You gotta know it, Ire. You gotta—shit."

Smiling against his carotid, she trailed her hand upward and tried to pull her guy down for a kiss.

"Later, baby," he said, catching her hand to lower it again. "Ash is worried. What you worried about, Ash? Tell my lady."

"Bluebell's the fucking superintendent's daughter."

"Aye." Her guy kissed her knuckles. "You questioning her loyalty?"

"No! Every ass is on the line—"

"We don't know what the fuck to—"

"Your first concern, Castor, should be walking out of here alive. 'Cause that is not guaranteed."

Leaving her hand on his ribs, her guy's slid beneath the cushion at their side. The click of a gun being cocked revealed the weapon to her. Whether or not the others knew before, she didn't care. Were they in a room of allies or did danger lurk?

Strange, even with the uncertainty, she wasn't afraid. Her heavy eyes closed, and she shifted to kiss his family tattoo. At the same time, her hand slipped between them and descended to the bulge in his pants.

Once again, her inhibitions fled. Using her whole body and the grip of her sure hand to stimulate them both, she only had to feel, not think. Parting her lips on the whisper of a moan, she pressed her mouth against him.

"Both targets are valid," Conn said to the guys, his palm running down her hair again. "I tell you to take him down, you take him down. We got a problem?"

"No problem, just be smart. The more witnesses—"

"Macushla belongs to me. Every inch of her body and ounce of her sense." Her? God, yes. "Her commitment is unconditional."

"If she plays you—"

"That an accusation, Castor?"

"She could be useful," a different male said. "Can we use her?"

"You don't think about her, look at her, or breathe near her," her guy snarled. "You've got a fucking job to do."

"If we take it before he gets to the dinner—"

"Then everyone gets the message," another of the guys said.

Conversation continued like she wasn't even there. The accumulation of her need took her higher until her tongue flicked his earlobe.

"Tastes so good," she breathed, caressing his ear with her lips. "Conn…"

His jaw moved in her hair. "Where is your kingdom?" The others, debating between themselves, wouldn't hear the murmur, but it awakened her. Snatching her hair, he yanked her head back, baring his teeth. "What's your fucking job?"

To support him. Oh, God, yes, she wanted to do that, exactly that. The man ruled her, every part of her, and it didn't hurt the myth to demonstrate exactly that. Choose to submit, that was what he wanted. The stronger the man, the more secure the family. Proving his power submerged her, proved his ability to rule the city.

Easing her body from his, she straightened, gathering her hair on her head as it went back, absorbing the glide of his fingertips up over her breasts and back down her cleavage.

Her guy. Her kingdom. Her right.

Slithering down to the floor between his feet, it didn't matter that they weren't alone, this was them. Everything was them. Good, bad, and explicit.

Warmed, enlivened, aroused, she kissed his abs, peeking up at his commanding stance, the certainty in his expression. This was them. All of them. Staking a claim, to the man and the building, she wouldn't undervalue herself.

His fingers twined in her hair as hers peeled back the waistband of his sweats to kiss the flesh beneath. Her right. Her territory. Licking him slow, she didn't meet any resistance, not that she expected any. No. It's about pride. And, suddenly, fuck, it all made sense. She wanted him even more. Inhaling, she sank his cock deep into her throat and sucked it free. Catching it with her hand, she only played for a second until it descended to tease her prize.

Fuck, she could blow him all day. Like this, with stuttering conversation in the background that was little more than white noise. Her guy, arms stretched along the back, feet set wide, this wasn't bravado or conceit, his pride glowed too.

Mmm… capturing him into her mouth again, she had some fun, relaxing into it, taking her time.

Didn't take long for his grip to clamp tight in her hair, holding her head steady as his hips lifted to force himself deep. She swallowed every drop. Her man. Her McDade. Her future. Her right.

That same grip pulled her up from the floor, returning her to his lap, almost boneless in her satisfaction.

In fact, she was so relaxed that sleep tugged at her again. God knew how long later, heavy footsteps on the stairs interrupted her semi-doze.

"Company?"

Niall's voice. Conn always had guys on site at Stag, but it was always reassuring to know Niall had her guy's back. Nothing to worry about.

"Aye."

Footsteps again, descending this time. Whatever Niall's question meant, he'd got the go ahead. More people, more talk, more whatever. It didn't matter so long as she was there, against him, breathing with…

Someone ascended the stairs, more than one someone.

"Ready to trade?"

Her eyes opened as her senses froze. That voice. Evander. Shit.

"You wanted in on the meet, this is it," Conn said. "What you bringing to the table, Vex?"

"Less than you if that tail's in play."

Fear. Dread. She'd been in the same room as Evander and Conn before. This wasn't the same. It was the first time she'd been so open, so vulnerable. Wearing only Conn's shirt, legs straddling his hips, her body was concealed from view. She couldn't move. If she moved, if anything—Evander would drink in every drop of the scene. Every drop of her near nakedness draped on her man. What if it angered him? If he thought to challenge Conn…?

"I warned you never to utter her name."

"Didn't say it, did I?" Evander asked with a hint of amusement. "Nice of you to offer him charity, Princess."

Conn tensed and her hands went to his shoulders. She wanted to calm him, to defuse the growing pressure.

"This is her house. Don't disrespect her."

"How much respect has she got? Bet she's wearing nothing under that shirt and here with your guys… Like cheap sluts, McDade?"

Her stomach lurched, but her own upset took a backseat to Conn's twitch of movement. She pushed up, just enough to lay a hand on his cheek and draw his eyes to hers. With a gentle kiss, she couldn't do more to beg his restraint.

"Bed," he ordered her.

Inside, she rejoiced at the instant sensation of liberation, but… if she left, who would remind him not to let Evander provoke him?

She couldn't argue with him. Wouldn't. Whatever happened, she trusted him.

With another kiss, which gave her cover for fastening some of the shirt buttons, she reversed from his lap, keeping the fabric closed over her body.

Going to bed meant passing Evander and the two men with him. Keeping her head low, she couldn't give Evander the chance to further needle Conn with some wink or whisper.

Except as she was about to pass him, he sidestepped into her way. Not completely, just enough that with his Manzani goon at her other side, the path was too narrow to pass without contact.

Probably exactly his plan.

What an idiot. In McDade territory? In Ire's kingdom? This wouldn't end well.

"Touch her and I'll kill you," her guy growled from the couch.

"That's why I hire muscle."

A Manzani goon grabbed her arm. And boom. One instant. So quick it seemed like the gunshot sounded after the guy slammed into the floor. Eyes fixed. Red liquid seeping from the side of his head. Oh… Conn had actually done it. That guy touched her and now he was dead.

Reflex had taken her a good meter from where she'd been before.

"Who's next?"

"Fucking asshole," Evander barked.

Another shot blasted and someone else hit the floor.

Whirling around, Evander was the target. Not dead, not shot in the head like the other guy, instead, he'd got a gut shot. The Manzani son slumped against the depth of the wall at the top of the stairs, cradling the blood seeping between his fingers.

"A shot there, without medical help, is one hundred percent fatal," Conn said, coming up beside her, concentrating on the shocked, angry, and God knew what else, Evander. Her lover's arm rose again, this time to take aim at Evander's remaining lackey's head. "Lady's choice. What do you want, Macushla? We let him bleed out slow or scurry into the dark for help?"

Life or death. The choice was before her. Evander "Vex" Manzani was vulnerable, in the perfect spot to pull the plug. To end his pursuit of her for good. How many times had she wished for that? Thought about what she'd do, how free she'd be, if he just vanished?

Without giving an answer, she took a steadying breath and walked away. Going into the bedroom, she went to the meter of bare wall between the closet and Conn's nightstand.

A snap from Connel's home language broke the air. A few seconds passed and then he was there, by the bathroom, looking at her. As he scrutinized her through the shadows, she reversed until her spine met the wall. Did he see judgment? Read fear? Lifting her hand, she beckoned to him.

Stalking over, his hands landed on the wall at either side of her head, gun still in his grip. He bent his knees to align their eyes.

"Macushla—"

Her fingertips met his lips. How could she feel all he made her feel without shattering into a million pieces? How did she contain it? Her toes left the floor to slide around his calf, rising higher, higher until he caught the back of her knee and coiled it around his hip. She boosted the other up for him to catch as she freed his cock and then he was inside her.

Exactly what she needed. Bliss came with an exhale that pushed her head against the wall. Her body bowed, pressing closer to his, aching with a deep need. Loving him was bigger than her, than them.

Yelping and gasping, she didn't hide the intensity of what he made her feel. He thrust into her while she levered herself with a grip on his shoulders, his neck, his hair. There wasn't enough room in her body for the desperate delight exploding within her.

Connel McDade was her everything. Nothing more or less. Whether he said the words or not—at least, whether he said them in the language she spoke or not— he put her above everything else.

A rumbling growl in his throat built until it became a roar of climax that almost matched hers.

And he stayed there, within her, breathing hard, the fog of humidity between them closed in another kiss.

"Let him live," she whispered on his lips. "Mo Grá. Because I want to keep you."

If they killed the youngest Manzani son, they'd be next. She'd take it if it fell on her, but him? Connel? The blood in her veins, the air she breathed, the universe. Without him, the world would cease to be. She wouldn't stand it.

They'd made their point.

THIRTY-FIVE

FROM WHAT SHE'D HEARD, Evander was carried out by his goon. The other guy, the body, she wasn't sure what happened to that. Conn's conversation with Niall was in their mother tongue.

Movement and voices seemed endless and then, in a single heartbeat, silence.

Calm came with it. Seated alone in the center of their bed, time ebbed and flowed, washing over her, cleaning away any glimmer of regret or uncertainty.

Without a sound, Conn materialized in the bedroom, coming to a stop at the end of the bed. One beat. Two.

"Need a drink?" he asked from the back of his throat. "A ride out of here?"

Something about him was different… or maybe it was something about her. Whatever it was, the change lingered on the tip of her tongue, she just couldn't pinpoint it.

"Cushla Machree—"

"I need my man," she said, tilting her head. "Why

the distance, baby?"

Dropping to the bed, he came to her, scooping his hand across the side of her head, sweeping her hair into a fist that locked at the back of her skull as his kiss crashed against hers. Forced onto her back, she clung to him, whimpering, pleading, grateful for all he was and that they'd found each other.

He ripped his mouth away. "I won't apologize."

"You have nothing to apologize for," she panted. "You don't say the words, but I feel your heart, Mo Grá." Killing for her, again, and inflicting a potentially fatal wound on a man for thinking about touching her, how could she not? "I want you to love me like that."

Just as she'd said about him wanting her. The depth of that passion, its potency, was a blessing, a gift. One she didn't feel worthy of.

"I'd have killed the worm," he hissed through gritted teeth. "Him near you—"

"I belong only to you; it's your right to protect me."

If only she could protect him with the same ferocity. How far did that go? Was she testing him with her risks or trying to embrace his world? This man, all of him, belonged to her with such purity of intention that her embrace would never be enough to repay him.

His lips brushed hers, slowly pressing harder until his fist dug into the back of her skull. They could just be there together, everywhere, whatever else happened in the world couldn't touch them in the intoxication of their kiss.

And that was the worry she hadn't faced.

He'd murdered a man for touching her. Wasn't the first time he'd killed for her, and she doubted Evander's goon was innocent. For all Conn gave her, she took and took, only digging him in deeper. One day, as Whisper said, they could face criminal action or injury.

Because of her. Some McDade illicit misdeeds might not be on her, but the list of those that were grew daily.

Shooting Evander wasn't something anyone would just get over. It wouldn't be forgotten. The man had been obsessed with her for years. Maybe seeing her with Connel broke the spell and changed Evander's perspective. Had she become a cheap slut? No, she couldn't let him into her mind like that, couldn't let him control any of their narrative. If anything, she feared being with Conn would fuel Evander's desire, not with any kind of love or genuine emotion, spite would be the source.

She turned her head to free her lips. "Mo Grá, will there be retribution?"

Evander wasn't just shot, wasn't just bleeding, he'd been humiliated in front of others. Who would pay the price for that? The immature egotist wouldn't let it go easy.

"Always, Macushla." His hand loosened to comb through her hair and his other arm locked around her waist to drag her up the bed beneath him, landing her head in the pillow. "For you."

But she didn't want to be that. "I don't want to be the cause of—what about your deal with Evander?"

His mouth didn't leave her skin. "Nothing's more important than this."

Was there anything more important? Submerged in him, in them, the future could be dark, but she couldn't bring herself to care. Except she had to care about him, about more than the way he made her feel and how he appreciated her. Support, that was her role. She couldn't just stand back and watch everything turn to shit.

Something within her, something—she pushed him back. "Connel." His curious frown required a beat. Breathing deep, she licked her lips. "I'm in love with you." When he tried to kiss her again, she resisted. "There's nothing in this world I wouldn't do for you. I know you say it all the time and prove it over and over and I'm…"

"Baby—"

"I'm not pulling my weight," she confessed a truth that startled her. "The words aren't enough, the words are useless, an insult, when stacked against what you bring to the table."

"That's my call."

Was it? He'd never ask anything of her. Never had, never would. He took protecting her and solving her issues seriously while she… how did she show her love?

"You could go to prison. For killing that man, for shooting Evander."

"I'd have killed him if you hadn't told me no."

"How does that make me good for you? I jeopardize your freedom. The family need you. Your job is to run things, to take care of your people. If loving me distracts you from that, jeopardizes your freedom…" The McDades would come to hate her. "You'll resent me one day, when you realize what loving me has cost you."

"It'd cost me more to lose you." Propping his weight on his elbows, his forearms framed her face. "If you walk out, if you leave me, it better be because you don't love me. It better be that you've figured out you're better than this, more worthy than my level. And you'd better hope I believe it, because if I don't… there isn't an obstacle I won't obliterate."

Desperation raced her heart. "What does that mean?"

"Only you can stop this. I'll never see you as anything other than mine. You are the only one with control."

Over him? Over them?

"I'm bad for you, for the family. How can you

give yourself to this? Your people… they'll see I caused this, that just by existing, I weaken you."

The twitch of his brow became almost… disbelief.

He rolled away, cutting all physical contact. "Then go."

Bewildered, the move took her aback. "What?"

"Go. If you mean what you say, go."

To prove that the family meant more, was that his point? Though she'd made her own. If all she did was damage, he'd be better off without her.

Lip service or a reality she believed? Conn meant more than her desire. No question.

She left the bed by her own side, something she couldn't remember doing while Conn shared it with her.

This man was a monolith who supported his family, ensured jobs and livelihoods. Was he always on the up and up? No, who was anyone to judge? Lives depended on him, hers included.

Going into the closet, she dressed quickly. Leaving Stag wouldn't be easy. Without it before, she'd spiraled. And this time Strat wouldn't be there to support her either. How had she become poison to the people she loved? Lach would be in her apartment. Was he next on her list of people to screw up?

She turned, tying her hair back, and came to a stop. Conn stood in the closet, just three feet away, and she hadn't heard him approach.

Driving his hands into her hair, he pulled her close, right into him until her face was against his chest. Her safe space. Him, she always craved.

"It's not possible to walk away from this," he murmured into her crown, his voice muffled by her hair. "We're a part of each other now."

"I don't want to hurt you, to be a liability for the family you love."

"A family you've defended. A family that values you. You've bled for us, Macushla. Stood up to the cops, stood up to your own blood. You are the core of us."

"The McDades belong to you. You're the core of them."

He pulled her head back to meet her eye. "And you are the core of me. Macushla…" His grip tightened as he shook her once. "Recognize your power. Accept it." Beseeching her, his frustration glowed bright. "Your father, your family, they underestimate you, baby. Here, with me, you are not at the bottom of the ladder. You rule here. Just like you did kicking your father to the curb. That power is yours."

"It does something to me," she admitted. "Being with you, being a McDade, it excites me. I feel like I belong—"

"You do belong."

"Would you have shot Evander tonight if I hadn't been with you?"

"You don't have to be around for him to talk about you or for me to defend you."

"Is that a yes?"

"Whether you're here or not, whether you leave our bed tonight, you will still be our McDade. You are one of us. We stand together. We fall together. Your name is ours and ours is yours. You wouldn't hesitate to go to war for our people, for our name. Why is it so difficult for you to believe we'd do the same for you? No one is to blame. We all know the risks and we're in it together."

"My brother's the only other man I thought would be with me no matter what."

He scooped up her hair to hold it in his fist in a ponytail. "Now you have an army of them. An army eager to please. An army you command."

"You command."

"And who commands me?" he asked. "Ask and it's yours." His eyes narrowed as his mouth came closer. "I'd fall to my knees for you, Cushla Machree."

"No…" the word was a whisper. Her eyes closed. "I want you to rise, to push the McDades higher than any other. I want you untouchable, invincible. I want you with me, always."

"I'm with you."

And as long as that was true, she'd weather anything else. Let their enemies come for them; they'd handle every storm together.

THIRTY-SIX

DALY OPENED THE CAR door for her just like any other day. The van that usually parked a few meters away, or on the opposite side of the street, pulled up right behind them. Another building stood before them, apartments, not like her grandfather's townhouse, not even close.

"Not much to look at, is it?" Daly said, his shoulder bumping hers as he took position beside her.

"Not everyone's lucky enough to have their own nightclub, Daly. Though…" Whatever she'd been about to say slipped away when the van's side door opened. Hock got out with Snuff. Did she need three—another two got out and then the door closed again. "How many people do you think we need for one guy?"

"Gotta be prepared," Hock said.

"Like the boss says."

"Like a boy scout."

Her gaze landed on Snuff. "Prepared? Yes. But believe me, honey, your boss is no boy scout."

The guys snickered. Her three guys did anyway,

the other two seemed more reserved. That one furthest away, why was his face familiar?

"Do these two talk?"

"If you need them to," Daly said and leaned in to speak near the top of her head. "Haven't you figured out that the guys who don't know Bluebell fear Bluebell?"

"Fear me?" she said and glanced at the building again. "They don't fear me, they fear what Ire will do to them if they upset me."

"Same difference," Hock said, striding on by to ascend the stoop.

The other guys carried her along with them in his wake.

"Got a gameplan?" Daly asked.

She pressed the buzzer. "I'm going to ask nicely."

"Think that'll work?"

"If I thought it was guaranteed, you wouldn't be here," she muttered under her breath.

The speaker crackled. "What do you want?" a guy barked.

"I'm looking for David Sneddon."

Daly shouldered her closer to the microphone as he crowded in at her back.

"Why?"

"Are you David Sneddon?" she asked, though his reticence was sort of answer enough. "I have a few questions—"

"Go away."

The crackling stopped.

"Guess he's happy to see us," she said, turning to the guys just as the door opened.

Her moment of hope that Sneddon had changed his mind vanished when Daly's tools in the lock clued her in.

He slipped the metal gadgets away. "Mademoiselle…"

"You pick locks?" she asked, going inside. "Is that like a prerequisite? I thought you'd be less… discreet."

"Trick is…" Hock led the way up the stairs, "be discreet in public, where people can see."

"Then behind closed doors…"

"Plausible deniability," she said, bobbing her head. "I get it. Smart."

"McDades are in the business of reducing our criminal footprint."

"Leave as little evidence as possible."

"Gives you more time to work. If nothing's out of place…"

No one would have reason to call the cops.

"There's more to this thug thing than I realized."

"Don't worry," Daly said, slinging an arm over her shoulders. "We'll get you up to speed in no time, Rookie."

"He's in 4D," she said when they got to the fourth floor.

Four apartments to a floor, so they didn't have to go far to find his door.

Hock, at the head, turned to the side and barged the door with one powerful shoulder, forcing it from the frame.

When she stopped, jaw loose, he shrugged. "What?"

"You didn't think to knock?"

"He was rude," Hock said like the motive was obvious.

It was done now, so when he pushed the door open, she followed him inside.

One guy stood in the middle of the living room with the TV on behind him; looked like they'd startled him out of his chair. The ferocious anger on his scrunched expression changed hue when the guys kept on coming. Yep, it wasn't just little her bugging him through a speaker, she had reinforcements.

The front door closed and the two unknown guys passed by her to grab who she assumed to be Sneddon and slammed him into the wall.

"Do we have to be so full on?" she whispered to Daly from the corner of her mouth.

"They're checking for weapons. After that…"

Hock spun the armchair. Snuff kicked a table out of the way and killed the TV's power by yanking its cord from the wall.

Satisfied, she guessed, her two extra thugs threw Sneddon into the chair.

"He's clean," one of them said, though the pair remained flanking him.

"What…? What is this?" the pale Sneddon asked.

She smiled. "Like I said, I have a few questions."

"You're… you're his…" Sneddon took in the scene. "Fuck."

"Yes," she said, still wearing that smile. "This may be a fuck situation for you, depending on how you cooperate."

"I'll cooperate."

"Great." She took a breath. "As I'm sure you were alluding to before, I'm Alderman McLeod's granddaughter."

Though he could've been aiming for one of the other numerous men in her life.

"He… he's dead."

"Yes." A "duh" seemed appropriate, but she refrained. "Murdered, to be precise. I'm sure you've seen the news. Though, I suppose, you know it better than anyone since you were the only other person in the building when it happened… You were the only other person present, weren't you?"

"I… I was on that night, alone, yeah, I… I didn't

see nothing."

"I don't care about things; I care about people. You were on security that night and your protectee ended up dead. Horton said you haven't been back to work. Whatever you saw must've shaken you up if you were traumatized. Just what did you see exactly?"

"I gave a statement to the cops."

It didn't bother her that Sneddon's attention darted from guy to guy. He should be aware of the threat, that was only smart. And it let her slip under the radar a little.

"Police statements are my brother and father's wheelhouse. I care less about what should be said, or what might be judged, and more about the truth. No one here is looking to secure a prosecution." Though the group at large hadn't actually decided on a collective course of action. "We don't care what you were doing, what else was going on, we care about who killed him."

"I didn't see nothing. No one. I didn't see no one."

"No one? Okay, take me through that night. My grandfather must've been at home when you arrived because the shift change is on the access log after my grandfather got home."

"You've… got the access logs?"

Her smile broadened again. "There's very little I can't get my hands on, Mr. Sneddon."

"Then what'd you need me for?" he asked, finding a little backbone. "You're not a cop, I don't have to say nothing."

"Seen the news, asshole?" Hock asked.

In fairness, he didn't seem like the type to even get close to the news channels.

"Do you know who she is?" was Snuff's question.

"I know him," he said, nodding at Hock. "And

that guy."

The guy to his left got a nod too.

Daly stepped up. "You know who we work for?"

"I don't know nothing about that," he said, waving both hands in front of him. "No way I'm going there."

Maybe he was smart after all.

"Their boss wants you to answer my questions," she said because it was true. "If you answer them to my satisfaction, we will leave, no problems."

"Don't answer them…?" Daly said. "That's a big problem. Big. One Ire'll take personally."

"I don't know. I don't know shit. She's a McLeod, not a McDade. I'm not saying nothing to a cop's kid."

"Do we look like a cop's family?" Hock asked.

The familiar side guy kicked the chair. Ah! That was where she knew him from. Pietro.

"She could've just paid you off the street."

Daly was incredulous. "Freelance? You don't believe she's a McDade?" He laughed, Hock and Snuff joined in, setting Sneddon off balance. "Please make me call the boss for confirmation. Please, man, 'cause then you'll really get to see us work."

"You can get Ire McDade on the phone?" Sneddon scoffed. "Yeah, right."

"She can get him on his back."

Snuff's joke maybe wasn't well timed, but the statement was true.

"Why would McDades care about the alderman? Not like they gotta worry about him talking. Guy's dead, what's he gonna say?"

Now that was interesting.

"Why would we be worried about that?" she asked. "Who was he talking to?"

"No one, he's dead."

Stranger Side Guy smacked the back of Sneddon's head.

"What did he know?" Daly demanded.

Another smack.

"He was asking questions," Sneddon said. "Something going on with the council."

"How do you know?"

"They were arguing about it."

"They? They who?"

"Him and Lupe."

The housekeeper.

"Thought she wasn't there that night."

"She wasn't, not later when… They were arguing at shift change, Horton said they'd been at it a while before I got there. Then Lupe stormed out, said she wanted no part of it. Said…"

His hesitation came with a dip of his chin. Familiar Side Guy grabbed Sneddon's hair to wrench up his head while Stranger hit him again.

And it was then she got the overkill of operatives. Conn wanted her guys to protect *her*. Her trio were there to protect and support *her*. She was their mission. The two new guys were for Sneddon's benefit; they were her supplemental thugs tasked with intimidation.

"Said what?" she demanded. "What?"

"That he was going to get himself killed." His breathing was ragged. "She said it wasn't his business that he was too used to being in control. That he wasn't invincible."

"How did you hear this?"

"Horton and me were on the first floor. They were up the stairs. Arguing in the hall."

So their words carried down the staircase.

"Did she name any names?"

"No, that was it, then she left."

"She isn't in the access log."

"She never is, hardly ever. She hates all the technology stuff, always complained about it."

"I don't understand. Security on the door, the camera, it takes a picture every time—"

"She goes in the back."

"The back?"

"You want to know anything about the alderman, Lupe's the only one who'd know. She knows everything."

"I didn't know there's a back way. He has a yard, then there's a service alley—"

"There's a tunnel, from back in Prohibition days. Needs a key, nobody has it, just her, not even your grandaddy. One place we were told never to monitor, her pantry entrance. Old man gave her whatever she wanted."

"Why would he—" The woman in his life, the constant. His anchor. "Shit."

Daly's voice came lower. "Same reason the boss gives you whatever you want."

Her grandfather's great love? The household staff. Lachlan was accepting while her dad would go nuts. No shock there, on either score.

"Why didn't you tell this to the cops? I read your witness statement, and you didn't mention the argument, or her leaving..." or the secret entrance. What other secrets were being kept? "Why lie?"

"You want to get a job in this town, you've gotta prove you're no snitch."

No snitch, though the omission could've led to them looking in completely the wrong place.

"Thank you, Mr. Sneddon. This has been useful."

"You good?" Daly murmured.

"Aye," she muttered, then remembered the thought she'd had in the shower, "oh, just one more thing, do you have your security pass?"

"My security pass?"

"If you're not working, you don't need it. With my grandfather gone, you won't have to go back."

"Yeah, I—but I—"

The guys closed in as the side guys hauled Sneddon to his feet.

"Bluebell gets what she wants," Hock said.

Sneddon was tossed to the wall. Familiar Side Guy held him there while Stranger Side Guy searched his pockets. Snuff went around searching the apartment, making a mess as he did.

"Hand it over. Make it easy on yourself."

"I don't have it. I… I lost it."

She wasn't buying that, and neither were the guys. Hence the blow to his belly and his wail of shocked, winded pain.

In the corner of her eye, the front door swung open.

Shit.

"Lach…" she said to her brother observing the scene.

"Is this what you are now? What Ire McDade has turned you into?"

Before she could reply, her brother stormed out. Shit. She couldn't let him go, not like this.

THIRTY-SEVEN

"YOU JUST RUN out on me?" she called, going after him.

"I don't know who you are anymore, Sersh," Lachlan tossed over his shoulder from the flight of stairs beneath hers. "How many guys you got in there beating on him?"

"It wasn't like that."

"You think he killed Henry, is that it? Why? What's his motive? He's only doing himself out of a job by killing his boss."

"No one was beating on him—Lach!"

Her brother got to the first floor and blasted out the communal door before she could catch up.

When she hit the street, he was on the other side, striding up the quiet block.

After a quick check for traffic, she ran across, hurrying until she was just a few feet behind him.

"You don't have to be there." Somehow her brother must've sensed her. "Only reason Ire wants you there is to make you an accessory. He'll use it to blackmail—" He suddenly spun on the spot, so fast she almost ran straight into him. "Is that what he's doing? This whole relationship is—or is it the alibi? He's holding something over you and—"

"I asked him for the backup. This is my meet, for me. Conn is protecting me. I wanted to talk to Sneddon, but I've never met him before and I'm not much of a force on my own. I asked Conn for help. For manpower."

Lachlan's focus rose over her head. "You're out of there and they're still keeping tabs on you."

Daly was a few paces behind her. Hock and Snuff were on the other side, but aligned with—shit, Lach was on the move again.

"Stop running away from me. Can we talk about this?"

"About what? You and your team of enforcers? Your gang of investigators, breaking laws and apparently limbs—"

"So you're allowed to investigate and I'm not? That's bullshit. Damn your skills, your badge is a liability in this investigation, you said so yourself. Being a cop, your investigation could jeopardize any prosecution that—"

"And you think beating on people will secure a prosecution? Or does Ire plan on murdering the perpetrator? An eye for an eye?"

"You won't even give him a chance to—"

"He's a criminal!" He stopped by a car and the lights flashed. "The man has murdered people. I may not have proof, but I know it. He's killed, tortured, maimed—this is not a good man. And now I have to see this? See what he's turned you into?"

"He loves me."

He opened the driver's door. "You should hear yourself. Hear how ridiculous you sound when—"

"He gives me the power to do what I need to do."

"That's right, I forgot, they're your family. Not the McLeods. Not me and Dad—the way you spoke to him yesterday—"

"I'd do it again." She folded her arms. "He better stay the hell away from me."

"Or what? He'll be next in line for your enforcers? Yeah, sure, McDade hasn't changed you."

"Dad and I never got along. That's no newsflash."

"This is just how McDade likes you: isolated."

"You're doing that yourself."

"I didn't toss Dad out on his ass. I didn't humiliate and embarrass him—"

"No, but he's been doing it to us for long enough. He doesn't like a taste of his own medicine?"

"He just lost his father. You can't even give him a second to grieve. Now he has to lose his daughter too?"

"His choice."

"Lose her to an evil that's spreading through the city, darkening the streets he loves."

Oh, yeah, now it was her turn to be incredulous. "Dad doesn't love this city. He loves his status in it. And I don't want to hear a damn word about him suffering when he's in a mess of his own making. If you didn't notice, in our meetings, he made no effort to communicate, to work with anyone, he showed no concern about finding his father's killer. Ever wonder why? You and I have wrung our resources, we're fighting for justice. What's he fighting for? Nothing. He hardly bats an eye."

"Why are you so desperate to judge him?"

"Why are you so desperate to defend him?"

"He works hard to make our streets safer—"

She laughed. "Shit, Lach, you keep on singing

that tune. You have no idea. No idea. And you say I sound ridiculous defending Conn?"

"Our father is family, blood. He has integrity. Loyalty to the people of this city. He's honorable, serves a noble purpose. He's—"

"On the take." Someone would have to tell him sometime. Though from the look on Lachlan's face, the shock equated with catching a bullet. "He's not righteous and noble, he's as corrupt as every other official out there."

"No."

"I'm sorry. I know how difficult this is, but—"

"McDade put this in your head."

Pity twisted within her. "It's true."

"No, he can't—he wouldn't—"

"He has, Lach. I'm sorry."

Though she wasn't really sure why she should be apologizing.

Lach's lips stayed almost static. "I don't believe it."

"It's true," she said again.

"I don't believe it!"

On that exclamation, he got into the car, slammed the door and sped off so fast he spun his wheels.

"So…" she said to herself. "That went well."

Daly was still behind her, maybe ten feet away. "You okay?"

"Strat's," she said. "Take me to Strat's."

Her grandfather was dead. She'd banished her father. And her brother would probably never speak to her again. Strat would be the most likely to forgive her… if he let her through the door.

They walked back to the car and van together, though the other guys loitered on the sidewalk.

"Sort it?"

"Sort what?" she asked.

Hock shook his head and raised a phone to his ear. "Can't get the boss on the phone."

Unexpectedly, he handed her a card. Sneddon's security card. Not so lost after all.

Snuff typed into a phone. She slipped the card into her purse and retrieved her cell to dial her guy.

"Why do we need him on the phone?"

Daly pressed disconnect on her line before she raised the device an inch. "Not that boss."

"We have more than one boss? Who else do we answer to?"

"You? Probably no one. When the rest of us need the boss, we're calling Niall," Hock said but shook his head. "Just ringing."

"He had business today."

"Yeah," Snuff said.

In her hand, her phone rang. Conn. No surprise.

She answered, wandering away from the group. "False alarm."

"You ring once and hang up, I send an army, Macushla," he said, clearly not impressed. "Where are the guys?"

"We're fine. We're safe. Just a miscommunication."

"Macushla."

Yeah, he wanted an explanation.

"The guys were trying to get through to someone. They said the boss, I thought they meant you. They didn't."

"Niall's in the middle of something."

"We figured that."

"What's the problem?"

"I don't think there's any—"

"Why did they need Niall?"

"Oh, I don't know." She stopped to pivot. "Why

do we need Niall?" Returning to the group, their reluctance was obvious. "Niall answers to this guy. If Niall can authorize it, I guarantee my guy can." She thrust the phone to Daly. "Talk to him."

Refusing wasn't an option, so he took the phone to his ear. "Sneddon lied. Me and the guys don't like it. We want to keep track—yeah." Another pause and a deepening frown. "Aye."

He handed the phone back with an arm out to herd her toward the Bentley. Hock opened the door and in she got.

"Conn?" she asked, unsure if he was still on the line.

"Your brother showed up?"

"How do you know that?" she asked, agog. "I was right there, Daly didn't say anything about—"

"You told him the truth."

She sighed. "I started to, sort of. I'm sorry, I know we should've talked about it first. There's only so many times I can hear our father is 'on a noble, selfless mission' before I want to take glass shards to my wrists."

"Not funny."

Yeah, not really. "I've never seen him like that, just… It's Armageddon in his world. I don't know if I did the right thing. Doing that to him when he—"

"You didn't do it. Your father did."

"We were in the middle of the street," she said and groaned. "I could've been more… tactful."

"You had to hit him with it, hard. He'd never have heard it otherwise."

"I'm not sure he did."

"Give him time to process. He'll have questions." Ones she probably wouldn't be able to answer. "Want me to talk to him?"

"God, no. He thinks pretty much everything wrong with the world is your fault right now."

"I wouldn't expect anything less, I told you that."

"I know." Her head fell against the backrest. "Now I have to call Strat. Not sure I'm ready for him to ghost me. Though he's entitled. Strat always answers when—"

"He won't this time."

"He won't?"

"We have his phone."

"Great, he'll love that. Not like I've never showed up at his place without calling first."

"He's not there."

"I asked the guys to take me to—"

"You're coming here, to the club. I want you here for the rest of the day."

"Why?" she asked with creeping suspicion. "Baby?"

"Questioning me?"

Her eyes closed. "No, I would like to see Strat though. Could I try Jagg's before—"

"He's in the basement."

That opened her eyes fast. "He's—Strat? Strat's in the basement? Stag's basement? Baby—"

"Guy knows how to pick his battles. You can talk to him here. Work from here. I don't want you on the streets."

He'd have his reasons. Trust not only came easily, it comforted her too. Even without knowing all the details, she didn't doubt her guy's intentions.

"Any chance you'll get a break for dinner?"

"I'll find something to eat."

Her smile quirked. "I can bring something to you."

"Good girl."

The line disconnected and her eyes closed again. Stag. Fine with her. But Strat? Oh, this may not end well.

THIRTY-EIGHT

"THIS'LL SHAKE the jungle," Hock said as they descended Stag's stairs to the basement.

"What?"

"Women only come down here when the boss is done with them."

"Or he's passed."

"Or that."

Leaving the stairs, they entered the basement's square hallway. "I've been down here before," she said.

Daly apparently remembered. "The only woman who ever went left and came out alive."

Snuff popped open the door to the right. "This is the boring room."

She heard the TV and computer games before following them in. Pool balls ricocheted, but the dozens of voices dwindled until silence reigned.

"Subtle entrance." That was a familiar voice. "You lost, Scamp?"

Men moved aside until her friend, seated in the far corner, in a Barca, just like he'd be at home, came into view.

"No, I'm here to see you, old man." She started walking. "The rest of you, ignore me."

Though there were whispers, no one had the balls to go back to their fun. She stopped in front of her friend. If he could still be called that.

"Talking to me?"

"You've got a room full of wise guys ready to take me out."

"Strat…" She sank to her haunches. "I screwed up. I do that a lot these days. You aren't used to it by now?"

"Get up from there and sit your ass down. Don't want the guys talking."

She rose to the chair perpendicular to his. "I don't care about the guys." Who were still quiet, because they still gawped at her. "Private conversation!"

"Give her a break, guys," Daly said from the kitchen she hadn't seen until that moment.

People relaxed and she threw up her arms. Direction from a male worked where hers hadn't.

Strat laughed. "Word is, you don't mind being watched. You put on a show with the boss last night."

Her head snapped around. "Who told you that?"

Damn, he read her fast. "What's the problem? Think these guys don't know you blow the boss?"

Panic stood down. "Right, that."

"Why? What else happened last night?"

Things. Things she didn't want Strat being an accessory to.

"You don't want to talk about what happened with us yesterday?"

"What happened with us?"

She sighed. "Strat?"

"I've got a daughter, Scamp."

What was this? The moral of the story? The

lesson to be learned?

"Yes, we've met."

"You can't help yourself. Just like her. Neither of you can."

"We're tenacious."

"You're stubborn. And you set my own son on me, just like Immie would've."

"Yeah, I told him not to let you leave his sight. Nice to know he took me seriously."

"Oh, he did." He pointed across the room to Ford and Jagg at a pool table. "Might have to give him a pass or he'll be on my ass forever."

"I can't apologize for wanting you safe."

"I wanted the same thing for you."

"Conn kept us both safe."

He shifted closer, elbows on his knees. "You told him about Jane Doe?"

"Yes," she murmured. "You were right. I should've told him from the start."

"He know where she is?" She nodded. "How did the Swerve meeting go?"

"The meet?"

"Yeah, gave all the details to Niall. Did Swerve go for it?"

"I haven't... do you think he—I didn't want Conn to go."

"Ire's gonna do what he wants, Scamp."

Sure, but she should've asked what—he wouldn't have told her. Trust. She had to trust him.

"He'll tell me later."

"And our Jane Doe?"

"Conn will take care of her too."

"Take care of her...," Strat asked, "or take care of her?"

The same words with opposite meanings. Either he got her out of the city with a new identity or she was dead in the ground somewhere.

"I trust him," was all she could say.

"So when am I getting out of here, gov?"

"Soon as I know we're all safe."

"Which could be never. Me and the boys are fine. We can take care of ourselves. Stuck in here, we can't look after Immie. I don't like her being out there on her own. It's not perfect, but ask the cop to…"

And he trailed off, thus proving she was an open—large print—book where Strat was concerned.

"We're…" she started, "having some issues."

"Heard about your outburst with Daddy. The cop pissed?"

"That and I told him."

"Told him…?"

"That Daddy Dearest is on the take."

Strat sucked air through his teeth. "Shit, Scamp, you on some truth kick?"

"I freed myself from one lie when I gave Conn his alibi. And talking to him about it all, Jane Doe and… other things…"

"I don't wanna know," Strat said, smirking. "Just be careful stretching those loyalties too thin. Whatever's going on, isolating you could be exactly what they want."

"They?" she asked. "That why you're being so forgiving about yesterday? Don't want to give the assholes what they want?"

"You know me too well, kid," he said, winking above his smile. "They'll come for your boyfriend next."

She snorted. "Good luck to them."

"If they can put a wedge between you and the McDades, you lose your protection."

"It doesn't matter. I'm not a cog in the Harvest deal."

"You're a pawn."

"A piece easily sacrificed?"

"A piece that can be used to manipulate others," he said. "Going public with your relationship did one thing for them: tipped Ire's hand. Now they know you're his weak spot."

"If they drive a wedge between me and him, I wouldn't be a weak spot anymore, would I?"

"How real is what he feels for you?" Even if they weren't together, or were at odds, Conn wouldn't want anything bad to happen to her. "Stay on your truth kick. Don't give the people you trust any reason to doubt you. And doubt those you don't trust, though I think you've got that covered after kicking your dad out."

After all they'd been through. The friendship… The trust…

She slid a hand over his. "I truly am sorry about yesterday. You were right and I was wrong. I need you with me."

"I'm with you. I'm always with you. You aren't used to that by now?"

Her head tilted. "Because you love me like a daughter or because my boyfriend would pull out your fingernails with plyers if you hurt me?"

He shrugged. "Doesn't have to be one or the other." And a groan, "You protect people; it's no surprise."

"Maybe I get that from your side of the family."

"Wanna be a Stratford? That's fine by me, but I'm not paying for the wedding."

"He hasn't asked."

"Strikes me as the kind of guy who'll tell, not ask."

Bullseye. "I'm okay with that."

"You'd marry him?"

"In a heartbeat."

"Strat!" a call from the other side of the room got their attention. "Boss wants you upstairs."

Which boss?

Strat stood up, straightening his pants. "Summoned to the warden's office." She jumped up next to him. "Think this is my parole hearing?"

She looped her arm through his. "Want me to speak on your behalf?"

Daly met them on their walk to the door. "Not you, Bluebell."

"Not me? What did I do?"

"It's business. Business the boss doesn't want you near."

"But it's okay for Strat?"

Daly's thinned lips tried to hide a smile. "He thinks of you different."

"I fucking hope so," Strat muttered.

"You get to hang with us."

Strat kissed the top of her head. "I got your back, Scamp."

Not to keep her guy waiting, Strat wandered on out with Ford and Jagg not too far behind. Three for the price of one.

She sighed and took Daly's hand. "Give me the basement tour."

"Not a chance," he said. "But I'll show you how to play GTA."

"Wow," she said, deadpan. "My life is complete. There better be alcohol down here."

"Biggs!" Daly called and the bartender rose. "Lady wants a drink."

Whatever was going on upstairs, she couldn't deny her curiosity. Yes, it was her job to be inquisitive, not like the men in her life didn't know that. When she asked questions, some tended to think it showed a lack of trust. It didn't. The truth was much simpler than that, she was nosy.

The Strat meeting couldn't take all day. She'd

play for a while and then slip upstairs to work on her laptop. Conn said he wanted her there; he hadn't stated how she should spend her time.

THIRTY-NINE

NOT ONLY DID she spend the day and night at Stag, Conn asked her to stay the following day too. For most of it anyway. He'd let her out late in the afternoon with her usual security detail.

"I don't want to scare this woman," she said, smoothing her hair as Daly helped her out of the car.

"Then you should've called."

"I didn't want to stress her out."

Though Lupe's employer, and possible boyfriend, had been murdered not so long ago. If the latter was true, stress wouldn't be the only negative emotion in her life.

"Or give her time to get her story straight."

Yeah, okay, maybe there was a lick of that too. It was just as possible she'd read the situation wrong and Lupe was nothing more than a housekeeper. Only one way to be sure.

"I have to look her in the eye. This is not a conversation for the phone."

"What difference does it make?" Daly asked.

"You're safer at Stag."

Suddenly everyone was hyperaware of her safety. If there had been a specific threat made against her, she was in the dark. To her, it was just a regular Friday. Or as regular as it could be given… everything.

"Some questions can't be answered with words," she said. "They can only be answered in person."

"Such as?"

She paused in sliding her purse strap up her arm. "Such as what kind of woman she is. Their relationship wasn't public, but my grandfather had influence and money."

"You think she was in it for the dough? She won't tell you that flat out."

"Of course she won't, but I'll know if her feelings for him are genuine."

"Your magical power?"

"Because I know how I'd feel if I lost Conn," she said, hesitant to meet his eye though she did. "One woman in love recognizes another."

She hoped anyway.

This street was a massive improvement on Sneddon's. Didn't say much. Given the caliber of person Sneddon turned out to be, his block matched his personality. Would the same be true of Lupe?

Well-tended flowers in terracotta pots lined the external stairs they ascended. On the other side of the communal door, curtains were tied back with lace. Nice. Apartment 2A.

Daly intercepted her finger on its way to the buzzer. "Better to ask forgiveness than permission."

Out came the tools and he picked the lock.

"It's rude."

"And if she pulls a Sneddon and won't let you in?"

Good point. Ignoring her rejection and forcing

her way in would be worse than slipping in to get a little face time.

The door opened and a waft of lavender, not her favorite scent, hit her. A lingering memory of her grandfather's foyer faded up.

At her side, Daly tapped 2A with a single knuckle. Not a squad with her this time, just him.

"I'll wait right here."

Which they'd negotiated on the sidewalk outside Stag before she got in the car.

Someone approached the other side of the door, she heard it, then silence. Peephole maybe? Good instincts. Wait, did that mean she thought of herself as an enemy, a danger?

The door opened until a security chain stopped it.

"Sersha?"

The slightly accented voice came before a woman peeked into the gap.

Her first emotion? Guilt.

"Lupe?" she asked for verification, yet recognized the woman's features. "I'm sorry to bother you."

"I'm sorry for your loss."

"And yours. Can I come in and talk to you for a minute?"

Lupe's eyes went from left to right. "Are you alone?"

"I have a security guy with me, but he'll wait out here."

Lupe hesitated. "Okay," she said after a breath. The door closed to reopen and the short woman stepped back. "Come in."

Wall to wall carpet. Vintage furniture, fresh flowers. When she got a better look at Lupe, she set the woman's age around her forties. Huh, younger than she thought. Had Lupe imagined a future with Henry? Wasn't impossible. If she and Conn could do it, anyone could.

God, she felt awful. Sick at the thought of losing the man she loved.

"Thank you," she said, sitting when Lupe gestured. "I don't mean to intrude on you. I know you haven't been back to the house since…"

"Why would I go back? Henry, Alderman McLeod, he doesn't need a housekeeper anymore."

"You were more than just his housekeeper. You ran that house for him. Kept things together. You meant everything to him."

With a slight, quick shake of her head, Lupe's eyes widened. "No, my job was, I—Henry was always professional."

"That's a shame. I would've liked him to have someone special."

"He was a special man."

"My brother says you're a special woman." She smiled as Lupe's interest became acute. "I know all about falling for a forbidden man. For trying to resist the inevitable."

Lupe exhaled. "I was surprised, your relationship… was unexpected."

"To everyone. Conn and I included."

"How did it feel…? The world finding out?"

Telling the truth, that it had liberated her from so many chains, seemed cruel given that Lupe would never have that chance with her love.

"It's been bumpy."

"Your father, Ronald, how has he reacted?"

That question required an eye roll. "Not well."

"Did you expect him to take it well?"

"I was more worried about Lachlan. My father has never been a fan of mine; I was never going to please him. My brother? I value his opinion. Disappointing him was difficult. You and Grandpapa never thought about going public?"

Another moment of reluctance passed. "Only when I lose him does the world learn the truth."

"I'm sorry we didn't invite you to the memorial. If I'd known..."

"No." Lupe shook her head. "That was for show, I know that. Lachlan told me, something for the circus."

"We'll have something more intimate when it's over. When everyone has moved on."

Lupe took that with a pinch of salt and a single laugh. "Moving on...? Is so simple?"

Their eyes met and she saw it. The glint behind Lupe's gaze, a hollow something that had once been filled.

"Love doesn't have to be public to be real. It doesn't have to be accepted or sanctioned. What you and Henry had was real. I can't imagine what you're going through. The devastation. One thing I know for sure, if Conn was murdered tomorrow, he wouldn't want me apologizing to anyone or being ashamed of what we felt."

Startled, Lupe squirmed. "I'm not ashamed— I... I..."

She shuffled to the edge of her seat. "You can say anything to me. Anything. I'm good with secrets."

Maybe comforted, Lupe showed her first smile. "You must have to be with the McDades."

"Sometimes we need to be there for our men. To support them when no one else can. Grandpapa must've confided in you."

"Lachlan asked me about Henry's work. I told him—"

"Lachlan's a cop." She shrugged. "And he has that white hat that makes everyone feel guilty. You don't have to worry about that with me." Silence. Reluctance. "I spoke to David Sneddon."

That broke her resolve. "Henry wouldn't be told. No matter how many times I said he should stay out of it."

"Out of what?"

"Corruption was a poison. Is a poison. He felt a responsibility. As he was getting older, he said he wanted to leave the system in a better state than he found it. Crazy old man. I told him he was asking for trouble. That there was a reason no one had been successful in eliminating corruption in the city."

"You told him he would get himself killed." A meek nod was the response. "Do you think it was that? His work?"

"His mission. He got caught up, took risks."

"No one else was in the house that night. Just him and Sneddon."

"Video in the security office proves it," Lupe said. "The police told me that, but I didn't need to hear it."

"Why's that?"

"No one except Henry and I were ever allowed on the third floor. We were the only two with keys to his room."

"No forceable entry. Grandpapa opened the door to his killer. How can that be?"

Something poked at the woman by her. "All I could think was…"

"I'll take any theory. All I want to do is bring his true killer into the light."

"He'd been trying to make headway with some of his colleagues. He thought he was close with one or two."

"Allies or enemies?"

"I can't believe he'd be stupid enough to

welcome someone who'd hurt him. Someone must have turned on him."

"First, though, the killer had to get into the house without triggering security."

Distance grew in Lupe's gaze until her mind seemed miles away. "Do you believe in an afterlife? Heaven, paradise, reincarnation?"

"I try not to think about it."

"The people we love…" Lupe's eyes narrowed. "We never say what we should. We hold back until it's too late. I don't know if there's life after death. If there is, I hope Henry knows I… We were fighting. Our last words exchanged were in anger."

"Coming from a place of love, you were worried about him." And with good reason, it turned out. "Grandpapa was smart. Observant. Whatever you said at the end, he knew what was important. He knew how you really felt."

Lupe slid up the couch to take both of her hands. "He didn't always know how to express himself, not when it came to his feelings. Men can be…"

"Infuriating?"

Lupe laughed. "Yes. They can. Your grandfather was proud of you." That was—oh, uh, unexpected. "He didn't always understand you. Your father didn't either. But Henry, he wished you were closer. Interpreting him took time, but…"

"You became fluent."

"As you must be with Ire McDade."

She snickered. "I'm getting there… I think."

"Has he supported you?"

"I'd be lost without him."

"Value him. Each other, because you never know how long you have. Tell the people you love how you feel. Your grandfather would want you to know…"

"Want me to know…?"

"The chest in his office, you should look inside."

Sounded ominous. "What will I find?"

"Just look inside."

Hmm. "I'm learning so much about him. I can't believe how self-centered we all were. We took time for granted; we should've taken more of it for each other. I wish I'd known about your relationship while he was alive. You worked for him for ten years?"

"Twelve."

"And how long were you…?"

Lupe took her hands back. "Seven."

"Years?" That was… wow. "But you kept this place? Why didn't you permanently move in with him?"

"We didn't want people to know."

"Was that why you used the secret entrance?" Pushing too hard could break their rapport. Easy, slow steps. Calm, soothing. "Is there a chance anyone else had a copy of the key?"

"No," Lupe said quickly, clutching her own wrist. "I didn't sleep after… I desperately tried to think of anyone, of any chance… The key, the only key that exists, it's been in my sole possession for… years."

Didn't rule out someone making a copy. They'd have needed to know about the relationship, the key keeper, and had to steal it and return it without Lupe noticing.

The lock may have been picked. If the person was a professional, they would know not to leave evidence.

"Who knew about it? That the tunnel existed?" She hadn't. "Is it on the building plans or any public archive?"

"I don't know. I told no one. Henry and I—I would never—"

The tears in her eyes brimmed in a flash.

"I know," she said, standing up, taking Lupe's

hand to draw her to her feet into an embrace. "You did nothing wrong. You loved him and would never do anything to hurt him."

"But he's gone." Lupe's sorrow released, the visceral pain tightened her hold. "He's gone. Forever. And I don't know how I—how I'll—"

"You're not alone. Lachlan and I will be with you for anything you need."

"You can't…" Pulling away, Lupe wiped her eyes. "Your father can't know. Please."

That urgency bordered on panic, on fear. "I won't tell him. You have my word. We will look after you." She couldn't help being pissed. "You owe my father nothing and he shouldn't bully you into denying your truth."

"It will only hurt. Ronald does not need to be hurt by this."

"Do you deserve to be hurt? Do I? Why is everyone so determined to tiptoe around him? Why is he so precious?"

"He's… combustible."

"I lived with his tantrums. Lachlan could never tell me why the rest of us are supposed to yield to his petulance."

"He lost his wife—"

"We lost our mother." Defensive wasn't a good look. "I'm sorry. I lost less than Lachlan. He lost his mother. Our father disappeared into his work. And Lach was stuck with me."

"Your brother dotes on you," Lupe said.

"Always taking care of everyone."

"Family is important."

"And you are part of the family, so we take care of you too."

Didn't help her grandfather much. Family carried their own, and it had taken falling for the forbidden man to figure that out.

FORTY

FROM LUPE TO The Chronicler. Conn had released her into the world, and could pull her back anytime, so she'd make the most of current latitude. That and her conversation with Lupe was still percolating.

Steeple probably couldn't remember what she looked like. Some days she didn't either.

Lucy, like nothing had changed, leaped up the moment the elevator doors opened.

"Sersha!"

Leaving the elevator, Daly at her side, she slowed as the reception desk opened up in her view.

Flowers.

"Where did those come from?"

"Your admirer," Lucy said, touching a petal. "We haven't had any deliveries from him this week, then at lunchtime…"

"He's watching," she whispered.

"Huh?" Daly asked.

"Is there a card?" she asked Lucy.

"Oh, uh, yes…" Lucy dug around in the stems

and produced a tiny envelope. "Here it is."

Filled with dread, she took the card. This could be bad, and she didn't want to face it, but there was no turning her back on it either. She'd once neglected to tell Conn about a threat to his men; Daly bore the brunt of that mistake.

It couldn't happen again. Wouldn't.

She slipped the card from its envelope. Two words: "Bang, bang." A threat? The concerning thing was the picture in the corner. A shamrock. Must be leftover stock from March.

What did the shamrock mean? Was he acknowledging that she was one of the Irish or threatening her Irishman?

She moistened her lips and opened a hand in front of Daly, attention still trained on the flowers.

"Call your boss and give me your phone."

"My boss?" He retrieved his phone from an inside pocket. "Why can't you call him?"

"I don't have your boss's number." She snatched Daly's phone as soon as he unlocked it. "Wait here."

Striding into the empty interview room by the desk, she closed the door and dialed the contact.

It rang half a dozen times before the line connected.

"Aye?"

Good start, the right guy.

"It's Bluebell. If you're with Conn, can you get out of his earshot?"

A dozen seconds passed that seemed to drag for hours.

"Aye?"

Apparently, that word meant everything. Maybe Gaelic was his only fluent language.

"Evander sent flowers. Vex." Which, yeah, he'd know. "I'm at The Chronicler and... I'll tell Conn later, this is not me circumventing him, but if he hears—I need to be physically with him or bad things will happen. More bad things. Evander's sending a message."

"Aye."

"He's watching. His people. There haven't been flowers for days, then the day I show up at work… He's alive, which is good. This feels different. Don't ask me how I know, but this feels like a message for Conn, not for me."

"Aye."

So much for forging a friendship with her guy's best friend.

"Okay, forget it. I thought I could trust you to have his back. Obviously not."

She hung up, biting her tongue in the face of more frustration.

As she turned, the window by the door revealed Tulip over by Steeple's office, talking to another of their colleagues.

Personal, professional, where were the lines these days?

Her own phone rang.

"Whisper?" she asked when the line connected.

"High Class! So, Sugar, my guy got back to me. Nothing out of line on the surface, but he's going to keep digging. The logs don't show obvious signs of tampering. Means either there isn't any—"

"Or the tamperer was good."

"A professional. Would have to be. He's not giving it up; just his provisional assessment."

"Thanks. I appreciate it." She blew out a breath. "Hey, I might have a thing sometime—"

"What kind of thing?"

"Someone's asking questions, an ally, but I'm wary. If I have to deal with—"

"I'm there. Girls' night?"

"Yeah," she murmured, fixated on the animated Tulip. "Just between us for now."

"Roger that. I'll call if I get anything else."

"Thanks."

Rejoining at reception, Daly fell into step behind her when she started her next mission. The idea was to see Steeple, but avoiding Tulip would be impossible.

And, yes, the second Tulip saw her, she became a wolf on the hunt.

"Hang back," she murmured to Daly from the corner of her mouth.

He stopped while she carried on to meet a guarded, yet confident, Tulip.

"Sersha, hi. How are you doing?"

Sympathy, both sincere and patronizing.

"How are you?"

"Oh, she avoids the question. How is your boyfriend? Ready to meet?"

"You better hope not."

Curiosity glinted in Tulip's eye. "He's known for his volatility."

"You don't want to aim for Conn. The price on Nicki's head, that's your focus. Forget Ire."

Tulip closed in. "You have something for me?"

"Maybe I can get you a meet."

"Say when and where."

"Stay by your phone."

She wouldn't call, not that day and probably not the next. Her experience as an investigator dictated it was better to be led on by a source with a maybe than ghosted by one that gave nothing. The former at least kept the reporter playing nice. Tulip wouldn't step out of bounds while there was a chance she'd get the scoop. She may test the boundaries, but they could handle that.

Doing Steeple the courtesy of knocking on his door, she was already going inside when he granted her entry.

"How you doing?" Steeple's sympathy swerved the condescension. "The memorial service caused a stir."

"Oh, yeah? I didn't hear about that."

Her smile said otherwise.

He laughed. "You've got to be getting used to that. Drawing attention."

She sank into a seat opposite him at the desk. "It's easier to deal with as half of a pair."

"You just here to check in? You know you can have all the time off you need."

"I'm going to write it up."

"It?" he asked.

"It's the best solution for all of us. I'll write it, so I can control the flow of information and respect. The Chronicler gets something to print so we can't be accused of a coverup. And you can assure the higher-ups breathing down your neck that you have your mob-affiliated employee under control."

"I have been getting calls."

"From?"

"Everyone I ever met. People have questions. And they don't all mean well."

"I read the obit," she said, "the whole feature. Thank you."

"Your grandfather was popular."

"In some circles. In times of intrigue, the volume of the villagers rises. Next week something else will take over the gossip mills."

"That mean we'll get your piece before then?"

"I can give you something. Maybe we make a continuing feature for a few weeks." Although it was clear in her head, Steeple was a step behind. "My grandfather was murdered. Investigating the crime has taken us down a rabbit hole. This will not be a quick solve."

"Murdered at home," he said, serious. "Was it personal or professional?"

She stood up to head for the door. "I'll work on it today."

"Keep in touch."

Pausing, holding the handle, she asked, "If you hear anything…"

"You'll be the first to know."

For some reason, what he'd said just sank in. "Who's been calling?" Her interest piqued. "You said people had been calling. Anyone I'd know?"

"A bunch of people."

"You said they didn't all mean well."

He shrugged. "It's just a rumor. Like you said, the gossip mill."

"Steeple," she said, arching a brow.

He surrendered. "We got a tip."

"About the murder?"

"About you… You and Ire."

"A tip?" she asked. "We're together. What else is there to know?"

"I wasn't gonna mention it. I thought about calling, but—"

"Steeple."

"Is it possible there's… a flash drive?" A flash— ah. Oh, God. "Word is it's something juicy. I don't know what, but—it's nothing. I'm sure it's nothing."

"Who?" she asked.

"Who?"

"Who tipped you?"

"Anonymous caller. Said we should ask around because it's out there."

"Okay," she muttered.

"Mean anything to you?"

Sucking in a breath, she faux smiled. "Course not. Let me know if there's anyone with an unusual interest."

"No one specific has raised a red flag. I can forward the call logs… I don't always take them."

Sure, the man had a department to run.

"That would be great. Thank you, Steeple. Your understanding means a lot."

Some people in her life were a support. Others had questionable motives. Where did the truth lie?

FORTY-ONE

THEY PULLED UP outside Stag. When she got out, Daly nodded over the car at something, someone. Lachlan. On the other side of the street, getting out of a vehicle, her brother headed their way. Had he been waiting for her? For how long?

"Can we talk?" he called.

When he reached her, she side nodded then followed her head in a turn to go into the club.

"We can go back to your place," Lachlan said as they traversed the tunnel.

"This *is* my place."

"You giving up the apartment for good?"

"I'm surprised you haven't moved into the bedroom already."

"Thought about it, but considering what you've done there…"

"Change the sheets, flip the mattress, buy a new one," she said, pointing at a stool while going behind the bar. "What do you want to drink? Coffee? Liquor?"

"The club's not open."

"I wasn't planning to charge you, but I can get a bottle from upstairs, if that would make you feel better."

"Why don't we go up there? Scared Ire will see us together? Is he home?"

"If you mean here…" She chose whiskey. "I have no idea." Two fingers each. "Did you come to talk to me or to him?"

"Trying to judge how much he trusts you."

"He trusts me."

"That why we're down here instead of in his office?"

She pushed his drink to him. "Ah, that's why you came? To snoop? Want me to show you his underwear drawer? There is a man behind the myth. He has a toothbrush too."

"I came to talk about Dad."

"Let me guess?" She swallowed a mouthful of warming liquor. "I'm wrong. Making things up. Listening to bad people who mean me harm?"

"No, actually…" He seemed unnervingly calm. "I came to hear you out."

Huh, well, now she had to regroup. "Have you talked to him? Dad?"

"You mean have I leveled your accusation at him? No. Because the first thing he'll ask is who laid the charge at his door."

"Listen, I'm not interested in making a case. You believe me or you don't. I won't try to persuade you either way. Your relationship with Dad is your relationship. I have this information; I shared this information. Done."

"Why? Why tell me?"

"Because you're my brother, I love you, and I don't want you to be blindsided when this comes out. Which it will eventually." Maybe another of them would die first. "And I was angry with you when I said it. I shouldn't have blurted it out in the street like that. You don't know how difficult it is to listen to how incredible Dad is when some part of me suspects he was aware of the attack before it happened."

"The attack? What—" The surrounding air crackled. "You don't mean…" His head shook shallow and slow. "No, shit, Ser, is this what Ire's putting in your head?"

"This is the problem with honesty, right here. You're so determined to hate him that you close off to everything I have to say. This is not coming from Conn, this is me." Folding her arms, she rested them on the bar to lean closer. "The day you got me into Records, Dad came to me asking for information."

"What information?"

"He wanted to know who I'd seen with the McDades. Who I'd seen with Conn."

"While you were investigating your McDade story?"

"Right." The precise truth didn't make any difference to the story, why confuse things? "I wouldn't tell him because I have professional integrity and would lose all my credibility to—it's not a revelation, I never talk about my work."

"How does that tie Dad to the attack?"

The gravity of what she had to say would incriminate more than their father. "It was what they wanted. The men who attacked me. They asked the same questions. They wanted the same information. The information Dad failed to get from me." His lips thinned, but she could see his mind working. "Lach—"

"All this time, you knew what they wanted, who they were." And judging by his tone, he deemed that a betrayal. "Why didn't you tell me?"

Looking at him now, she couldn't remember. "What could you have done?"

"If you'd told me who wanted the information, it would help us track the assailants down."

"At that point, the only person I knew for sure who wanted that information was Dad."

"When did that change? Who do you think is paying him off?"

"Silvio Manzani." An astounded scoff. "Look, this is pointless. You believe it or you don't."

"What proof do you have? Bank transactions? Surveillance pictures? An incriminating recording?"

"I'm not a cop. My evidentiary threshold is lower than yours. I haven't printed anything in my paper, this is not a case. This is me, just me. I believe it's true."

"Because Ire McDade told you. He offer Dad a bribe?"

"Why would he?"

"Because he's a businessman, right." Frustration tightened his jaw. "You can't ask me to take this on faith."

"Okay, don't. Just don't say I didn't warn you. If this all comes out and I'm right—"

"I'll get an 'I told you so,' is that it?"

"I take no pride in this, Lach. And I'm not interested in lording it over you. Lying to you hurts us both. Please, if you don't believe me, that's fine, just don't forget I told you. Stay on alert. If he knew about the attack on me, I can't trust him to have my back. That means I don't trust him to have yours either."

"I can take care of myself."

She sensed he'd probably want to end that with some comment about trusting their father not to hurt him. If only she had that confidence.

Sweeping her hand over the bar, she caught his. "All my life, you've looked out for me. I know your love for me is real and genuine. You'll always be my brother, I love you. Honesty is all I can give you."

"It's a lot to take in."

"It is. You always wanted his approval. Believed him to be some larger-than-life hero. I never had a chance at getting his acceptance." Which made it easier for her to come to terms with the truth. So much mess, such a small family. "My instinct is to apologize."

"For not telling me the truth about your attackers?"

"That was a dark period. It screwed my head up. I shrugged it off, even when Conn called me on it."

The angle of his chin shifted. "You talked to him?"

"I talk to him every day."

"Talk to him about important things. You didn't tell the rest of us the truth, but he knew, didn't he? You confide in him?"

"Yes. Which you'll probably say is a mistake."

"Does he help?"

"Help?"

"From my perspective, the guy's a violent mobster."

"Maybe change that perspective, Lach. Forget about whatever he does or doesn't do for a living."

"And instead?"

"Think of him as the man your little sister loves. The man she's planning a future with. The one who takes care of me. There's nothing he wouldn't do for me, Lach. He loves me. Why can't you trust my judgment?"

"I'm here," he said, gesturing around with his free hand. "That's progress."

Baby steps. If each man did their part, maybe they'd end in middle ground.

A bunch of McDade guys piled in, bringing noise with them.

"Club'll be opening soon," she said. "You get your wish, want to come upstairs? There's no food here, but we can order in. You'd be amazed how fast they deliver."

"Wonder why that is."

When Biggs split from the entering gang, she crept around the bar. As they approached each other, Biggs squeezed the back of her neck.

"Lookin' for a job, Bluebell?"

"I'm not allowed to mix with the masses."

"I remember. Doesn't matter anyway, you're needed upstairs."

"Have I been bad?"

"Only if the boss is lucky."

"Biggs, this is my brother Lachlan."

"I know."

"And I know you know, but this is formal introductions."

Their eyes met and though his lower lip curled around his teeth, Biggs eventually clucked his tongue and offered a hand.

"Biggs," he introduced himself.

She held her breath and almost whooped when after a quick glance Lachlan put his hand in Biggs' to shake.

A knock from above brought everyone around.

Up there in the office window, Conn zeroed in on her, beckoning twice with two straight fingers.

"He looks pissed," Lachlan said.

She and her brother crossed the club together.

"He's in work mode. He takes work seriously."

"Will you get shit for letting me in here?"

"He's my partner, not my jailor. Want to come upstairs and say hello?"

When they stopped at the bottom of the office stairway, she got his answer.

"Another time. I have things to do." He kissed her head. "Take care of yourself. Call if you need me."

Her brother departed, hopefully lighter than he'd arrived.

FORTY-TWO

WITH A BRAIN SWITCH from sister to girlfriend, up the office stairs she went. If Conn needed her for anything urgent, he'd have called. Maybe he just missed her. Not that he'd admit that out loud if they weren't alone.

And they weren't. Well, she was alone with one guy in the office, not her guy, his best friend.

"You have a temper," Niall said to her.

Offended, her jaw loosened. "I was worried about my man. Sorry for giving a shit. If I'd called and told him direct, he could've blown the wheels off this thing without anyone there to dial him back. I thought your job involved protecting him, helping him make choices. I didn't know I wasn't allowed to talk to you."

Which was weird because Conn let her in on everything else. Nothing was off-limits, until Niall got involved.

He came a step closer, his volume low. "When I don't say much on the phone, there's a reason. Listening ears. People we don't trust. I'm in an unsecure environment or enemy territory."

That sucked out some of her gusto. "Oh."

"Aye. We need to be allies. My job is to protect him. The family. You." She blinked in surprise. "Secrets and discretion."

"What secrets?"

"You practice hanging on to your reins, girlie. I'll deal with the grown up stuff."

This guy lived to irritate her. It wasn't malice though. Weirdly, it almost felt like… was he teasing her? She had a brother and knew exactly what needling someone sounded like. That or he was testing her. Would she run to "daddy" and put a wedge between the men? Sorry, Niall, not her style. The more people watching her guy's ass, the higher the chance it would come home to her.

"What's going on?"

Connel had passed through the curtain without her hearing a thing.

"Evander sent me flowers at The Chronicler with a message," she said. "I think it was for you, not for me."

"What message?"

She took the card from her pocket and handed it over when he sauntered up. After he read it, he handed it straight to Niall.

"Maybe it's nothing, but I thought that before and—"

"Find out where he is," Conn said to Niall. "Time to finish it."

She snagged his hand before he could walk away. "I need to talk to you about something else. A few somethings else actually."

"Can it wait?"

"No," she said fast. Whether it could or not, she needed time to defuse some of his increasing anger toward the aggravating man attempting to provoke him.

"I have to talk to you now. Alone."

The word was enough to prompt Conn to nod Niall out of the room.

"What's wrong?"

"Lupe, the housekeeper, is the woman, she's the one."

"Your grandfather's side piece?"

"No," she said, leading him to the couch. "I think she was his whole piece. She speaks of him with love, she's genuinely heartbroken, and she's pissed he didn't listen to her."

They sat and she slid in close, laying her arm across his torso as she rested her head on him.

"Some women don't understand men know better."

And if she was in the mood to pick a fight, he'd cued it up. She wasn't.

"She says there's no chance anyone got the key for the tunnel, and she doesn't strike me as a liar. Or a woman who'd endanger the man she loved. They talked freely, I guess that's what you get after seven years. They never went public with their relationship, with how they felt about each other." Something he knew, but something that plagued her thoughts. "Seven years, Mo Grá."

"We're public," he said, reading her mind.

"That could've been us. When I think what could—"

"Macushla."

"I know. Sorry. Lachlan knew about them; I don't know how long. She's adamant that my father shouldn't ever learn of their relationship. Why is everyone so worried about his opinion?"

"He's head of your family now."

Sickening thought. "He can't damage or punish her. She has her own apartment. I suppose she'll need a job, but surely he can't block her chance with employers."

"He can." Yeah, maybe she'd been kidding herself. Much as she didn't like it, her father had influence. "Put her on payroll."

Taken aback, she tipped up her chin. "Here?" Actually… "You know, that's not a bad idea."

"She works here and progresses to other sites when we're sure we can trust her."

Because one conversation didn't warrant full access. Absolutely not. And that faith was on her shoulders. Better that others got to know Lupe and concurred than her judgment of character alone should be the deciding factor.

"Thank you."

"What did your brother want?"

"To talk," she said. "I told him Dad might have known about the attack beforehand and that I think he's in league with Silvio Manzani."

"He'll confront your father."

"Maybe. He's still absorbing," she said. "I just hope he keeps his focus. His job is dangerous. I couldn't bear something happening to him now because of something I said."

"Your father did this."

As he frequently told her. "I know you're right. Just feels like my family is coming apart at the seams."

"This is your family, Macushla." And with him driving, she had no concerns about them staying on track. "I have something for you," he said, kissing her head then getting up.

"Like a present?"

"A gift."

Wasn't that the same thing?

As he went to the desk, she continued. "I told Steeple I'd write about my grandfather. Keeps the media off our backs if we're doing something exclusive for The Chronicler. Although we don't know much yet, I'll start with a piece about his life. A retrospective type thing—" She stopped when he held up a flash drive. "Is that…?"

He tossed it across the room to her. "The complete police investigation up to now." Okay, not the flash drive she expected. "Should help with your piece."

"Yes." Turning in her hand, she showed him a smile. "I thought it was something else." He crooked a brow as he leaned on the front of his desk and folded his arms. "Apparently, we're out there."

"We?"

"Our sex tape."

"How did that happen?"

"I don't know. It could just be a rumor. Steeple said someone called to tip him off."

"Who?"

"Anonymous. Of course."

"Want me to track it down?"

She sighed. "We have so many more important things to worry about, Conn. It's not like the city don't know we have sex." One side of his lips sloped up. "I know, we've come a long way."

Sauntering over, he stopped in front of her. "Aye."

She stood up. "We don't know how long we have with the people we love." The atmosphere closed in as she grew more somber. "Lupe said it and she's right. You know I love you. Do you know how devastated I'd be to lose you? Don't answer that." Conn would be pragmatic about it, she wanted to talk and him to listen. "I love you and I need you to know that even if we're in a fight or pissed off with each other, I still love you. Whatever we say, in anger or grief, it's nothing to how devoted I am to you." She blinked and met his serious eye. "And if something happens to me, if I leave you without getting a chance to say goodbye, know my last thought was of you and how much I'm going to miss what we'll never have. But I'll be so grateful, I am so grateful, for every second we've spent together. Promise me you'll remember that."

"You won't leave this life before me."

"We don't know that. We can never know that. Baby—"

"I won't let it happen." Cupping her face, he pushed it back and stooped lower. "You hear me? I won't let it happen."

Her guy had power and influence in a lot of areas, especially in the city. This, life and death, he didn't have a say over that. Not a complete say anyway.

That he wouldn't acknowledge it, that he was so adamant, was touching in itself. He just couldn't imagine a world without her in it.

"Is Strat still here?"

He brushed her hair from her face and ran his thumb across her chin. "He's with the guys."

"Here or…?"

"Somewhere else."

Okay, not informative. Her questions about what her friend did with her flash drive would have to wait.

Slipping her hands under his jacket, she stroked his hard body beneath his shirt. "Whisper had a guy checking out the logs, you know, the digitized whatever."

"Mm?"

"Nothing suspect yet. He's not done though; he'll keep digging."

"Feel like we're getting somewhere?"

"He was my grandfather and I miss him. But I don't think I really got it, the gravity of… When my mom died, I was too small to remember much. The grief was more curious than visceral. What did I miss out on? I had no idea."

"Seeing Lupe changed that."

"Exactly," she said, searching his eyes. "They were part of each other's lives every day. Some part of me can convince myself Henry is still out there because I didn't see him all the time. But Lupe, she's lost her world and I feel that. Wasn't exactly the same, but when we ended us and I was without you…"

"It'll never happen again."

Closing her eyes, she sank her arms around him to hold herself tight against him. Life without him just didn't bear thinking about.

The office door opened. She heard it and tried to pull away, but Conn held her in place.

"We've gotta go over those numbers." Niall's voice. "When Bluebell's—"

"She's working in here today."

Leaning back, their gazes met. "I am?"

"Be grateful."

Oh, she would be. For every second they spent together and to him in the night. He listened. Understood. Took on board her concerns and her happiness. Being near him, being with him, there was no better reality.

FORTY-THREE

HER PIECE WAS coming together. The police investigation made for interesting reading. Not that she'd include anything from it in her introductory article. It had to be real, to contain some humanity, but she wouldn't give the world her vulnerability.

Nope, that belonged to the man at the desk.

Work went on around her. Her perch on the chesterfield kept her immediately out of view of anyone who came in. They'd notice her when deeper inside, but Conn never offered an explanation. Why should he? Her being there, around him, with him, was the most natural thing in the world.

Sure, it might take his people, friend and foe, time to get used to her. That was their problem. She had no intention of going anywhere. And although Conn didn't dilute or censor anything those in the room said during their meetings, she wasn't paying much attention. His work was his business, and she trusted him to take care of it.

With her laptop on her knees, she edited the

introduction and read through a few more lines. The office door opened, but she didn't look up. Just someone else who—

Swerve.

Shit. Unexpected.

Niall and the other guys present stiffened with wariness, on alert, ready for anything.

Their guest put something heavy in the middle of Conn's desk, right in front of him. Keeping her head down like she was working, her eyes tracked him backing off a step.

"To replace the one you lost," Swerve said.

"Lost?" Conn asked.

What was it? Oh, with a slight lean, she saw it. Whiskey. McDade whiskey.

"Yeah, the arson report wasn't specific, but we hunted it down. The glass of the incendiary matches the McDades' signature brand of whiskey. Subtle."

Her lips pulled back in a grimace. Thank God no one was looking at her.

"The Carlyle fire? I don't give a fuck about your hotel," Connel said. "That bullshit's a Manzani mess."

"This is your warning. First and final. You come for us, Irish, we come for you."

Swerve didn't wait for an answer and strode on out.

"What the fuck is that?" Niall asked his boss.

"They're chasing their tail," Connel said. "If they're gonna cause trouble... find out who set that fire and why. Maybe their cause matches ours."

"Or they're setting us up."

"Then you know what to do."

"Uh... excuse me..." She raised a flat hand and the half dozen guys turned to her. "It might've been me."

"What?"

"The fire at the Carlyle..." She slipped her laptop

onto the couch at her side. "I started it. The Carlyle fire was me."

Everyone's attention swung around to Connel whose cool gaze stayed locked on her.

"Okay." Niall broke the silence. "So it was us."

"If there's going to be payback—"

"Up security at every site," Conn said, "guys go out in doubles or groups. Take inventory. Everything gets restocked. If they want a war, we'll give them a war."

"Heard," Niall said.

"Now get outta here. All of you."

After they were alone, he waited just a breath. "Why?"

"It was an accident. A sort of accident." She stood up. "All I meant to do was create a distraction. It's not my fault their electrics were shot or that they used dodgy building materials."

"The Carlyle is the Manzanis primary site for their girls." Their working women, trapped under the Manzani boot. "Why did you need a distraction?"

She went around the desk to prop herself against it at his side.

"It wasn't for me, it was for Imogen, Strat's daughter." She filled her lungs. "It's a long story. Basically, investigation for an article led her to the Carlyle. The Manzanis, under Silvio's purview, it turned out, were making snuff movies there. Imogen wanted in."

"For the snuff movies?"

"No, because the stars of those movies, the ones being killed, weren't hookers." Not that it made a huge difference. "Women were going missing; she was looking for the abducted women—"

"That's where you found Jane Doe."

"Yes."

"She was their next star."

"I couldn't leave her there. The building was on fire and she was padlocked inside it. We had to bring her out."

"We? Imogen was with you?"

"Yes, though no one except Strat knows that. I told Imogen to deny all knowledge, that if anyone asked, she met me at the hospital after it."

"Why? That puts all responsibility on your shoulders."

"I couldn't let anything happen to Imogen."

"You protected her."

"I know more about the Manzanis than she does. And I have relationships there. At least if anyone came after me, I had the Evander card to play. They'd have killed Imogen without hesitation."

"It was her story."

"No one asked me to take the heat," she said. "It was my decision."

"You should've come here."

"If I'd come here, I wouldn't have wanted to leave."

"I'd have—"

"I didn't want to ignite war between the families." She exhaled. "Best laid plans… Looks like it's ended up that way anyway."

"I'll handle it."

"You always say that," she said, sliding along the desk, guided by his hand on her hip. "I make these messes and then you—"

"This is your kingdom."

"What will happen?"

"Whatever needs to happen."

"Mo Grá, I live to support you."

And these messes wrought more complications.

He reared up between her legs, planting his hands on the desk behind her hips. "This is my job."

So it was her job to support him and his to clean up after her?

"Have I got time to be grateful now?"

He shirked his jacket and slid both hands up her thighs, pushing her skirt to her hips.

"You were a naughty girl."

Connel McDade, the only man in the world who could turn arson into an aphrodisiac.

"Our enemies know we're powerful," she said, heart hammering. "They should fear us."

His mouth drifted closer. "All of us."

"Are you mad?"

"Proud."

Somehow, she'd known that. "Mo Grá…"

Their lips met, lingered for a second, then with one powerful plunge, his tongue forced its way deep. Yes. Being with him, lounging in their lust, life was surreal. How could she be so in love? So dependent and yet so strong in his protective shadow.

The door burst open and she grabbed his shirt in both hands, keeping him against her, away from any nearby weapons.

Niall and Whisper occupied the space at the top of the stairway, crowding each other, trying to get in first.

"Score's has gone up."

"The club?" Conn asked, loosening her hands. "In Miami?"

"It's ablaze!"

Her guy, cool and unruffled, simply asked, "What does he want to do?"

"Beeks is frantic."

"Score says let it burn," Raze said as he sauntered in, no crowding for him.

People moved away from him like shoals of fish in the unseen current. No one would dare get in his way, probably even his wife. No, second thoughts, Whisper would crowd anyone.

"Yeah, 'cause he'll never go back there now."

"A phoenix rises from the ashes," she muttered.

"He sure does," Raze said, fixed on his cousin. "Helluva coincidence, don't you think?"

Was that a reference to the Carlyle? He hadn't been in on the conversation they'd just shared.

"Heavy handed of Silvio," Whisper said, like she was trying to figure it out too. "Why strike there and not here? If we're burning each other's shit, seems practical to start local."

"No," Conn said under his breath. "This isn't Manzani work." His short exhale signaled he was pissed. "Fuck!" Okay, maybe pissed was an understatement. He tensed to action, nodding at his lieutenant. "I want Madison Byrne here within twenty-four hours. No excuses. If I have to send someone, I'll mail her back to her father in pieces, starting with the pretty ones." Next was Whisper. "You're going to the prison. I want you in front of Biz."

Whisper laughed, folding her arms and cocking a hip. "Damn, you are smart."

"Score's on his way north."

"No," Conn snapped at Raze. "Tell him to head west. Clancy's got a few miles in him yet."

"Nero wants it to burn," Whisper said, brimming with impressed excitement. "If he can't have it, no one can."

Razer laid an arm over his wife's shoulders. "Next stop Burl?"

"No," Connel said. "He's irrelevant."

Whisper whooped with her next laugh. "Daddy won't like that at all. Not even a courtesy call? I love it." Whisper pushed her shoulder into her husband's body. "Did it just get hot in here?"

"To get back in," Conn said, ignoring the

Doherty, "Burl has to prove he controls Biz."

Everything was connected somehow. Except, she couldn't figure out…

"Silvio sent his men to Miami. Doesn't it follow that he'd be in on this? Responsible for this?"

"Whisper's gonna find out."

"From the horse's mouth."

"Will he accept a visitation request?"

"Not many people visit him," Whisper said.

"He wants in on the action, to swing at us. Damn right, he'll accept the request."

Her guy spoke again, this time to his lieutenant in their native language.

Whisper pouted. "You know that's rude." Conn and Niall carried on. "Doesn't it piss you off, High Class?"

"No, it turns me on."

Whisper's shoulders rose and dropped in an exaggerated sigh. "We don't know what's good for us. Damn our McDades."

"We should've seen this coming," Conn said to his cousin like no one else was in the room. "All the bullshit is connected."

"You think Biz is…"

"Trying to take power with one risky swing."

"In cahoots with Silvio Manzani? He can't trust him."

"We can't trust anyone," Conn said. "There's been too many distractions. We forge the path, we don't follow others."

"You sure about this?" Raze asked.

"They've come for your brother first; the rest of us will be next. You want Biz to represent your name? The McDade reputation?"

"No. Fuck him."

"By the time we're through, he'll beg to

surrender his name."

The McDades weren't quitters. Her guy had a plan, at least the beginnings of one. Parker "Biz" McDade wouldn't know what hit him.

FORTY-FOUR

"YOUR OFFICE BIG enough?" Strat asked, approaching.

In the central VIP booth of the club, in the middle of the day, she'd spread herself out across the circular table.

"It's quieter down here."

His attention tracked around to the office windows above. "A lot of rumors flying around."

"Oh, yeah?"

Strat slid in at the far end of the booth. "What's coming next? How's he doing?"

"Emotionally or tactically?" she asked, and he shrugged, laying both arms along the top of the seat. "I don't know. He didn't come to bed last night."

"Your bed or anyone's bed?" Her head fell to the side and he laughed. "Okay, Scamp, no yanking your chain, I got it."

"That's the kind of question I'd expect from Lachlan."

"Ire needs an outlet." Her friend grew serious. "A lot of pressure on him. The mood trickles down from the top. Someone needs to be on top of that."

On top of Conn? Is that what Strat meant? If the words were judgment, she didn't appreciate them.

"It's not like the guys aren't used to him having a temper. Except this time it's…"

Gazing toward the office, all she wanted to do was take the weight of responsibility from his shoulders.

"It's…?"

She exhaled. "He's angry at himself."

"How do you know?"

"Because he's working flat out. Barking orders. I don't know, it's in his voice, his stance, it's… he's his own harshest critic."

"Aren't we all? Though, for the rest of us, getting it wrong doesn't mean—"

His almost distracted tone halted when clarity hit his expression. Had he forgotten who he was talking to?

"So that's what the guys are talking about? It's treason to speculate about the demise of the king."

"No one wants that, believe me. Biz? Who the fuck wants to work under that fuckturd? But you can't deny the asshole's fucking serious if he's working with the Manzanis and the Byrnes. Says something when a guy's only way out is to work with his enemy to screw his own people. It's like the fucking apocalypse. You hear Madison Byrne's on her way into town?" She'd known that was coming. "He talk to you about her?"

"He doesn't need to talk to me about her. I'm not his keeper and the family takes priority over everything else, everyone else."

"Protect the top, that's good," Strat said. "I almost believed you."

Her shoulders dropped and she slid closer as he did the same from his end. "I hate it. Of course I hate it. The man I love is… I can't ask him not to, we're talking lives here. The Byrnes want to kill Nicole McDade. Conn has to handle it."

The buck went all the way to the top, and she had to accept… She didn't want the visual and couldn't think about it.

"Biz wants her dead. His wife, his choice," her friend said. "McDades don't work for him anymore and Score would never do it. Harsh of Biz, seeing as she's standing by the fucker. Any other woman would get a divorce and split with the cash."

"Nicki isn't capable of looking after herself."

"Yeah."

"And women don't leave McDades. Not those McDades anyway."

"Not those McDades? That mean you can leave Ire?"

"I'd never want to." Life with Conn was the only future she could see. Her friend accepted that, better than her brother. "It makes me sick that to save Nicki's life, he'll have to…"

Her stomach clenched, desperate to rid itself of the nausea.

"Nicole is only family on paper. Why does Ire care if she's dead?"

"I'll tell you who doesn't care. Whisper," she said. "I think she'd do it for free, if it didn't mean giving the Byrnes a win."

"Does Nicki think there's a chance Biz will get out and they can be together again?"

"He wouldn't have her."

"Putting a price on her head is a damn clear message. What the fuck does he have to be pissed about? She never testified. Did she help the feds or something?"

Her eyes flicked away, lips parted, her teeth still together beneath. This was Strat. She trusted him with her life.

"On the QT," she said, leaning in. "Like most

classified QT, our throats will be slit in our sleep for sharing this kind of QT…" His head went back in a quick nod of understanding. "She was fucking Burl." The prolonged blink from her friend was more than surprise. "Trying to get pregnant, though Burl had her on birth control she didn't know about."

"Fuck." Sinking back, he ran a hand through his hair. "It's a Greek tragedy."

"Irish, but yes. It's fucked up. Not all crimes were broadcast at the trial."

"That's a fucking mess any guy would want to keep a lid on. No wonder he wants her dead; I'm surprised he hasn't put conditions on collecting."

"Conditions?"

"Like making it hurt."

Torture. Pain. Biz wouldn't think twice about what his wife endured. He'd only see the humiliation.

"Haven't heard anything about Burl being punished for it."

"No, 'cause he wouldn't," Strat said. "It's fucked up, but even Biz wouldn't…" Wouldn't he? Brother had turned on brother before, would son turn on father? "He might. The problem is Burl's better at it."

"It? The game?"

"And doing what needs to be done." Strat splayed his fingers on the table. "If Burl heard Biz put a price on his head, he'd have his son slaughtered before sundown."

"If he has the reach."

"Heard Raze hit the road. Running for his life?"

Not a chance with that guy. He was a weapon all on his own.

"Backing up Whisper," she said. "She's going to the prison."

"For father or son?"

"Son," she said. "Conn and Raze met about it

late last night. I went in to say goodnight and they clammed up."

"You wanted to hear the details?"

"He would've told me if we'd been alone." Or she'd asked. "With Whisper not there either it…"

"Was guy time. They're McDades. Blood. Score should be pulling his weight. Kinda got everyone into this mess."

"Biz started it," she said, oddly defensive. "What was he trying to accomplish setting Score up for murder?"

"Exactly what he wants to achieve now. Biz wants to be head of the family, even from inside prison walls. Not impossible, it's been done before. Anyone mention Clancy?"

Burl's brother. The cousins' uncle.

"Conn sent Score that way. Clancy has a network, but the guy's not… Losing his daughter took his appetite for power." From the way Conn told it anyway. "Doesn't mean he'd turn his back on his family."

"Smart move. Score's traveling with a wife, a kid, and his brother's best friend. And a lawyer. He can't keep them all safe alone. Though it's not like the McDades are safe on the west coast."

"Shit, Strat…" Her elbow landed on the table at the same time she scooped a hand around her forehead. "This is coming at him from all angles. I'm overwhelmed and I don't have to do a damn thing."

"Yes, you do." Trust her friend to be so stoic in his support. "You have to keep him sane. No one else is gonna look after the guy. No one else would dare try right now with the mood he's in. From what I hear, he's earning his name and a helluva lot more."

"He has Niall. This is the first time we've—there's always trouble, but this is huge and… I don't want to overstep my bounds."

"Oh," he said, pushing down the seat slightly. "Then, man, did I get your relationship wrong. Go upstairs and pack a bag—better actually, do you have stuff at the loft?"

"Stuff?"

"Clothes, passport, money, enough to get you through a few days. If Whisper and Raze aren't there, we can be in and out of the loft without anyone knowing. Gives us a head start."

"Why would I need—" Horror blocked her throat for a few seconds. "You want me to run?"

"Fuck, yeah," he said without shame. "Your family aren't laying out the red carpet for you these days. If this Ire guy's a lay, why the fuck should you deal with the bullshit in his life? You're not in it for the long haul—"

"I didn't say that."

"I'll get you somewhere safe. We've hit this bump before, Ire did his thing, whatever, the past's the past. You can't stick around waiting for Vex to bail you out. We have to get you outta the city."

Vex. Seemed there was always a balance somewhere. As she revealed one secret to Conn, there was another to be hidden from Strat or Lachlan.

"No. I'm not leaving. I would never leave Conn. Why would you…" His slight smile killed her words. He didn't expect her to leave, he was making a point. "My job is to support him."

"Yes, it is. Babe, if you're scared of him, what chance do the rest of us have?"

"I'm not scared of him. Right now, he doesn't need to be worrying about his relationship on top of everything else. We're fine. And when he needs me, I'll be waiting for him."

"Okay," he said, unconvinced. "Don't forget who your friends are, Scamp."

"You'll be my first call if I need to run for my life."

"And if he splits…"

"He wouldn't," she said, shaking her head. "It's about pride."

"That's usually what gets men like him dead."

They'd get through this test. Conn's ability far outweighed that of his cousin Biz. No, she hadn't met the guy, but she didn't need to. She'd always have faith in her man.

"On another subject…" Quick pivot. "What'd you do with the flash drive?"

"Flash drive?" His fingers paused mid scruff scrub. "From the alley?"

She nodded. "You found it, right?"

"I…"

The hesitation shivered through her spine. "Strat?"

"Yeah, you told me to get it, to hide it, that's what I did."

"Okay," she said, relieved. "That's what I figured."

"Why?"

"You don't want to know." Trepidation crept in. "You didn't look at what was on it… did you?"

"No, but now you've got me curious."

She smiled. "You and the rest of the city. If someone gets their way, everyone will lay eyes on it eventually."

"Lay eyes on what?"

"Conn and me," she said, figuring it was smart to prep the guy, just in case he thought to satisfy his curiosity.

"Conn and you, what—" The way his attention leaped to hers wrung a laugh from her throat. "Shit, babe. Someone's got it? Who?"

"I don't know."

"Why would you…? Was it voluntary?"

"Let's just say our beginnings weren't as pure as you might think."

He scoffed. "Never put Ire McDade and pure in the same sentence." And her friend didn't need long to put the pieces together. "That's how he got you. Taped it, threatened to leak it."

"Didn't play out the way it should've, from either of our points of view."

"You're sitting there chill. You're okay with—"

"Do I want the whole world seeing me and Conn like that? No. But, seriously, look around, McDades have bigger fish to fry."

"Doesn't have the same clout when you're public, and your dad's not high on his righteous high horse anymore."

"There was a time I'd have stood up for the McLeod name. I did stand up for it."

"Or lay down for it," he said, not polite enough to disguise or restrain his snicker. "Come on, if you can't laugh…" Her hand dropped to the table and his expression hardened. "Tell it different if he forced himself on you."

Her friend would laugh if, in retrospect, there hadn't been a hardship to the intimacy. If there had, if Conn had touched her without consent, Strat wouldn't think twice about putting a bullet in the man himself, consequences be damned.

"It was never like that. I always wanted him, to be with him. Our first time was spontaneous." Her tongue tasted the corner of her mouth. "Hormones and hellfire, for me anyway."

"When did it change… for him?"

"Conn figured it out before I did. He's smarter than me."

"He made a smart choice. You make him look smarter than he is."

Spoken like a true friend.

"Bluebell!"

The easygoing call came from the tunnel, where Biggs and Daly emerged.

"Your brother's here," Daly said. "Want him in?"

"Yes, I want him in."

She'd be pissed about the request for confirmation if she hadn't already thrown a member of her family out that week.

Daly gestured and Lachlan appeared from the shadows of the tunnel behind them. At least he hadn't been left on the street.

"Need drinks?" Biggs asked.

"No, we're good," she said and smiled at her brother. "Lach doesn't like drinking our stock when the club's closed."

"Our license is good," Biggs said, but carried on past the bar.

Daly caught up with his friend. "Maybe he thinks it's stealing if he doesn't pay."

"If he wants to give me money, I'll take it."

The two laughed; even Strat smirked.

FORTY-FIVE

"I'LL LEAVE YOU two to it," Strat said, sliding along to leave the booth.

"Not for nothing…" her brother started, "Immie thinks you're avoiding her."

Strat stopped. "Me?"

"Yes, you," Lachlan said. "Jagg told her you're into something and Ford won't tell her what."

"Shit," Strat muttered. "Another damn reason…"

To disapprove of the relationship. Her friend conveniently forgot one obvious fact about his tenacious daughter.

"Imogen's a reporter. An observant one," she said. "I'm surprised she lets Jagg away with anything."

Whatever he muttered next, she wasn't sorry to miss it. He moseyed off the same way as Daley and Biggs.

"Those guys don't know where the door is."

Yes, her brother was fishing.

Smiling, she linked her fingers and set them on the table. "There's more to this place than meets the eye."

"Oh, I bet there is," her brother said, coming to a stop behind the end booth opposite hers so they were twelve to six.

When his eyes moved across her papers, she semi-stood to scoop them closer. "My sources like their privacy. You did come to see me, right? Your sister? What can I do you for today?"

"You offer full services?"

"At Stag? Are you planning a birthday party? Want a stripper?"

"There's a lot of chatter on the streets," he said, ignoring her quip. "A lot of movement."

"I wouldn't know anything about that."

"I hope he's keeping you out of it, sis. I really do." Her brother couldn't help but care and she had to love him for it. "Spoke to Lupe."

Ah, a more likely reason for the visit.

"She's a special woman."

"Funny, that's what she told me I'd said to you." No denial, she just smiled. "She doesn't want Dad to know."

"'Cause he and I are bosom buddies who tell each other everything and braid each other's hair. Lupe told me already. The secret's safe."

"That what you tell Ire?"

"Lach," she half whined, half warned.

"The shit that's going on, the players that are moving onto the scene… Sersh, you could get hurt. You will get hurt if he doesn't—"

"He will. You don't have to worry about my safety or the McDades security."

"At the top of the food chain? Maybe not. That doesn't mean stability within the family. Do you know there's a price on Nicole McDade's head? Word is her incarcerated husband put it there." Time to practice her poker face. Whatever she did got her brother exhaling an incredulous laugh. "You did know. How long have you known?" Nope, she wouldn't say a word. "This is the people you're dealing with. Men hiring hitmen to take out women they once claimed to love. Why are you still here? You're smarter than this."

"My relationship is not the same as theirs." For one thing, she'd never cheat on Conn, especially not with a member of his own family. "Conn keeps me close to keep me safe."

"If Biz makes a move to take over—"

"We'll be ready for it."

"It's dangerous, Sersh. Did you hear about the fire in Miami? Score McDade's nightclub, gone." Lachlan gestured around. "What stops Stag being next? You sleep here, right?"

"Why are you so—"

"Because you're my little sister." Concern bubbled beneath his impatience. "I can't look after you if I don't have access."

"You have access. You're here."

"Not that kind of access."

"What other kind of access is there?"

"Access to the full picture, the full truth. You're hiding things from me."

"And you've never hidden anything from me?" she asked. "You're not the only one who wants to protect their sibling. There's nothing to worry about. Conn knows everything. He has my full truth."

"I don't trust him."

"I got that."

"I want to talk to him."

"No." Not like he'd never brought that up before. "There literally couldn't be a worse time. He's busy."

"Plotting the deaths of his own family members?

Nicole McDade's in the city."

She said nothing, just waited. Eyes locked to her brother's. Protecting Conn and the McDades was her reality. Some little part of her though, a corner that craved her brother's happiness, that part wept. She'd always trusted Lachlan and this, the way things had been between them, didn't feel the same anymore.

"I will not be your source."

"You think that's why I care? A case?" His head shook once. "What if you're standing next to her when someone takes a shot?"

That wouldn't happen.

"Conn would never let me be caught in anyone's crossfire. I'm safer here with the McDades than I have ever been in my life."

"You talked to Dad?"

"No, and I have no intention of talking to him." Though the reminder did stoke some of her annoyance. "You think the McDades will get me killed? You know what's more likely to get me killed? Dad fucking around with the Manzanis. You don't think that makes me vulnerable? If they want to make a point, what's to stop them putting a bullet in either of us? Maybe Grandpapa got dead because he asked the wrong questions. Maybe he got dead to prove a point to our father."

"You think the Manzanis are behind the murder?"

"I think if I didn't have Conn protecting me, I'd be out there in the wind. You're a cop. People notice when a cop gets dead. Me? I'm a reporter who pokes her nose where it's not welcome. Easy to off a meddlesome journalist, people sort of assume we deserve it."

"Dad would never—"

"He's not the man you think he is. He doesn't deserve your loyalty."

"Who does?"

Did she? Was that his target? Shimmying out of the booth, she couldn't stay on her ass when her brother's mood was ramping up.

"Lachlan, if you don't want to be here, if you don't believe me and you think Dad is innocent, why did you come?"

"I have to believe I'll get through to you. When you were a kid, at school, I never told you who to hang out with. I always assumed you'd—that you were smart enough to sense danger. It's in us, that gut instinct—"

"Not according to Dad. According to him, I don't have it. I'm useless and a liability to—"

"Why do you hate him?"

"Why do you love him?" she asked. "He's never given you any recognition, never supported you when it counted. He's so fucking self-centered—"

"And you think Ire is Mr. Selfless and—"

"Lachlan, this is the man I'm with, the man I choose, the man I love. No one is asking you to love him too. Nothing has to change between us. I'm still your little sister. Still Sersha. You've always loved me. Are you saying that me being with Connel changes that? That you don't love me, can't love me, if I stand with the McDades?"

He couldn't—they wouldn't… She'd known he would be disappointed and had never once considered cutting him from her life. Was that what she was facing? It had never occurred to her that Lachlan, her big brother and protector, might cut her from his.

"Time's up."

Hock's deep voice broke their stare. Snuff loitered near the entrance as Hock moseyed over.

"Time's up?" Lachlan asked.

"Time to go, Detective."

"Hock, he doesn't—"

"No one raises their voice to Bluebell." Shit. Had

they been heard from upstairs? She'd chosen her spot knowing Conn would see her and know where she was if he needed her. Could be choosing the central spot in the echoey cavern would be responsible for severing her connection to her brother at the most crucial point. "Time to go."

She exhaled. "We should take a breath. I'll call you."

"Sure."

Lachlan put up no fight. Hock didn't even get close. Her brother turned and stalked out. The McDades were fighting to stick together at the same time the McLeods were falling apart. And with dire circumstances weighing her guy down, she couldn't talk to him about it. She couldn't distract him. His head had to stay in the game; stay in staying alive.

Surrounded by people, she'd never been so alone.

FORTY-SIX

ALL DAY. All night. Fifty hours he'd been in that office. Working. Shouting. Meeting. Negotiating. Threatening. Guys were afraid to be in there and she didn't blame them.

Lying in the dark felt wrong. Stag was home, yes, but without her guy, while he was dealing with trauma, she couldn't settle to sleep. She shouldn't be relaxing, thinking about recharging while he was still going full throttle.

As far as she'd witnessed, he hadn't eaten a bite or drunk anything more than whiskey during his sit-in. If her guy wasn't taking care of himself, someone had to step up. Like Strat said. Man, that guy somehow always knew the future.

How useful would Conn be running on empty? With threats closing in around them, he had to keep his wits. Continuing like he had would be a recipe for disaster and one she'd acknowledged, so couldn't hide or deny that awareness later.

Getting up and wrapping herself in their sheet

had purpose. Connel didn't have to say he needed her. Her job was to support him and she wasn't doing that alone in their bed.

"I don't care if you have to tie him to the bumper and drag him here," Conn barked at someone as she descended the stairs. "Just get him in this office!"

"Boss."

Movement, people. The ragged edge to her guy's voice was more than frustration. He knew what he wanted to do and didn't give himself a break. After so many hours on the go, his mind would be slowing, his actions laboring. He needed her, this was exactly her role. Thus she swept the curtain aside to join them in the office; her arrival went unnoticed by her guy seated at the desk.

"What's your fucking excuse?"

Twenty guys loitered around the office, standing, waiting their turn like peasants in the king's court.

Tension hung heavy in the air, so thick it stuck to her skin like humidity in summer heat.

At the opposite end of the desk, on his feet, Niall's concern bled from his gaze to hers for a flicker of a beat. Guy had probably been standing there for days. If Conn didn't sleep, Niall wouldn't either.

Few people had the right to interrupt the man at the center of all focus.

With the sheet trailing and not a hint of hesitation, she slid a hand onto his shoulder to gain his spotlight.

"Fucking speak," he said, still concentrating on a goon, as she swerved her hips around his knee to sit on his thigh. "What the fuck…"

Connel slammed his fist on the desk. Those on the other side jumped in unison. Still, her love didn't acknowledge her presence. Whatever he needed, she'd be patient.

The cigar box was close, maybe too close. Her eyes met Niall's again. He got it. Just like her. Conn's frayed edges could do them all harm. Time to claim the limelight.

"Baby…" she whispered, sinking lower, sliding a hand the width of his chest as she trailed her lips to the side of his neck.

"I'm sick of the fucking excuses, sick of this fucking bullshit!"

Anger reverberated through him. If he didn't kill someone soon, he'd give himself a heart attack.

"Mo Grá," she murmured, massaging his chest. "Come to bed with me, baby."

Wriggling in his lap, she aimed to soothe. Kissing the angle of his jaw, his stubble, her lips snaked their way to the corner of his mouth expecting to tempt his into reciprocating.

Instead, he grabbed her jaw, painfully tight. "Desperate for it, striapach? We're at war," he snarled. "I have no time for whores. You want it? Niall…" His eyes burned into hers even as he called for his lieutenant. "Line up the guys, Bluebell's taking them for a ride. They'll take turns with the bitch all night. How many guys can you take in one shot?"

Slamming her hands to his chest, she shoved, but he put up no fight against her surging to her feet.

His arrogant laughter rumbled low. That sinister sneer wouldn't triumph. If he wanted to play games, she'd play them right back. And she'd be damned before letting him pierce her armor in front of an audience. Rather than being a relief, she'd been humiliated. Who did that help? Did he feel better? She sure didn't.

"Why take up valuable office space?" she drawled. "Let's find out who can get me off the fastest. Can anyone beat the boss's personal best?"

Before she could take a step, Conn snatched her

wrist and yanked, pulling her face down to his.

"You open your legs for another man," he snarled from between his teeth, "I'll put a bullet between his eyes."

And so she was vindicated. "That's what I thought."

Jerking her wrist free, she spun on her heels to march upstairs.

It might be her job to support him, but it wasn't her job to be the subject of ridicule. Her kingdom? Maybe not so much.

Changing into her clothes, she went down the spiral stairs into the club, bypassing the couple of security guys more interested in ogling the young clubbers than doing their job.

Given her security guys had to rest and follow Connel's commands, it wasn't a surprise her car wasn't waiting by the curb. She was supposed to be in bed, asleep, little chance of that after what just went down.

Cabs lined up though, so she slipped into one and gave an address a street away from the loft. Whether the driver recognized her or not, she didn't care. She did care about leaving a trail to Conn's private space. People were watching her now, just like he'd said, her name was his.

What could she do, honestly? Connel was wound tight because he thought he'd missed something. He took on the responsibility of herding his family this way and that, ensuring everyone's safety. Hence his reason for forgoing sleep. She wanted to be there for him, to help. Did that mean providing an opportunity to blow off some steam? Yes. Did it mean putting up with public humiliation? No.

She was mad, yes, and wanted an apology. But that wasn't the time to demand it. Conn had enough on his plate, and just like she'd told Strat, he didn't need relationship drama in the mix. Rather than leaving her Stag bed, she should've stayed put and would regret being the reason he took his eye off the ball. She wouldn't be the cause of further upset for the McDades.

It was about pride.

Discovering his cousin was coming for his spot from a prison cell must sting deep. Was Biz's intention to run the family, or was he more interested in letting Conn's accomplishments disintegrate?

In the empty loft, alone, as far as she could tell anyway, she put her phone in her nightstand charging dock. Given their spat, being in their bedroom didn't feel right. It could be perceived as gameplaying if she slept in the room under video surveillance. If he didn't want her around, she wouldn't force herself into his line of vision.

She lay down in one of the guest rooms instead.

Bed didn't feel any better there than it had at Stag. Maybe she should've gone back to her apartment. Crashing Lachlan's life wouldn't be fair. If he'd moved into her bed and made changes, she wasn't going to usurp the place back. Plus, her brother didn't need any further reasons to disapprove of her relationship. Every couple had bad spells, but…

Closing her eyes, she rolled onto her side, back to the bedroom door. Nothing she could do about it now. Sleep. Breathe in. Out. Sleep. It shouldn't be so hard. Why was it so difficult to settle?

"You don't belong here."

His voice cut through the darkness. The impact of it bedded itself deep in her chest.

Conn.

"No?" she asked, staying still. Was this the end of them or his idea of an apology? "Where do I belong?"

Without warning, he scooped her up into his arms. They went through the dark apartment and up the stairs to their room. Only then did he lay her down in the middle of their bed. Before he could rise, she snagged the back of his neck.

"Macushla." He took her wrist to draw her hand away. "You're lonely."

"I'm worried about you."

"Everything's under control."

"I know." Even if it wasn't and there was stress on him, he wouldn't tell her, not now. Except she had to know. "Lie down with me."

Without resistance, he stripped and got into bed beside her. His hand skimmed across her stomach, holding her down as his lips sought hers. Yes, they could kiss, but when his hands and mouth got more demanding, she pulled away.

"You need to sleep."

"I need to show you the truth."

She accepted another kiss, a short one, then swayed away from the next. "I know the truth." Her hand slid onto his jaw. "I miss you, Mo Grá, but it's my job to support you. My job to make sure you get everything you need. Sleep now. We'll make love when you're rested."

"At the club, in the office—"

"It's okay," she whispered. "We'll talk later."

Yes, she'd been embarrassed, but he was under an inordinate amount of stress. Once he'd slept, and they got back to an even keel, she wouldn't hesitate to tell him his behavior had been out of line. Though given he'd come to her, not just in Stag's bed, but to their home, it was a good bet he got that already.

The guy was taking whacks from every quarter. She'd be safe for him, just like he'd be for her. The man killed for her. He went to any lengths for her. Sometimes it wasn't all about her, that was something he had to be taught. His needs were as important as hers. More so when he had family, blood and kin, depending on him.

"I forgot," he murmured.

"Forgot what?"

"That you're the most important thing in my universe."

"No. The family is your priority. I didn't come to you to—it wasn't about me. I'm worried about you and the family. You haven't been sleeping, eating, taking care of yourself. To be at your best, you need to be at your peak."

"To be at my best, I need my woman happy."

"Your woman is with you." Her fingers trailed down his body. "Always."

"Biz won't give up easy."

Was that his way of telling her things would be like this for a while?

"Let's just see what he says to Whisper. Maybe he has a proposal."

"You think I should accept his terms?"

"I think him laying them out gives you an idea what he truly wants."

"Know your enemy."

"He's your cousin. That gives you some insight. You have Score and Razer on your side. We're strong." His fingers drifted down her cheek and up to the hair at her temple. As his lips moved in a whisper, the foreign words didn't need meaning for her to understand. "I love you too." She kissed him slow. "I don't care how many hours you go without sleep or how many times we argue in public, I'm here. I'll always be here."

"It's about pride—"

"I know, you—"

"Not like it used to be," he said, speaking over her, continuing his previous thought. "I don't want to let you down."

"And I don't need you to prove anything to me. I love you no matter what you choose. No matter what happens."

"Work is autopilot."

"Focus grounds you, I get that."

"Hurting you…"

"Distracts you," she said. "I'm sorry, I didn't intend to disrupt your momentum."

"You are my pride, my strength, Cushla Machree."

"And you are mine." Easing him onto his back, she tucked herself against him. "Sleep, Mo Grá. Recharge."

The fight would still be there tomorrow. And with him ready and alert, she didn't doubt the McDades' chance of coming out on top. They had the right man at the helm, he'd guide them to victory.

FORTY-SEVEN

HER PHONE WOKE her on the first ring.

Awake, she lunged over the bed to grab it off the nightstand in the same move she slung her legs out of bed. She didn't know the time but did know Conn's sleep couldn't be interrupted.

"Hello?" she answered in a whisper when she got to the closet.

"Sersha?"

It couldn't be—she took the phone from her ear to check the screen. "Dad?"

"Are you alone?"

"What?

"We have to meet."

"Meet?" Opening Conn's top drawer, she checked the time on his many watches. "Are you insane? It's three thirty in the morning."

"This can't wait. Your brother's life depends on it. Meet me at your grandfather's in twenty minutes. Alone. Come by yourself. Alone."

"Dad, I—"

The line disconnected. A second later, she was staring at the screen again. Had that just happened, or had she dreamed the whole thing?

Why her grandfather's? Because she wouldn't be dumb enough to rock up to her father's house? Henry's house was the closest safe and private neutral territory. That was her guess.

With curiosity stirred, and concern for Lachlan alight, there was no way she'd ignore the request.

What did a person wear to a middle of the night clandestine meeting with a duplicitous parent?

Jeans.

She couldn't trust her father. She didn't. Zipping her pants, she opened Conn's underwear drawer.

"Shirt or tee-shirt?" she asked, grabbing boxer-briefs and turning to toss them to the man she'd sensed in the doorway.

"What does he want?"

"I don't know, but he said Lach's life depended on us meeting."

"Alone?"

"That was what he said." Many times. She retrieved a bra. "A meet at Grandpapa's."

"Threatening your brother is the quickest way to blind you, Macushla."

"I can't take the risk."

"That's what he's counting on."

"We go in, hear him out. Walk out any time."

"You want me with you?"

She paused, startled by the unexpected question. The opposite hadn't occurred to her.

"It's only my father. If you don't want to come, I can handle him alone."

Sauntering over, he brought his body up against hers. "What do you want?"

"I want you with me," she said because it was the

honest truth. "I want you to sleep and be rested, but will you really sleep if I go do this alone?" And there was another reason. "If my dad's mixed up with Silvio, and we don't know if he knew about the attack before it happened…" She sighed. No, she wasn't afraid. Not exactly. The unknowns instilled sensible wariness. "I'll only come home and tell you everything anyway. Going together saves time. And if my dad needs help, you're more equipped to offer it than I am."

"Your father won't accept help from me."

"Would you give it?"

"If you asked."

He got to dressing so probably didn't see the smile tug at her lips. Conn and the superintendent may be at odds, but her guy cared about her first and spite second. He'd help her father not for his sake, for hers.

He tucked his shirt into his pants. As he turned, she caught his belt before he could buckle it.

"You're holding up the McDades, the Dohertys, now I'm asking you to support the McLeods too."

He slung one arm around her waist, forcing her up and against him. "Maybe we cut out the middleman and give you the McDade name."

Hope and excitement spurred her to her tiptoes. "Just tell me when."

"Cushla Machree." He kissed her slow, ending by smacking her ass and giving it a squeeze. "When we get home."

They'd kiss some more, or he'd give her his name?

"Should I call Daly?" she asked, fastening his belt.

"Car's downstairs and we've got a squad of six. We need more?"

"You're what I need." She coiled her arms around him. "So long as I've got you, nothing can hurt me."

"Then we let the First Team sleep and take this on the road ourselves."

When he intended to go, she tightened her hold to bring him back.

"Mo Grá…"

"I've got you, baby," he said, kissing her head. "Come on. Let's get this over with."

Their bed waited, lonely, as it had been for too long. Her father really picked his moments. Whatever he wanted, he better be quick about it, she'd missed having her guy all to herself.

FORTY-EIGHT

HAD SHE THOUGHT of her grandfather's as a neutral location?

In the car, they weren't too far from their destination. She really didn't want to be dealing with more of her father's bullshit. He better not embarrass her in front of—who was she kidding? Of course he'd embarrass her.

She sighed. "I wish we were going to the club."

That none of this was happening and their lives were carefree. So many dreams.

Conn kept texting but threaded his free fingers through hers. "I'm on a promise when we're through here. Focus on that."

What did that mean? "You're getting more sleep when this is through."

Typical her father should call and inject himself at one of the worst possible times. They didn't need the extra aggravation right now. No, not them, Conn. Conn didn't need the extra aggravation.

"You're laying down and spreading 'em wide

when we're done here, Macushla."

Well, that was their agreement, after sleep came sex. She brought their joined hands to her lap, guiding his arm over her. God, it felt good to be with him, sharing air and space with him. Being in proximity balanced her thinking.

"What about tomorrow?"

"What about it?" he muttered.

"Will I see you?"

He stopped texting and a second passed before he put the phone down to slide a hand onto her face.

"You've woken up lonely enough."

"I'll always be waiting for you, with you," she said. "Don't ever worry about my loyalty or our relationship. I'm always with you. Always yours."

A guarantee she wouldn't retract. Even with Madison Byrne on her way into town. With him bogged down in work, she wanted to be a source of strength for him, present or not.

"And if you're in trouble?"

"You're my first call," she said, understanding why he needed to reiterate that with so much else going on.

"Where are you always safe?"

"With you," she said, stroking the back of his hand. "You know it's the same in reverse, right? That I'll always be safe for you. And if the time comes and you want to cut ties, I'll be with you then too."

The angle of his whole body shifted. "Cut ties?"

"If we have to get out of Dodge fast. You don't need to explain anything to me. Just come get me, tell me it's time to go."

"You're betting against me."

His air of harsh incredulity reminded her of the night they'd met.

"What? No!"

"You expect me to fail."

"No, I didn't say—"

"Your job is—" The car stopped.

"Conn, I—"

But he was already out, on the sidewalk, his men approaching from behind.

Damn. She shouldn't have said a word. What an idiot. That wasn't the time to—she'd called Strat out for contemplating their king's demise and she'd just blurted it out. Conn did not need that. Her job was to support him and instead, she'd put doubt in his head. If she couldn't believe in him, as he thought, how could he have faith his people would foresee success?

Dingo held the door open. She'd sat there so long that he ducked to check on her. "You coming?"

Her father was the one in the building, so yes, she didn't have a choice.

Slipping out of the car, leaving her purse on the seat, her discomfort didn't bode well.

"You got it?" Conn said to the guy who seemed to be taking instructions.

She didn't like strangers having their back. If they'd had Niall there, Daly, any of her guys, she'd have some certainty that they knew what they were doing. Though the men present now were strangers to her, these were McDade men too. Loyal to a fault. They'd have to be or Conn wouldn't have them on his detail.

They just had to get through this meeting. Their familiar people, their First Team, deserved their rest. With some sleep, they'd be better equipped to do their duties.

Without a word, Conn linked their fingers and led her up the external stairs.

"Conn," she said, wishing they had more time.

He produced something from his pocket and flashed it at the door. Sneddon's security card. Good.

The last thing she'd want to do was knock and wait for her father to grant them access. Was security still downstairs or would they be alone in the building?

The hallway was dark. Shadowy. Cold.

The front door closed behind them and she nestled closer to her guy. A light up ahead beckoned, dim, warming the crack between the office door and its frame. Okay. This was it.

Conn didn't need her to direct him. With all the confidence in the world, he strode on down there and into the room.

"McDade."

Her father's voice near the fireplace.

"Superintendent," Conn said.

She peeked around his arm. And, yes, her father was by the unlit fireplace, a hand on the mantle.

"What's he doing here?" her father asked. "I said alone, Sersha."

"I heard you," she said, moving to her guy's side. "And this is what alone gets you."

Conn took control. "What's this about?"

"Family business."

"Conn's specialty," she said. "Where's Lach?"

"We have to talk. Alone."

Her father turned his back. Did he expect her to send Conn away or send him to the hallway?

Like he read her mind, Conn didn't consider either.

Irritation in his air, her father spun around wearing a glare. "He shouldn't be here."

"You don't make the rules, Superintendent," Conn said. "If you have something to tell us, talk. Otherwise, I'm taking your daughter back to my bed."

"Don't you see this, Sersha?" Her father gestured at Conn. "Why can't you see it? How he uses you—exploits you."

So much for Conn's warning working long distance.

"Is that why I'm here? To hear you criticize my relationship?" She tightened her hold on Conn's hand. "Take me home."

"No!" Her father bounded toward them, stopping by Henry's angled desk with the window behind it. "We have to talk, Sersha. We have to do it without outsiders."

"Conn isn't an outsider. You get both of us or we leave."

They'd achieve nothing if her father kept throwing up objections.

"Our family…" Like he'd just decided Conn was no longer there, her father's eyes drilled into her. "We have a special position in this city. People respect us. They follow our example."

"I'm not interested in being worshipped."

"It's not about worship, it's—" Sealing his lips, anger flared her father's nostrils, but he held onto it. "We need to consider what's best for the city. Not what's best for us."

"Meaning?"

"The man you…" He swallowed what appeared to be a bad taste on his tongue. "He doesn't want what's best for the city. His family is not—heritage is important."

"History? Is that what you're selling?"

Conn edged to the side, closer, putting his arm in front of hers. "You called the meeting to demand inside information," her guy said, stating what it would take her father all night to clarify. "You want to know the McDade position, our plans. You thought she'd be weak enough to turn on us if you could get her alone. Tried that before, Superintendent, and it ended with her in the hospital. That won't happen again. I'll take down any threat to her. Including you.”

"That was your fault,” her father snapped. “You didn’t protect her in your territory.”

"It’s her territory too and she’s never in danger now that she’s safe behind the McDade shield.”

Maybe not totally safe, but safer than she had been before the world knew about her and Conn.

"You better hope that’s true.”

That sounded like a threat and she didn’t like it. Neither did Conn.

"Say that again,” he growled beneath his breath. "We’ll lay son next to father.”

"Recruiting me was never going to work, Dad.” If they didn’t walk away, the situation would become grave. “I won’t turn on Conn, on the McDades. I wouldn’t then and I definitely won’t now. The McDades are my future.”

"He’s manipulating you,” her father barked. "How can you be so stupid? So naïve? He’s using you to get to me!”

Her lips curled just before a laugh escaped. "Wow, and I’m stupid?”

"Sersha—”

"He doesn’t need you!” Dropping Conn’s hand, she put herself in front of him. “You are irrelevant. Unimportant. Insignificant.” Her sneer startled her father, not that it stopped her. “What is it you think you can give? What is it you think we need? You don’t take up any space in my man’s head. None. No McDade gives a shit who you are or what you think. We don’t need you. And that’s what you hate. You want us to covet your help. You want Conn to need you, but he doesn’t. He doesn’t need you. I don’t need you. You have nothing we need.”

"Which gives you no bargaining chips,” Conn said, sliding a stable hand onto her shoulder and around to grip her throat, drawing her back against him. "Sersha's loyalty is not for sale. She won't deliver on the promises you made, promises you can't keep."

Sound from the hallway interrupted the moment. People. What was happening? Person. Just one judging by the footfalls. The door squeaked and those feet came closer.

"Ire."

Her inhale wasn't quite a gasp, but the last thing she'd expected was…

"Silvio," she whispered as he passed them and stopped by the fireplace. "What the hell is going on here?"

FORTY-NINE

"YOU SAID YOU'D deliver your daughter alone," Silvio, Manzani Don, said. She still couldn't believe that she was looking at—the don's eyes traveled down her body and back up slowly. "I see the appeal."

God, nausea, that examination, the intensity of Silvio's scrutiny peeled her clothes away from her skin, wheedling much deeper than Evander's typical leer.

Conn exhaled a sound of amusement, though not quite of laughter. "Your father knew he wouldn't persuade you," her guy said, skimming his hand down her arm to link their fingers again. "You played your ace too early, Superintendent."

This was dangerous. Much graver than any threat her father could present alone. The head of the McDade family stood with the don of the Manzanis. Were Silvio's men outside with theirs? Shit. So much for discreet.

"It was meant to be a private meeting," her father said.

"Why is he here?" she asked, looking at her father, nodding to Silvio. Despite her awareness of the truth, her father hadn't expressed it. "You want me to turn on the McDades, while you're clearly in league with the Manzanis?"

"Now your world comes tumbling down," Conn murmured behind her.

"Your father and I have been working together for some time," Silvio said, putting another smile on her face. The expression prompted confusion in his frown. "Did I say something funny?"

"Actually, yes." Angering Silvio wouldn't be smart, but she just couldn't hold it in. At least she hadn't laughed out loud. Conn squeezed her hand. "I know, baby, I'm sorry. It's just—the pristine superintendent is no better than a cheap, dirty street cop."

"Sersha—"

"Chastise me, Dad, whatever. Your high horse is a crock of shit. A special position in the city? Damn, you believe your own press. What you are is disgusting. A fraud. A phony. Say what you will about these men but at least they own what they are. You want my loyalty? You want my respect? Pick up the damn phone and get Lachlan here. Tell him to come here right now. Admit the truth to him."

Their true beacon of righteousness. Hers anyway. Though, the truth was, she didn't want Lachlan there. His responsibility to do the right thing would get him into serious trouble.

"This is nothing to do with your brother."

"Yet you got me here by threatening his life." Her gaze cut to Silvio. "Is that you? Did you threaten my brother to get my father onboard?"

"Your father is a reasonable man."

"Meaning he'll do anything for green," Conn said. "You can buy the superintendent. His children don't fall in line so easy."

"My son has a fascination for your woman."

While addressing Conn, Silvio's eyes did that undressing thing again. "How quickly would you flip, if I took her to him right now?"

"Seen your son lately, Director?" Conn asked. Silvio snapped from the perusal. "Get your own house in order before you come for mine."

Evander and his father weren't close, they didn't have trust. That didn't mean Silvio would accept his son being injured, shot, by an enemy. If Evander was smart, he'd be lying low rather than admit to his father he got shot by Ire McDade while conspiring against his own family.

Turned out Evander got his insecure ego from his father.

Silvio turned on hers. "Once again, you disappoint, McLeod. You fail to deliver."

"We have the votes," her father said, a thread of desperation in the back of his throat. "We don't need her."

Her. Like she was some repulsive stranger.

"Her power is greater than yours," Silvio stated, his lip curling in disgust. "You have nothing to offer."

The don started for the door, halting for just a moment to lock eyes with the guy behind her. She held her breath until he carried on out. The door closed and then they were alone with her father again.

"Can we go home too?" she asked, guiding Conn's arm around her waist.

"Now see…" The purr of pleasure in Conn's voice was more than a little smug. "You're in trouble, Superintendent."

"Trouble?" she asked, watching panic flicker behind her father's eyes. "He's in trouble."

"Nothing to offer the Manzanis and the McDades don't want him."

"I have plenty to offer," he barked. "Plenty to

of—"

"Your influence hasn't paid off. Feel the desperation? There'll be a price on your head by morning."

"What are you—"

"Working with The Director protected you." Another of Silvio's names. "Now you can't collect the votes—"

"I can. There's time—"

"We got Blakely."

Cold dread settled over her father. "No, you—"

"With a little help from my woman." His, not her father's daughter, not a McLeod, a McDade. Shit. Pride. The delectable weight of it enveloped her in satisfaction. "You took money from Silvio promising you could deliver him the council. Instead your father brought scrutiny and your daughter proved her allegiance elsewhere. Like she said, you are irrelevant. Nothing more than a liability. A loose end. The Manzanis won't leave a loose end."

She'd lost her grandfather and now her father could be in danger of losing his life. Where did that leave them? How did she feel about…? Seemed cold to think her father had made his bed, but was courtesy enough of a reason to ask Conn to step in? Could the McDades take on another battle? Protecting her father would prove difficult if the Manzanis were determined.

Lachlan.

How would he feel if something happened to their father?

"There will be other votes. Other situations with—"

"Except you've proved you can't deliver. Why would the Manzanis rely on you again?"

If the Harvest deal was in the bag for the McDades, their territory would grow. Their influence would spread. Her guy, providing he could deal with the threat from within, would build strength upon strength.

No doubt Biz wanted the Manzanis to win the vote. From prison, he couldn't offer much in the way of support or influence. No, Biz was up to something else. Maybe Silvio would exact a price for this defeat. Would it be enough to disrupt their bargain, whatever the details?

"They can't hurt me. I'm Superintendent!"

"How did position help your father?" Conn asked. "He died within these walls for standing with integrity. You'll fall without yours. Someone was willing to put a bullet in him for—"

"He got in the way! Asked questions that were— he caused trouble!"

"Doing the right thing," Conn finished his sentence. "Standing up for something."

"If he had stayed out of it—"

"What? Did he find you out? Find out you were—"

"He wouldn't hear me! Wouldn't hear what was best for the family, for the city, for—"

"You. Let's not fuck around, Superintendent. You wanted money."

"I wanted to win!"

"To prove you were—"

"My father wouldn't listen!" Just like she wouldn't either. The man was losing control of his own family; he couldn't run a department if he couldn't keep his own people straight. "He needed to listen! He'd be alive if he'd just listened to me!"

Spinning around, he shoved half the contents off the mantle, scattering them across the hearth and floor.

"You feel that, Ronald," Conn murmured, though not to her. "Feel yourself losing your grip? It's over. You're through."

"No," her father exhaled. "No. No!" Spinning around, he swept something up from the mantle. It wasn't until the silencer barrel was aimed right at her that the firearm took shape. "You will listen to me, Sersha."

"I'm listening." Her hands opened and arms rose when Conn tried to move around her. "What do you want? You want me to listen? I'm listening."

"You're a McLeod."

"Okay." Appeasement could be their only hope. "Whatever you want."

"Macushla." Conn yanked her hard, forcing her behind him. "You want to aim that at someone, aim it at me."

"You took my family. You took my authority."

"Aye," Conn said, head held high.

What the hell was he doing?

"Now you force me to hurt my own daughter. Sersha, get out here. Move over." He gestured with the weapon and she stepped out, but Conn went with her, using himself as a shield. "Get out of the way!"

"You shoot, you better kill me, Superintendent. The second you pointed that at my girl, you signed your death warrant. I told you, I warned you, Macushla is the primary McDade concern."

"You corrupted her!"

"Aye, you're fucking right. Every damn night, I corrupt her over and over," Conn snarled. "I've fucked your little girl every way a man can. Think a man like me hears no? She's my whore. Begs for it, begs on her knees, worships my cock every fucking minute."

She needed him to stop. "Conn!"

Conn wanted to redirect her father's anger, to put himself in the firing line and save her. She couldn't breathe. He had to stop. How could she make this stop?

"Doesn't matter now. The McDades will come for you," Conn growled, taunting him. "Put a bullet in me or her, they'll make it their mission to take you down."

"I am Superintendent!"

"This city is run on power and influence, not job title. You couldn't convince your own daughter to stand with you. Your father fought against your pathetic authority."

"And died for it. He wouldn't listen. I talked, I told him; he wouldn't listen to me!"

The quiver in her throat hit with a clarity that fired heat behind her eyes. "It was you," she whispered, inching aside to look her father in the eye. "We knew you knew but… He let you in. His son. He welcomed you into his sanctuary and—"

"He made his choice! He wouldn't keep quiet! He found out Silvio and I had an arrangement—"

"He learned you were dirty." God, a lump rose in her throat. "You killed your own father. You killed him for…"

Being righteous. Being right. Standing up for himself and the city.

FIFTY

"SILVIO KNOW YOU murdered your father?" Conn asked. "Maybe you'll catch a break and they'll squeeze another couple of miles outta you, old nag. They'll dangle this over your head, and you'll pant like the little Manzani bitch you are. You roll over for him too? You like playing his whore?"

Her father must've killed her grandfather in what she could only imagine was an anger-fueled frenzy. And from the looks of it, that same craze had ahold of him again. Gritting his teeth, Ronald pulled back the hammer.

"No," she said, leaping around Connel. "You don't have to do this, Dad. We'll... we'll fix it. I'll fix it!"

"How?"

"I..." Damn, she needed a minute to come up with something. "I—" An idea. "I'll write it!"

"Write it?"

"An insider look, an undercover piece, another exposé. This time from inside City Hall. We'll figure it out, all the details. You went undercover to, um, weed out corruption. Without knowing who you could trust, you couldn't discuss it with colleagues. We'll tell them only we knew, you and me. Silvio's lost the Harvest deal anyway, what does he care if you name and shame his allies? They haven't done him any good. This will shake things up, get a fresh batch of guys in there. Teach the old ones a lesson."

"Silvio won't—"

"We don't have to say who they took bribes from. We'll keep the Manzani name out of it. Evander listens to me, and I have a relationship with Helios. I can do this. I can pull the Manzanis back for you. I can protect you."

No mention of the fact that Evander could be dying of septic shock at that moment or that Hell could be liberated soon and start a mission to grab power for himself. No, her father had killed once, in this desperate state, he wouldn't hesitate to do it again.

For a second, Ronald seemed to consider it. Then his scrutiny narrowed on her guy.

"He won't allow it. He won't let you."

"I make my own choices, Dad." Believe it or not. "Connel supports me in whatever I choose."

"You'll support her?"

"No," Conn said, deep and stern.

Fuck, what was he doing? "Baby…" Turning to him, she kept her back to her father, desperate to meet her lover's gaze, yet he wouldn't yield. "We have to think of the family. Of what's best."

"It's about pride, Macushla." Why wouldn't he look at her? His cool stare stayed locked over her head on the man threatening them. "Ronald, here, is done. He's a snake who doesn't deserve our time or our loyalty."

Maybe not, but he was the one holding the gun.

"We'll figure it out. Together. As a family."

"He's not family. Not mine. Not McDade.

Which are you, Macushla? McDade or McLeod?"

Was he asking her to choose? An ultimatum? He couldn't. In the car he'd… They were supposed to be a unit, able to trust each other no matter what.

"Mo Grá—"

"Decide!"

If there wasn't a gun in the equation, the choice would be so much easier.

"You don't take her," her father sneered. "Don't take my child from—"

"Your child is my woman. She'll write the story I tell her to write. She'll write the truth. That you're a sniveling weasel. A sorry excuse for a human. So weak you had to kill your own father to—"

"Enough! Sersha!" Pivoting a half turn, she loathed the weapon still aimed at them. "You'll write my story."

"McDade or McLeod," Conn murmured next to her.

"You write mine," her father said. "I don't want to hurt you. I don't. But you know the truth now, you know that—I can't let the city down. It needs me." Talk about arrogance. "I value it more than anything. It's a sacrifice I had to make, I prioritize the city." His position. His reality. His status. "Don't make me hurt you."

Her eyes blurred though the obvious angle of the weapon was pointed her way. He'd killed her grandpapa and now she knew the truth of his crime. Guilty not only of taking bribes from the Manzanis, her father was a murderer too.

"Why did you have to kill him? Why did you—"

"Because the city is more important than blood." Except he wouldn't give himself up for it. "None of this would've happened if—you should've listened to me. I told you. I asked you. If you'd just told me the truth, told me who you saw and—"

"Turned on a family I love?" The McDades. "No." That meeting in the stairwell, of her and her father, was the watershed. At the time, she hadn't realized it; now it seemed so obvious. "You're not in control, haven't been in control. You're dancing to a Manzani tune and expecting me to do the same."

"This is about the city!"

"This is about pride!"

What gets men like him dead. How right Strat had been. Except her father wasn't done. How many people would he take with him before he fell?

"You can't understand," her father spat.

"I understand!" Anger burst out of her. "You're a coward! A useless, lying—"

"No—"

"Weak—"

"No—"

"An embarrassment. You're spineless—"

"No!"

His arm straightened and Conn moved fast, shoving her down to the floor with one quick action. A short pop jolted the air. What just…?

Her man turned as she tossed her hair from her face and—blood.

There was blood on Conn's chest.

"Oh my God," she gasped, scrambling across the floor, climbing up in a crouch.

Like nothing had happened, her guy caught her against him, balancing her weight with his strength.

"Mo Grá."

Conn's focus landed on her father. "You should've finished me."

"If she moves, I will."

"No!" she shrieked, pressing herself against Conn while speaking to her father over her shoulder. "No more, please."

"You have to learn, to know there are consequences," Ronald said. "This is your fault, Sersha."

"You fucking—"

"No," she said, using all her power to prevent Conn from crossing the room.

Another shot burst and she screamed when the round whizzed past her ear. "No, stop!" Forcing Conn backwards, she pushed him to the massive oak framed couch to sit him down and straddle him. "Baby…" Ripping fabric from a pillow, she pressed the material against the wound. "Sit still."

"I'll rip him fucking open—"

"Baby—" With her hands on his shoulders and her knees squeezing into him, she fought to keep her guy steady. "Please…"

She fumbled for the phone in his pocket, grabbing it out to—

"Give it to me," her father demanded, closer than before though still out of reach. The angle of the weapon shifted to point at Conn's head. "Give me the phone."

"He needs help!"

"Give me the fucking phone or I end him right now."

Swallowing, eyes on Conn, she couldn't believe he smiled as her shaking hand put the phone in her father's. He threw it to the floor and stamped on the screen, then kicked the pieces toward the fireplace.

"Cushla Machree," the murmur left her guy's lips.

Heated tears streaked her cheeks. Her man. Her life. Her reason for breathing was in peril and she had no idea what to do. They needed Niall. Needed Strat. Needed a hospital. Life was seeping out of him, staining fabric and skin. The long, thick, red blot grew and sank, soaking the thin cotton of his shirt. Each second was valuable, they needed to get out of there before the damage was irreversible.

If her father didn't let her get help, if he didn't leave or release them, her guy wouldn't survive. How many bullets were left in that gun? If she screamed at the top of her lungs, would their men hear from the street? Were Manzanis still out there? If they were, and rushed to the scene, would Silvio finish what her father started?

She couldn't breathe; grief and panic swallowed her. Conn needed her to be strong, needed her support, like was her job, and she was helpless so long as that gun was aimed at her lover's head.

"Mo Grá," she whispered, seeking strength in him. "Mo Grá. Mo Grá. Please. I… Help me."

When his next words were foreign, she closed her eyes, letting the tone of them wash over her, absorbing their power.

Her fire burned for her man. "I will not let you do this." Pressing Conn's hand to the fabric on his wound, she leaped up, putting herself against the barrel of her father's gun. "I am taking him out of here. The only thing that will stop me is a bullet. So do it. If that's what you're going to do, do it."

"You're going to write the story, just like you said."

"No," she said, shaking her head. "McDade. I choose McDade and I will always choose McDade. You're deranged! Insane! A complete—"

"You write it or he's dead!"

"You'll never get out of here! Our people are right outside. They'll take you down and I'll—" He grabbed her arm, muscling her aside as she fought for freedom. "Let me go!"

Again, his arm straightened and there was Conn, under threat.

"Stay down, McDade," her father barked.

The gun blasted and she braced, though had no idea what the bullet hit.

"No! No, I'll do it!" Getting between the men, the danger was too palpable to risk. "I'll write the story! I'll do anything you want."

Anything to help her guy.

"Turn around." Holding her breath, she did as he said. "Hands behind your back." Cool metal and the snick of a lock, handcuffs. Her own father just cuffed her. "Go stand over there!" He gestured to the furthest door in the corner, one that led to the back of the house. "Go now!"

Hands at her back, she went that way, trying to be subtle about testing the restraints. They wouldn't give. Her father knew what he was doing when it came to subduing prisoners.

All she could do was watch as he tossed another set of cuffs at Conn.

The gun swung around to point at her. "Put them on," her father demanded of Connel. "Hands around the frame. Do it or I kill her."

Growling words in his native language, Conn clipped a cuff to one wrist and then the other, following her father's instructions.

The saturated fabric was gone from his wound, relieving the pressure, so the blood ran free.

Beads of sweat on her lover's brow and the lack of color in his face triggered her own life force to dwindle. Without him, there would be nothing. She couldn't lose him.

"Mo Grá? Mo Grá! Look at me! Baby, please!"

"He's done," Ronald said, marching over to block her view.

Throwing open the door, he shoved her into a short hallway. Desperate for hope, to help, anything, she screamed until her lungs burned.

Ronald pushed and pushed. "Quiet!"

Maybe the Manzanis were out front, but maybe they weren't. She had to take the chance; Conn would never scream for himself.

"No! No!" she objected, struggling. "Where are we going?"

Her father wrestled her through another door. "Out the back. Go!"

The pulse of her blood pumped fast and hot. "The back?"

"A passage that takes us far from the house before we hit the streets. Your McDades will never know we're gone. Ire will bleed out while his men watch the sun rise."

Bleed out. Her man didn't have long. With no one there to tend to him or keep him talking, he'd pass out and then…

Why had she answered the phone? Why had she asked him to join her?

Connel "Ire" McDade was a formidable monolith, or he had been until he met her. In him, she'd found her purpose. Her truth. Her need. Now that was gone, life faded from her soul as it would be fading from him. What was the future without Conn lighting her path? Pointless. Futile. Miserable. She didn't want tomorrow, not if it meant waking without him, waking lonely. All of this was on her. What had she done?

TO BE CONTINUED…

Thank you for reading this tale!
If you can, please take the time to review.

~

Ask your local library for more Scarlett Finn novels!

~

For all things Scarlett Finn
check out:

www.scarlettfinn.com